Karen Deaken walked apprehensively into the farmhouse, staring about her warily. Her hair was straggled and she had been crying. She looked crumpled and small beside the huge-bellied, bearded man who had brought her from Switzerland, through the same unhindered crossing at Basel. At once Levy crossed the room towards her.

"You mustn't be frightened," he said soothingly. "Everything is going to work out all right. I promise."

"Fear never hurt anybody," said the bearded man, whose name was Solomon Leiberwitz.

"Stop it!" Levy said to him. To Karen he said, "Don't worry."

She looked at him. He smiled. She responded, nervously, then realized what she was doing and straightened her face. "What do you want?"

Levy gestured towards the bench alongside the fireplace where Tewfik Azziz sat. "For the moment," he said, "just for you to sit next to him, over there."

"What for?"

"We want to take your photograph," said the Israeli. "Together."

Look for these other TOR books by Brian Freemantle

THE LOST AMERICAN
THE VIETNAM LEGACY

DEAKEN'S WAR
BRIAN FREEMANTLE

TOR

A TOM DOHERTY ASSOCIATES BOOK

DEAKEN'S WAR

Copyright © 1982 by Innslodge Publications Ltd.

A TOR Book

Published by Tom Doherty Associates
8-10 West 36 Street
New York, N.Y. 10018

First TOR printing: March 1985

ISBN: 0-812-58252-7
CAN. ED.: 0-812-58253-5

Printed in the United States of America

DEAKEN'S WAR

Prologue

Home leave had been the reward for the original concept and then for all the training and preparation, but he had been away so long that they were practically strangers and it had not been the success they hoped. She had wondered if he would mention it, to bring it out into the open, but he had not. She stood just inside the bedroom door, watching him pack, and wished she could feel greater regret at their parting. He was a good man and she wanted to love him. But his ambition frightened her: it seemed to consume him.

"How long will it take?" she asked—a recurring question.

"I've allowed for two months," he said. "But it could be much shorter: maybe just weeks. It depends on their reaction being what I predict."

"I hope it's short," she said.

"Frightened?"

"Of course," she said. "Shouldn't I be?"

"This could establish me completely . . . mean a lot to us."

"It is going to mean a lot to us," she said heavily. He hadn't always been a callous man.

"Sergei's place at the academy will be automatic," he said, anxious to stress the advantages.

"He is clever enough to have got in anyway," she said.

He looked around the small apartment. "And it'll be nice to get somewhere bigger."

She came farther into the room, wondering how long it would take her to get to know him again, when he was back permanently. All his documentation was on the bed beside his suitcase. She picked up the South African passport, smiling at the stiff official picture. "Rupert Underberg," she said. "That's a good name."

"He's got a boy, just like us," he said. "Two years younger."

She frowned, imagining something she didn't know. "You've met him?"

He shook his head. "Just borrowed his identity for the last year."

They walked to the door together.

1

The crammer's school for the very rich was off the Basel to Zürich road, sufficiently close to Zürich for the lake to be visible from its expansive verandahs and stepped walkways. Here, after the struggle of prep schools, privileged children of ambitious parents were force-fed to make university entrance, just as, to the north at Strasbourg, geese had corn thrust down their throats to make pâté de foie gras. The product of Strasbourg was frequently on the dining-room menu at the Ecole Gagner. Its students were frequently on the acceptance lists of Oxford and Cambridge and Harvard and the Sorbonne: only by sustaining maximum results could it remain the best and charge maximum fees.

The main building had been created in the seventeenth century in the style of a walled, turreted castle with crenel-lated battlements by a Frenchman who had pretensions to a military life without the stamina to make it possible. The high walls and the single drawbridged entrance to the dormitory area remained, giving the Ecole Gagner added attraction. They meant it was secure. Even so, bodyguards were an accepted feature in the school precincts. Six were assigned to a Kuwaiti prince. The son of a rancher who owned ten square miles in Paraguay had three. So, too, did Tewfik Azziz.

The regimentation at the Ecole Gagner would have pleased its military-minded architect. Everything had its order, from mealtimes to recreation to examination times. And vacation times. The longest holiday was in the summer, always starting on the Wednesday of the second week in June and not ending until the last Thursday in August: the principal considered the extended relaxation necessary after the workload imposed through winter and spring.

Most boarding schools have a travel officer. Reflecting the importance of its pupils, the Ecole Gagner had a department, staffed by four. Here, as with everything else, the precision was absolute, timetables agreed and adjusted weeks in advance to fit parents' requirements, and usually the convenience of private aircraft. Azziz's departure was scheduled for noon. His father had brought the *Scheherazade* into harbour at Monte Carlo and the Alouette helicopter, which had its own pad and hangar at the stern, could make the journey to Zürich and back to the yacht in under four hours, with the inconvenience of road travel only necessary from the school to the airport. The school's closeness to the tight-packed foothills prevented its having a landing pad of its own.

Azziz's car left the school grounds at eleven. All three

bodyguards were with him. The American, Williams, who had been a Green Beret officer and then a contract employee for two years with the CIA, rode in the back alongside the boy. One Bedouin drove, the other sat beside him in the front; from their clothes and demeanour it was difficult to tell that they were Arabs, or had, ten years earlier, been desert tribesmen.

Obediently the driver kept to the speed limit crossing the ancient bridge, only accelerating slightly along the winding driveway through the outer grounds beyond; to the left were the playing fields, skating rink and covered swimming pool. The gateman was waiting at the boundary wall. He looked in, smiled and then operated the electrically controlled outer protections.

The car turned right, onto the main road, almost immediately picking up the river Limmat; from the hills it was possible to see the lake into which it fed.

"Looking forward to the vacation?" asked Williams. With the boy safely aboard the yacht, he would have two clear months to himself. His sister was expecting him in Houston by the end of the week.

"Very much," said Azziz. He hadn't found it easy, achieving the examination grades. But he had managed. He knew his father would be pleased. It was important always to please his father.

"When do you sit for Cambridge?" asked the American.

"Immediately I return. They think I'll get in without any difficulty." The boy knew that the assessment had already been sent, along with his end-of-term report, to his father. It was going to be a pleasant holiday.

The road began to fall away for the final descent into Zürich; from the elevation it was possible to distinguish the newness of the Bahnhofstrasse set against the tangled parts of the old quarter. The driver was familiar with the route and turned away towards the airport, missing the congestion of the town. Azziz detected the black spot of a helicopter and wondered if it were his; it was too far away to see the markings.

"We're in good time," said Williams, as the car turned onto the slip road to the airport. He wasn't a good flyer and put a travel pill surreptitiously into his mouth. He hoped Azziz hadn't noticed.

There was a separate car park for the private section, away from the main airport complex. When the car halted all three men turned instinctively towards Azziz. This was a mistake. So, too, was leaving the doors unlocked. All four opened simultaneously, the ambush perfectly coordinated.

"Move and he's dead," said a voice.

The .375 Magnum was against the front of Azziz's head, so all three men could see it; fired from that close, it would have decapitated him. The three remained motionless. It took only moments to disarm them. Williams had a Colt automatic in a shoulder holster and a short-barrelled Smith and Wesson against his leg in an ankle strap. The Arabs each had a Smith and Wesson, both long-barrelled.

"Take me too," said Williams. His head was tilted awkwardly because a pistol was hard beneath his left ear.

"Don't be stupid," said the man who had first spoken. He was short and slightly built, olive-skinned and crinkle-haired.

One of the Bedouin said "Pig" in Arabic. In the same language the spokesman said, "Tell his father that; tell his father we're the worst pigs he can imagine." He came back to Williams. "You listening?"

"Yes," said the American.

"Tell his father to wait until he's contacted. And then cooperate. If he tries anything, with the authorities or any people like you, we'll kill the boy. You got that?"

"Yes," said Williams again.

A fifth man appeared in the doorway with a gunlike object in his hand. None of the three men recognized it as an immunization compressor which injects without the necessity of a needle. There was a hiss as the man fired against the necks of the American and the driver and into the hand of the second Arab. Unconsciousness was almost immediate.

"They're not hurt," said the curly-haired man to the boy.

Azziz looked fearlessly across the car at him. "Get this gun away from my head," he said. "It hurts."

The man nodded and the pressure was relaxed.

"You won't be harmed," said the man. "Not if you do what you're told. You're going to get out of this car and be taken to another. If you try to attract any attention, we'll shoot your legs away. You won't die, but you'll be crippled for life. Do you understand?"

"Yes," said Azziz.

"All right," said the man. "Now get out."

The boy got out of the car, fully aware for the first time of the number of men who had crowded around the vehicle, shielding what was happening from anyone else who might have entered the car park.

"You're idiots," said Azziz. "Do you have any idea what sort of man my father is?"

"We know exactly what he is," said the man. "That's why we've got you."

The Liberian-registered and appropriately named *Bellicose*, a freighter of 25,000 tons, sailed from Genoa in ballast, making easy passage with the coast of Italy and France always in sight until it reached Marseilles. Captain Sven Erlander let his first officer go ashore to arrange the loading, while he completed the official record from the rough log. He was still working on it when Raoul Edmunson entered the cabin.

"Going well," said the first officer. "Plenty of stevedores, too."

"Anything awkward?" asked the captain.

Edmunson hesitated. "I always think arms shipments are awkward," he said. "I don't like them."

"Neither do I," agreed Erlander. "That wasn't what I meant."

"It's all crated," said the first officer. "And the general cargo is already loaded."

"Good," said Erlander as he completed the log. The last entry recorded was the visible passing of Monte Carlo, where the *Scheherazade* was expectantly at anchor. The helicopter pad was still empty.

2

Like cigarette odour or the smell of garlic on the breath, the overnight argument was still there, a barrier neither was prepared to cross. Richard Deaken moved politely but unspeaking about the kitchen and Karen manoeuvred with equal good manners and matching silence in the opposite direction, in a dance that neither enjoyed nor properly knew the steps. She set the table, as she always did. And he put the brioches in the basket and then laid the bread alongside; it was always his job to go to the baker just off the boulevard Jacques Dalcrose for morning bread. Just as it was to brew the coffee. He concentrated more than was necessary upon the filter. He heard her sigh. Deaken removed the filter and the coffee residue with elaborate caution, almost as if it might explode, and then carried the pot to the table. He put it between them, without offering to pour for her. She reached forward impatiently, splashing some into her cup so that it spilled into the saucer. Deaken realized it was childish not to have done it for her. Karen used a tissue to clean the saucer and then turned it between her fingers into a tiny brown ball. Deaken carefully ensured he finished pouring well before the rim of his own cup, so there was no spill; he should have bought a newspaper on the way back from the baker, to create a physical division between them.

"This is fucking ridiculous."

"Yes," he said. She wasn't referring specifically to this morning but to many before. And nights. And days. And weekends. Things had been going badly for a long time.

"I mean—why?"

"I don't know. It's ridiculous, like you said."

"Do you still love me?"

"You know I do."

"Then why?" she pleaded again.

"Ridiculous," he repeated. They were still dancing, more intricately now.

"It needn't be."

Deaken regarded their arguments like some juvenile game of Scrabble, a limited number of words arranged before them to create into a pattern of familiar sentences or phrases.

"We can't afford a baby," he said—the most familiar phrase of all.

Karen crumbled a brioche between her fingers, until it became a scattered pile of crumbs and dough. "We can't even afford this fucking bun!" she said.

"You know I'm right."

"Shall I tell you something . . . ?" She raised her hand way above her head, so that bread debris rained down between them. "I'm fed up to here . . . I'm utterly and absolutely pissed off . . . with this bloody affectation."

"You don't have to swear."

"I'll swear as much as I fucking well like!"

She seized her coffee cup with both hands, making a barrier between them. He thought she was beautiful, even though she had only scraped a comb through the blonde hair and coloured her lips. Anger flushed her face; she looked young and innocent and flustered. He wanted to reach out and touch her. He didn't.

"It's not an affectation," he insisted. He didn't want to argue any more with her.

"Then tell me what it is!"

"We've been through it all before."

"Richard Deaken, on the run again."

"I'm not running away," he said. "I work here in Geneva because I want to . . . because I think it might have a future for me. And because to have stayed in South Africa was impossible. You know that."

"You don't work here," she persisted. "You go into that dingy bloody office and make chains out of paperclips all day. Why the hell maintain all this crap about being a lawyer for the underdog? We're the only underdogs in the entire country. The Swiss are too bloody expert at making money."

"Maybe I should try to join a firm," he conceded. Deaken wondered how long it would take other trained lawyers to recognize his problem, if he did join a group of partners: to realize that his trial nerve had gone, so that he couldn't remember the construction of a brief or the points of defence or prosecution or seize, as he had once been able to seize, the mistakes and errors of the other side and turn them to his advantage.

"You'd better, before it's too late," she said. "There's no point in having an international law degree and the reputation you have, unless you use it."

Deaken started eating a brioche, not because he wanted it but because he needed something to do. It was difficult to swallow. He should have sought psychiatric help before now; before it had become so bad that he didn't think he could ever again appear in open court, and had tried to bury himself in the anonymity of civil ligitation.

"Would you need money to buy into a firm?"

"Almost certainly."

"We haven't got any."

"Sometimes they'll let you pay it off from salaries and fees, once you've joined."

She reached across the table for his hand, an impulsive gesture. "I don't mean to bitch," she said.

"I know."

"I *do* love you. I know how good and successful you could be . . . It just seems letting everything drift like this is such a waste."

She never accused him of failing her, even during their fiercest arguments, but he believed she felt that he had. "Maybe I'll look around," he said.

Karen put her head doubtfully to one side. "Promise?" she said.

"Not today," said Deaken. "I've actually got a client today. I'll start tomorrow."

Karen stood and swept the crumbs she had created into her napkin and then cleared the rest of the breakfast things from the table. "I've been thinking," she said, from the sink.

"About what?"

"Getting a job."

She turned as she said it, conscious of the effect it would have. She lifted a rubber-gloved hand against any outburst, washing bubbles dripping onto the floor in front of her. "I'm not trying to start another fight," she said quickly. "I'm bored with nothing to do. Honestly. And it would help; you've got to admit it would help. Financially, I mean."

"I said I'd look around," said Deaken tightly. Switzerland was packed with doctors and psychiatrists; maybe it wouldn't take long. He wouldn't tell Karen; she had once thought of him as strong and forceful . . .

"That's got nothing to do with it," she said. "Why on earth shouldn't I work?"

"Because I don't want a wife of mine having to," he said, recognizing as he spoke the same pride that kept him from telling her of his fear of a breakdown.

"That's rubbish!" she said. "I might have to soon." She dried and creamed the hands of which she was so proud and began shaping her nails with an emery board.

"Wait. Please," he said.

"What for?"

"Let's see what I can find."

"Haven't we waited long enough?"

She stared up from her manicure and for a moment Deaken thought his wife was going to continue arguing. Instead she made a half shrug with her shoulders and went back to her filing. He got up from the table, took a cloth and began wiping the crockery she had stacked into the draining tray. He was alongside her, but she didn't look at him.

"Why don't we meet for lunch?" he said.

"We can't . . ." she began and then stopped. "What time are you meeting this client?" she said instead.

"Eleven."

"What about?"

"I don't know. I can't imagine that it'll go on until lunchtime." Nothing had lasted that long, from the time he had arrived in Switzerland.

"Why don't I ring you around twelve thirty, just in case?"

"Fine," agreed Deaken. They had returned to the elaborate politeness of an hour before.

Because he was meeting a new client, the first for a month, Deaken wore the better of his two suits, the one with least shine at the seat and elbows. He returned to the kitchen from the bedroom for a cloth to give his shoes a final buff. When he straightened, Karen came forward and adjusted the knot of his tie. He reached out for her, feeling the stir of excitement at the touch of her body beneath the thin housecoat.

"Maybe today will be the big one," she said.

"Thanks," he said.

"What for?"

"Being kind."

She stretched up to kiss him. "Twelve thirty," she said.

"I'll be waiting."

Outside the apartment Deaken hesitated, at once aware that it had grown hotter since he had been out for the breakfast bread. He set out towards the water, turning left almost immediately up the rue de Rhône and then right, along a cross-street to take him to the avenue Pictet de Rochemont. It was too expensive an office, even huddled as it was like some afterthought atop the grander suites of bankers and accountants, but Deaken had wanted an impressive address. A mistake, he thought—like so much else. He went in through the main entrance, with its smoked glass and potted plants and uniformed doormen, feeling like an interloper, and took the lift as far as it would go. He emerged on the eighth floor, where the offices were already diminishing in size, and walked up the stairway to the top floor, which had been added at some time like icing to a cake. Here the flooring was linoleum, not marble or cork or tile, and the windows fronting the corridor had the smeared look of glass cleaned once a week by a charwoman with little enthusiasm. Deaken's office was the fourth along to the right but he stopped at the second because it was the one that Elian Fochet occupied. When he entered she was bent over a newspaper crossword.

"Anything?" he said.

"An offer for an out-of-hours answering service, without which no successful business is supposed to be able to operate, and a handout from American Express on the benefit of taking cards against the firm for employees' use," recited the woman. She hesitated and added, "Everyone got the same."

"Thanks," said Deaken.

"You've an appointment at eleven," she said. Elian Fochet was mousy-haired, absolutely flat-chested, and wore butterfly spectacles that had gone out of fashion years before. Deaken thought she looked exactly what she was, the shared secretary/receptionist for a group of people hanging on by their fingertips to some pretension of business. He wondered if she was a virgin.

"I know," he said.

"Do you want me to serve coffee?"

"No, thank you," said Deaken. Her coffee was appalling.

"It won't be any trouble."

"No, really."

She offered him the circulars but he shook his head. She threw them in the waste basket.

He continued on to his own office, unlocked the door and stood at the entrance. The cheap carpet still looked presentable. So did the couch along one wall and the matching chair in front of the desk. He could have got away with the imitation black leather chair, high-backed and padded-armed, behind it, but the desk was ply and looked it, despite the attempt to disguise it with varnish. The inset, too, was clearly plastic and not leather. Nothing he could do about it now though. From a bottom drawer of the desk Deaken took a duster and wiped the desk top, then the sparsely filled filing cabinet and after that the windowsill. He slanted the venetian blinds, lessening the light coming into the room, and then looked over his shoulder. Better, he decided. Not much better. He dusted the telephone which rarely rang, returned the cloth to its drawer, and from the one above took out his clean notepad; there were six pencils in a cup to the right, all needle sharp. That's how he'd occupied the last hour of the previous day.

It was ridiculous to continue like this. He had to do

something. And do it soon. The erosion of self-confidence had been insidious. A run of bad trial results—not surprising considering the sort of trials they were—and he had suddenly decided to take a rest. Expand my experience in civil litigation, he'd told everyone. Except that he hadn't been offered any civil litigation and doubts about his own ability had intensified, until now he wasn't sure if he could handle a case even if it were offered. Help, he thought, that's what he needed. Professional medical help. There would be no reason for Karen to know he was having treatment. Easy enough to arrange appointments and sessions during the day.

What about the real cause of the rows and their increasingly strained relationship? He was frightened of parenthood, Deaken admitted to himself. Of seeing Karen balloon into awkward ugliness, nine months of worrying whether the child would be born properly formed and not with some mental or physical disability. Was he unusual, thinking like that? Unnatural even? He knew Karen was determined to become pregnant; just as he was determined against it. Get the job settled first, he thought. The baby could come later. *Richard Deaken, on the run again.*

Because of the glass fronting he was aware of the shadowed approach, even before the peremptory knock on the door. Deaken just managed to stand before the man got into the room. He was tall and broad-shouldered, with clipped fair hair and a sun-tanned, open face; the sort of man to play rugby or tennis, Deaken thought.

One look encompassed the room and Deaken knew the shading from the venetian blinds hadn't worked. Shit, he thought.

The man offered his hand. "Rupert Underberg," he said.

The contact was dry, businesslike; for the first time Deaken put the name in possible context. The accent was bland but there could have been the slightest trace of South Africa.

When Underberg sat in the chair indicated, Deaken realized his face was almost completely shadowed in the effort to put the office in better light. Deaken glanced at his wristwatch. Underberg was ten minutes early. The man looked again around the office, more critically this time. Deaken had no doubt he could manage lunch with Karen. He would probably have time to plait several yards of paperclips. Except that he didn't have sufficient for several yards. He normally collected these from incoming mail. It was thoughtless not to have accepted the brochures from the answering service and American Express this morning.

"You didn't make it clear in your telephone call what exactly it was that I could do for you, Mr Underberg," said Deaken.

"I didn't know then," said the man. "Now I do."

"What is it?"

"Negotiate for me," said Underberg. "Negotiate something very difficult. And special."

Deaken felt a spurt of interest. He took one of the painstakingly sharpened pencils from the coffee cup, wrote "Underberg" on the pad, underlined it twice and then looked up.

"Why don't we talk about it and I'll see if I can help?" he said.

"Oh, I think you'll be able to help."

Deaken inscribed a third line beneath the man's name. "How?" he said, mildly irritated by the man's attitude.

"Do you know Adnan Azziz?"

Deaken frowned briefly, then he remembered. "The Saudi Arabian?"

"Arms dealer," continued Underberg. "The biggest."

"Yes," said Deaken, "I know of him."

"He kills people," said Underberg. "Not directly; he never does anything directly."

Deaken leaned forward over his desk, hand against his forehead to shield his face as much as possible from the other man. The words had an ominously familiar ring. He

had appeared in civil-rights trials, either as the leading
defence advocate or as the supporting advisory counsel to
lawyers of the country, in Germany and America and
Chile and Nicaragua and Turkey and Ireland and South
Africa. And so often his involvement had begun with a
meeting like this and with words like these. Not me, he
thought. I can't do it anymore. I've lost the enthusiasm,
I've lost the anger. I just want to be left alone.

"I don't think this is for me," he said.

"Oh, yes, it is," said Underberg.

Deaken's apprehension tightened.

"I know all about you, Richard Deaken," said Underberg.
"I know that in South Africa your father is a leading
member of the Nationalist government, a predicted cabinet
minister, which he would have been much sooner if it
wasn't for the embarrassment of having a famous son. Up
to a year ago there wasn't a better-known civil-rights
lawyer than you anywhere in the world; not many people
simultaneously get the cover story in *Time* and *Newsweek,*
you know. What's happened in the last year? Lost your
taste for fighting?"

"Who are you?" demanded Deaken.

The man smiled, baring his teeth again, and stretched
back in the chair.

"The man you're going to work for."

"Get out," said Deaken.

"You're going to negotiate for me with Adnan Azziz,"
said Underberg, his voice measured and confident.

Deaken stood up. "Please get out of my office."

Underberg settled farther in his chair. "We have information that Adnan Azziz has completed an arms deal
worth something like $50,000,000 with terrorists in An-
gola and Namibia. It goes beyond RPG rocket launchers,
up to wire-controlled tank and antipersonnel carrier missiles,
which we presume the Soviet advisers intend to operate,
because the SWAPO guerrillas certainly haven't got the
ability. Thousands of AK-47 rifles and tens of thousands

of rounds of ammunition. And not just communist weapons. We know there are crates of American Armalite rifles, again with tons of ammunition . . ."

"I don't want to know," said Deaken. He was still standing and felt vaguely ridiculous.

"It's important that you know," said Underberg, like a patient schoolmaster.

"I've already told you I won't take instructions," said Deaken with growing exasperation. "For God's sake, get out of my office."

"It's for a massive assault in Namibia," continued Underberg, as if the lawyer hadn't interrupted. "We think it's timed for mid-July. We've no definite date, but we know that's the month. We'll find out soon enough."

"For what?" Deaken's question was automatic, without proper thought.

Underberg's teeth showed, in his piranha smile. "To stop it happening, of course," he said. "It's scheduled to be their big show, the one that will finally sway public opinion against South Africa in favour of the United Nations' initiative. They're even going to invite the world's press, to report it. Only it won't quite be the story they expect."

Deaken sat down. Underberg obviously had no intention of leaving, and there was no way he could make him.

"We've infiltrated SWAPO up to here," said Underberg, putting his hand beneath his chin. "We're going to mount a counteroffensive they couldn't imagine possible and annihilate the whole movement in one decisive battle." He shifted, trying both for effect and a more comfortable position in the cramped chair. "Because we're going to have helicopters and tanks and guns and rifles and missiles and they're going to be grabbing for bows and arrows and spears."

"You said they'd purchased $50,000,000 worth of weaponry," said Deaken.

"Which they're never going to see," said Underberg. "You will get Azziz to deflect the shipment."

"Don't be ridiculous."

"Everything's been thought out very carefully, Mr Deaken. It'll work, exactly as we intend it to."

Deaken shook his head. This wasn't the sort of job he had hoped to impress Karen with at lunch.

"Azziz has a son of eighteen," said Underberg. "A very attractive, if indulged, child. This morning he was kidnapped on his way to join his father for his summer vacation."

"Jesus Christ!" erupted Deaken. "You know I can't listen to any of this. You're mad."

"No," said Underberg. "Just determined."

"I could have you arrested the moment you leave here."

For the first time the man's amusement seemed genuine. "It'll take the police or any other force hours to get here, even if they believed you. By which time I could be halfway across Europe. I understand your attitude . . . I really do. I actually feel sorry for you."

"I told you once to get out," said Deaken, burned by an awareness of utter impotence. "Now I'm telling you again. Get out of this office. I don't believe a word you've said, but I still intend informing the police." He snatched at the telephone, immediately aware that he didn't know what number to ring; the instrument growled demandingly in his ear.

"Put it down," said Underberg. "No one can get through to you if the receiver is off the rest."

Deaken remained with the receiver held before him. Underberg reached over the desk and depressed the telephone rest. The growling stopped. "Put it down," said the man again. "Please."

Slowly Deaken did what he was told.

"Thank you," said Underberg. He looked at his watch. "No harm will come to the boy," he said, his voice even and conversational. "You're to assure Azziz of that. If he does what we want, his son will be released unharmed and quite safe."

The telephone jarred into the room. Deaken jumped. It was too early for Karen, far too early.

"Shouldn't you answer it?" said Underberg.

Deaken obeyed.

"Richard," said a voice he recognized at once as Karen's. "I'm with two men. They came to the apartment just after you left and said you wanted to see me . . . so I went . . . they've told me to telephone you . . ."

Deaken tried to swallow, against the sensation in his throat.

"I've come a long way in a car . . . I'm frightened," said his wife's voice. "What's happening, Richard?"

They drove fast, anxious to cross the border, the speedometer needle registering the permitted maximum on every road, although they were cautious never to exceed it and risk interception by the police. The bodyguards had been under observation for two months, but their body weight was still only an estimate; the reduced Oblivon inoculation had been carefully measured against that body weight, but there was always the possibility they would recover earlier than the scheduled hour. And that they would ignore the instructions and raise an official alarm, sealing off the country.

They chose Basel.

As the Citroën joined the queue of vehicles edging into France, the curly-haired man arranged an anorak across his lap, covering the Magnum he wedged against Azziz's knee.

"We'll be watching you, not just from both sides but from the front as well," warned the man. "The slightest mistake when we come to the check and I'll blow your leg off."

It was the height of the holiday season and the busiest time of the day, when the customs officials were under the greatest pressure to keep the tourist flow moving in both directions. The passport checks were cursory.

"Very good," said the man, as the car picked up speed and began to descend into France. "I'm glad your people did what they were told."

"Take the gun away," said Azziz. It was an order, not a request.

The man did.

"Where are we going?" asked the boy.

"Not much farther."

"My father will pay, you know. Whatever you ask for, he'll pay."

"I hope you're right."

The tension lifted from the men in the vehicle now that the border had been crossed. The driver still kept within the speed limit.

They went through St Louis and then, almost at once, Huningue. Mulhouse was already being signposted but they turned off the main road to Rixheim.

Three of the men, keeping Azziz between them, got out at the farmhouse. The driver kept the engine running, using the gate entrance to make his turn and go back towards the main road.

It was a square, three-storey, yellow-brick building, with white shutters freshly painted and strapped back alongside each set of windows. It was no longer a farm. The surrounding fields were rented to a neighbouring farmer and the main house given over to holiday rentals; a boule set was neatly arranged at one end of the gravel drive and the immaculately clipped lawns through which they walked were set with a garden table and chairs and a canopied swing seat. Everything was new and white-painted; the canopy and seats were striped bright green. The thick oak door led immediately into the main communal room. It occupied almost half the ground floor and was dominated by a huge open fireplace at one end; racks and spits of a curing system were still in place. There were vases of flowers on the central table and on the large open dresser and sideboard. As they entered, a man emerged from what was clearly the adjoining kitchen. He nodded towards them but said nothing.

Azziz stood by the central table, looking around him curiously. He was a black-haired, deeply brown-eyed boy, tall and athletically slim; already his father's London staff were inquiring about stabling facilities for his polo ponies in the Cambridge area. He held himself disdainfully erect.

"What now?" he said.

"We wait," said the only man who ever spoke.

"You talked in Arabic at the airport."

"Yes."

"But you're not an Arab."

"No."

Momentarily Azziz's demeanour faltered. "Israeli?"

"Zionist."

Seeing the boy's alarm, the man added, "You won't be harmed, providing your father does as we ask."

"How are you called?"

"Shimeon," said the man. "Shimeon Levy."

"A good enough pseudonym," said the boy.

"It's my given name," said Levy. "I'm not afraid of people knowing it: they will soon enough."

Captain Erlander returned from the port office by eleven. Edmunson was aft, on the gangway deck, supervising the loading, and the captain turned away from the bridge approach, going towards the stern.

"How is it?" he said.

"Another six tons," said the first officer.

"An hour then?"

"Give me two, just in case there's a holdup."

"Three-o'clock castoff," decided Erlander. "The forecast is good so we can clear the Strait by midnight."

Erlander saw the other man frown and smiled at the doubt. "Dawn then," he said. "I want to get rid of this cargo as soon as I can."

There was a workers' café in the docks and from one of

its windows a man had patiently watched the loading. He was dressed in overalls, like other customers, but appeared uncomfortable with his dress and his surroundings. He was an African. His name was Edward Makimber.

3

Richard Deaken sat hunched forward over the desk, staring fixedly at the other man. He was sick with anger and impotence, the feeling of nausea churning through him, sour in his mouth. He was aware, too, of something else. He was frightened.

"Where is she?"

"Not in Geneva."

"Bastard!"

"Don't be stupid," said Underberg. "I give you my word she won't be harmed . . . or bothered in any way."

"What good is your word?"

"It's all you've got."

"Why?" pleaded Deaken desperately. "Why me? If you've got the boy, why not deal with Azziz direct?"

Underberg shook his head. "It wouldn't work half as well. It's been carefully planned."

Deaken looked away from the patronizing, self-satisfied man. Think; he had to think! Like the trained lawyer he had once been; still was. Christ, he was frightened!

"It won't work," Deaken said. He took up one of his sharpened pencils, tracing squares on the paper in front of him as he arranged his argument. "Let's say I get through to Azziz. And let's say he believes me and diverts the shipment. So what? He'll have met the demands, he gets his son back and then all he's got to do is assemble another shipment. You said yourself he's the biggest there is; he's got the resources."

Underberg laughed. "But that's precisely *why* you're involved. Why we've got your wife."

Deaken thought how he would like to smash his fist into that face, not just once but over and over again.

"A second shipment doesn't matter," Underberg said. "I've already told you the SWAPO buildup is underway for an assault in July. Once it's stopped, there won't be time for Azziz to arrange another. But he'll try something, he's the sort of man who has to. Which is why you're so essential. We need someone in the middle. Someone who can report every move. We don't want to negotiate in the dark."

The emotion surged through Deaken, making him shake; his legs were tightly together, feet braced against the floor, his hands pressed against the desk top.

"It would be natural for you to try and hit me," anticipated Underberg, in his even, unmoved voice. "I'd feel the same way myself, if I were you. But don't try it—I'd knock the shit out of you."

Deaken's eyes flooded at his own helplessness. "Don't hurt her," he begged. "Please don't hurt her."

"I've already promised you that."

Deaken pushed his hand across his face. Where was the cohesion to his thoughts, the logic that had made him best of his year at Rand University? "How do we keep in touch? Where do I go?"

Underberg reached into his inside pocket. "There's an air ticket to Nice. The evening flight," he said. "Azziz is in Monte Carlo . . ." From an opposite pocket the man extracted an envelope. "Money," he said. "We know you haven't got any and you'll need it . . ." The third item was a single sheet of paper. "Telephone numbers," listed Underberg. "The first is a public kiosk on the quayside at Monte Carlo, the Quai des Etats-Unis. The second is of the Bristol Hotel. If you haven't been to Monte Carlo before, it's on the boulevard Albert."

"There's got to be more than that!" protested Deaken.

Underberg shook his head. "Contact will always come from us, never from you. Be by that quayside kiosk at noon every day. If it's engaged for any protracted length of time, or broken for some reason, then go to the Bristol at four the same afternoon and we'll call you there—nothing will ever go wrong with the telephone system of a hotel like the Bristol."

It made them absolutely secure, Deaken realized. "I want to know something," he said.

"What?"

"Does my father know anything about this?"

"Nothing," insisted Underberg. "And there must be no contact between you—we'd know, if there were. You'll be watched, all the time. You won't know, but we'll always be around."

"When will I get Karen back?"

"When we're satisfied."

"You control me as long as she's safe," said Deaken. "If anything happens to her, your pressure goes . . ." He stopped, unsure of the threat. Then he said, "If anything does happen to her, I'll hunt you down. Wherever and however, I'll hunt you down and kill you."

"Of course you will," said Underberg calmly.

Karen Deaken walked apprehensively into the farmhouse, staring about her warily. Her hair was straggled and she had been crying. She looked crumpled and small beside the huge-bellied, bearded man who had brought her from Switzerland, through the same unhindered crossing at Basel. At once Levy crossed the room towards her.

"You mustn't be frightened," he said soothingly. "Everything is going to work out all right. I promise."

"Fear never hurt anybody," said the bearded man, whose name was Solomon Leiberwitz.

"Stop it!" Levy said to him. To Karen he said, "Don't worry."

She looked at him. He smiled. She responded, nervously, then realized what she was doing and straightened her face. "What do you want?"

Levy gestured towards the bench alongside the fireplace where Tewfik Azziz sat. "For the moment," he said, "just for you to sit next to him, over there."

"What for?"

"We want to take your photograph," said the Israeli. "Together."

4

Adnan Mohammed Azziz was a man conscious of his importance and content with the security and respect it accorded him. He was one of a number of men—another was his country's oil minister—born outside the dynastic hierarchy of brothers and cousins of the Saudi monarchy, but accepted within it and even accorded the honorary title of Sheik because he was a successful traveller, in both directions, across the bridge between the isolated, religiously dominated court of Riyadh and the commercial elbow-jostle of the West. His unique and peculiar empire had been founded by his father, who by camel pack had supplied the weapons that enabled Ibn Saud to surge in from his nomad's camp, storm a desert fort and establish his as the predominant family in a kingdom where oil was yet to be discovered. The father had taught the son and Adnan Azziz had been a diligent pupil, not just in a goatskin tent, but later, after the oil came, at Oxford and then the Business School at Harvard. A dynasty created by arms never forgets their necessity, even when the tradition changes from muzzle loaders and Lee Enfields to radar systems, missiles and supersonic jet fighters. Azziz served his country well and himself better. With seemingly inexhaustible funds at his disposal he arranged payment by percentage of what he purchased, and began his very first negotiation fully aware of the commission that would be available from the grateful manufacturer. He was neither greedy nor careless, remembering his father's teaching that a man fortunate to enjoy curds every day misses them all the more when they are denied him. He traded hard but always fairly, never leaving dissatisfied the seller with whom he dealt or the purchaser for whom he acted. Another of his father's teachings was that the gold merchants of the souk frequently began as copper beaters: Azziz applied for and was granted court permission to act for others, expanding his expertise and influence to the benefit of his country, and his fortune to the benefit of himself.

It took him twenty years to become the largest and most successful independent arms dealer in the world. In so doing, Adnan Azziz became a truly international man, as comfortable in a *galabeeyeh* in his palace overlooking the Red Sea near Jedda as he was hosting a cocktail party, at which he only ever drank orange juice, in his penthouse on the corner of New York's Fifth Avenue and 61st Street or in his Regency town house in South Audley Street, running parallel with London's Park Lane.

But he was most comfortable of all aboard the *Scheherazade*. It was a large, white, elaborate and sophisti-

cated yacht, 4000 tons in weight, diesel-powered and with
a crew complement of fifty. They were as specialized as
the vessel in which they served. Six men were employed
to operate communication equipment equal to that of American naval cruisers and necessary to maintain constant and
uninterrupted liaison with Azziz's world-spanning business
links; part consisted of two computers and a location-and-
fix device programmed for orbital navigational satellites.
The fifty did not include the ten-man team necessary to
service, maintain and fly the stern-housed Alouette nor the
immediate legal staff, at least two of whom were normally
in constant attendance wherever Azziz was domiciled at
any time.

They were led by an American named Harry Grearson,
who was with Azziz when the panicked telephone call
came from Zürich airport. The open emotion came
entirely from Switzerland; the nature of his business had
taught Azziz complete control, even when being told of
the abduction of his only son. His voice kept to a mono-
tone when he recounted the conversation to Grearson in
the stateroom of the yacht.

"Who are they?" Like his employer, the lawyer remained quiet-voiced.

"There was no indication, apart from the fact that they
spoke Arabic as well as English," said Azziz. He was an
imposing man, tall and full-bodied, the stature increased
by the fact that the weight was not indulgence but muscle.
He wore white ducks, a blue short-sleeved shirt and was
completely naked of any jewellery, even a wristwatch.

"You've informed the police?"

"No," said Azziz at once. "We were warned not to."

"That's a mistake," said Grearson.

"Better this way," insisted the Arab. "I'll meet the
demand, whatever it is." Tewfik's mother had died in
childbirth, and despite taking three more wives, as Azziz
was allowed by Moslem law, his four other children were
all daughters.

"What have you told your people to do?"

"Fly back here, so I can question them more fully."

"There was nothing left in the car . . . no note or letter?"

"Apparently not."

"It shouldn't have happened, not with three of them."

"I know," said Azziz. "So do they."

"Would any Arab faction have cause to attack you?"

Azziz shrugged. "I don't know of a particular reason. I supplied the Shah, so the Iranian fundamentalists could regard me as an enemy."

"They don't have the organization," judged Grearson.

Azziz lifted the internal telephone, dialled the communications room and asked to be told the moment the Alouette radioed landing instructions.

"It could be purely criminal, without any political implications," said Grearson. He was a lean, grey-haired man who wore rimless glasses which he was constantly adjusting, arranging them back and forth along the bridge of his long aquiline nose. He never wore anything but a business suit; today it was dark blue and waistcoated and seemed incongruous in the surroundings of the yacht. "Do we get him back ourselves?"

"We'll need someone," Azziz agreed.

"Who?"

"Professionals," decided Azziz. "Soldiers. But not yet. Let's see what they want. It might not be necessary."

The internal telephone purred softly. Azziz listened, without talking, and then said to the lawyer, "They're here."

Led by Williams, the three men who had failed to prevent Tewfik Azziz's kidnap came single file into the stateroom. The American was clearly nervous, the Bedouins terrified.

"Once more," demanded Azziz. "What happened?" The voice was still quiet.

Williams started hurriedly but Azziz stopped him at

once, ordering him to begin again; and this time neither Azziz nor Grearson interrupted. When Williams had finished Azziz told the Bedouins to recount their version in Arabic. It took longer, because of the two men's fear and because they interrupted each other in the telling.

When they finished Azziz interrogated Williams and the Bedouins, to ensure the stories matched and that nothing had been missed.

"Eight men then?" he said.

"That I counted," confirmed Williams. "There could have been more in charge of transport."

Remembering Williams's Green Beret service, Grearson said, "Any indication that they were military?"

Williams thought about the question. "Obviously it had been carefully planned, but I didn't get a marked impression of drilling."

"The medical gun is intriguing," said Grearson. To Williams he said, "The three of you recovered almost simultaneously?"

Williams nodded agreement. "Within a moment or two of each other. About an hour."

For Grearson's benefit, Azziz said, "I've asked about any accent in the Arabic that was spoken. They say it could have been Palestinian or Jordanian: maybe even Iraqi."

Grearson grimaced. "Too wide," he said.

"No liberation group would have cause to do it," said Azziz. "I've supported them, with both money and weapons."

"I'm sorry," said Williams. "Very sorry."

Azziz looked steadily at the man for several moments. Then he said simply, "Yes."

"I think we should inform the police," said Grearson again.

"We'll wait," said Azziz.

"For how long?" asked the lawyer.

"As long as it takes," said Azziz with Arab fatalism.

It was another five hours. The package had been delivered by hand to the harbour office at Monte Carlo and was brought back in the yacht's tender, doing the evening mail run. Grearson saw that Azziz's hands were quite steady as he slit it open. It was a coloured Polaroid picture of Tewfik Azziz and a woman neither of them recognized, sitting stiffly upright on a bench alongside what appeared to be a wide fireplace. A flash had been used in what must have been quite strong sunlight, so the picture was overexposed.

"Just a photograph?" queried Grearson.

Azziz turned it over. "A name," he said. "Richard Deaken. With what appear to be some letters of qualifications."

Grearson took the photograph. "It's a lawyer's degree," he identified immediately. "Several, in fact."

While Grearson was examining the picture, the Arab opened the second letter to arrive that night, scanning it briefly. "It's the school report," he said softly. "They're confident of his getting into Cambridge."

As he spoke Richard Deaken was disembarking at Nice airport from the evening flight from Geneva. Six hours had elapsed since the confrontation with Underberg and he still felt confused.

They had been identified to each other when the photograph was taken and separated immediately afterwards, both locked in separate bedrooms at either end of the house. In each a securing bar closed the outer shutters across the outside of the windows, which had been screwed down so that it was impossible to open them, even slightly. Into the frames, steel bars had bean newly fitted. A portable toilet was set in the corner of each room, and each had a washstand, with a flower-decorated bowl and matching pitcher. The wardrobes were empty, except for hangers.

When they were fetched for the evening meal, Karen was sitting on the very edge of the bed, staring towards the

door. Azziz was asleep, so he was the last to enter the
downstairs room. Only Levy sat down with them at the
table.

Azziz stretched up to look into the tureen and said, "Is
this meat kosher?"

"No," said Levy.

"I want to be sure."

"Don't eat it if you don't want to," said the Israeli.
"There's plenty of cheese and fruit."

He offered the dish to Karen. She had combed her hair
and applied some fresh lipstick but her eyes were still red.
She hesitated and then ladled a small amount onto her
plate; it was lamb, flavoured with just the right amount of
garlic. Levy helped himself and then pushed the tureen
towards Azziz. The boy stared at a piece of meat he had
manoeuvred onto his ladle, and then served himself.

The wine was local, in an unmarked bottle. Levy gestured towards Karen's glass. She hesitated again and then
nodded. Indicating a jug, Levy said to Azziz, "I assumed
you'd want water."

"Why is Mrs Deaken involved in this?" demanded
Azziz.

"Her husband is necessary," said Levy. He broke some
bread from a stick.

"What's happening to Richard?" she blurted.

"Nothing," Levy said gently. "He's working . . . doing
a job, that's all. He's quite safe."

Azziz put more of the stew onto his plate, then looked
across the table at the man. "Is it new Jewish strategy to
fight with women?"

Levy pushed aside his plate, cut a portion of goat's
cheese and then took an apple to eat with it. He looked
down, concentrating upon peeling the fruit. "Our argument isn't with you," he said. "Nor with Arabs even, not
directly."

Azziz frowned and said, "I don't understand."

"It's not necessary for you to," said Levy.

"How long are you going to keep me here?" said Karen. She wished her voice had been stronger.

"No longer than we have to," said Levy. "A few days I hope, that's all."

"And me?" asked Azziz.

"The same."

After the meal there was coffee, freshly ground and as good as everything else. They remained at the table to drink it.

"Tomorrow there will be some books," promised Levy. "And games. I'm getting a backgammon set." He looked at Karen. "Do you play?"

"No," she said.

"Pity." Levy turned to the Arab. "You'll be allowed out into the garden to exercise. Watched, of course. And not together."

"One acting as hostage for the other?" seized the boy.

"Yes," said Levy simply. "We don't want to hurt you, either of you."

"Unless absolutely necessary," goaded Azziz.

"I won't argue with you," said Levy. "There's no purpose in it."

He summoned Leiberwitz to escort Azziz back to his room. He took Karen himself. At the bedroom door he said, "I know you came away from Geneva with nothing. I don't want you to be embarrassed—if there's anything you need . . . anything personal, make a list and I'll get it for you."

"Thank you."

"Even underwear," he said. "I'll get it myself."

She thought he was more discomfited than she was.

"Don't be afraid, about the men I mean," he said. "You won't be troubled."

"Thank you," she said again.

"I wanted you to know."

"This isn't what I expected," she said.

"Nor me," admitted the man.

5

The *Scheherazade* was arranged like a gaudy ornament on the skyline, lit brilliantly overall; there was even some form of underwater illumination so that the hull was visible along its entire length. Because of the lighting, Deaken had seen the tender cream away from the side of the vessel while he was still linked by radio telephone from the harbour master's office to Adnan Azziz. Away from the yacht, it merged into the blackness of the intervening sea. Deaken became conscious of the telephone bank and hurried to it; the number he had been given earlier that day in Geneva was the second box from the left. He looked hard at it, then lifted the receiver. Nothing appeared wrong with it. He turned back towards the most obvious quay steps. Almost at once, the tender emerged from the darkness; there appeared to be a crew of three and a man in civilian clothes. As Deaken looked the man stood up and moved to the side of the vessel that was being brought against the harbour edge. Grey-haired, thin almost to the point of gauntness, official-looking, thought Deaken. He waved unthinkingly, self-consciously stopping the gesture half completed. There was no response from the tender. Two crewmen fended off, making no attempt to secure. The helmsman kept the boat expertly in place by reverse and forward thrusts of the engine.

"Deaken?" said the man in the suit.

"Yes."

"Grearson. Mr Azziz's attorney."

Deaken stepped awkwardly into the boat. At once it moved away, putting him further off balance. Deaken held a side rail and offered his hand. Grearson looked as if it were holding something offensive.

In silence they travelled towards the *Scheherazade*. They were so close it seemed to dominate the skyline now. Deaken thought it looked more like a liner than a yacht. There was a stepped walkway, wider than stairs in normal houses, let down from the side, with a flat landing stage at the bottom, three feet above the lifting sea. The tender coasted perfectly alongside. Deaken followed the other lawyer out as awkwardly as he had boarded; as he climbed he saw the davit hawsers dangling ahead, ready to lift the tender. The winch had whined into operation by the time he gained the deck. Deaken looked around expectantly but, apart from the crew waiting to ease the tender into its cradle, it was deserted.

"This way," said Grearson.

Deaken followed obediently, aware of a clumsiness in the other man's walk: it was not a limp, more the cautious stiffness of someone nervous of pain. As soon as Deaken went inside the yacht, he was aware of the smell. Cigars, clearly, and perhaps perfume or incense. Combined, it was an odour of richness, luxurious richness. The inner companionways were deeply carpeted and the panelling a dark, heavy mahogany. Where there was metalwork, it gleamed from constant polishing. The companionway led to a landing that crossed the width of the ship and from it, in a double-sided descent of steps, ran a stairway that reminded Deaken of the circle approach in a cinema or theatre. It was, indeed, an approach culminating not in walkways along a lower deck but in a large set of double-fronted doors, highly polished and dark wood again. Grearson, who was still in front, knocked and entered immediately, leaving the door open for Deaken to follow.

The young lawyer stopped just inside the door. Only the roundness of the portholes showed they were aboard a ship. Deaken guessed a hundred people could have gathered in the stateroom here for a reception without the slightest impression of overcrowding. Padded seating, in white leather, around the bulkheads was broken intermittently by tables from which flowers spilled in profusion. There were larger easy chairs and couches, again in masculine leather, arranged around the room, and two small writing bureaux with a third, lower table upon which were grouped four telephones. There was no colour differentiation; they were all white. To Deaken's immediate left there was a bar area, with a steward in attendance, a glitter of glass and chrome and four high-legged chairs. The carpeting throughout the entire area was white and long-tufted.

The man who stood waiting in the middle of the room dominated it, not because of his height and barrel body but from the way he held himself. When he was young, Deaken had attended government and diplomatic functions with his father and seen the same demeanour: it was always from politicians or leaders who were long established, who considered themselves unchallengeable.

The man was as severely dressed as the American lawyer, in a dark grey, single-breasted suit in some material that shone slightly, but not from overwear. It was probably silk. Like everything, it went with the perfume of wealth.

"I am Adnan Azziz," he said. The English was entirely without accent.

"Richard Deaken."

"Yes." The voice was expressionless, neither hostile nor friendly.

"There's a mistake," said Deaken desperately. "A misunderstanding . . ."

"We've obeyed your instructions," cut in Azziz. "Tell me what you want."

"They are not *my* instructions," exclaimed Deaken.

"I want my son back, unharmed," said Azziz.

Deaken was overwhelmed by a feeling of inadequacy. He was aware of his concertinaed, bagged suit and a collar that his tie didn't fit properly, the tie that Karen had tried to adjust for him that morning, the last time she had touched him and of his fly-away hair and of the stickiness of his skin, where he had sweated in fear of Underberg and then because he had travelled too far too fast on overheated aircraft and was confronting people he didn't want to meet. God, he thought; oh dear God!

"They've taken my wife," he said simply.

Neither man facing him made any response.

"Didn't you hear what I said!" demanded Deaken. "They've kidnapped my wife. This morning. To make me do this . . . come here . . ."

Azziz looked sideways to Grearson.

"I said we knew about you," repeated the American lawyer. He reached to one of the small tables and picked up what appeared to be a telex printout. "You were considered a radical at Rand University," he said. "After qualifying in international law you were actively involved with subversive movements . . ." He looked up. "Became famous through it," he said.

Deaken closed his eyes against the catalogue. It was like a criminal record, a list of previous convictions to be presented at every opportunity.

"No more," he said wearily. "I'm married now. Trying to establish a private practice . . ."

". . . in Geneva," picked up Grearson, still consulting the paper and wanting to show Azziz how efficiently he had assembled the information from just the qualification initials after Deaken's name on the photograph. "Operating there for a year."

"Listen," said Deaken. "Please just listen." Haltingly at first, anxious for some reaction from the blank, closed faces in front of him, Deaken recounted what had happened in Geneva, setting it out chronologically, as he would have done in court.

"A shipment to Africa?" queried Azziz.

"That's what he said."

The Arab looked to his lawyer again. Grearson shook his head.

"Surely you know about it?" insisted Deaken. "It's for $50,000,000, for God's sake!"

"Which is a comparatively small amount," said Azziz.

"It could be a subsidiary sale," said Grearson, talking to the Arab. "There would never have been an End-User certificate if it is going to Africa."

Deaken frowned between the two men.

"Check it, tonight if you can" ordered Azziz.

As Grearson moved to the telephone bank Azziz said to Deaken, "What's your wife like?"

"What?"

"Describe her."

Inexplicably Deaken felt embarrassed. "Blonde," he said. "She wears it short. Brown eyes. Doesn't use a lot of makeup—doesn't have to. Quite short, about five foot five. Slim, too."

From the table from which the lawyer had taken the telex sheet, the Arab handed Deaken a photograph. Deaken's eyes flooded when he saw her and he blinked. She was holding herself stiffly upright, legs tightly together, shoulders squared. There was a school photograph of Karen like that, back in the apartment. Except that there she was smiling.

"You knew," said Deaken, looking up to Azziz.

"Putting her in the picture doesn't mean she's a victim . . . it could have been done to support your story."

"Does she look like an accomplice?" said Deaken. "Look at it! Does she?"

Azziz took the photograph back. "No," he admitted after a pause.

"I want her back safely," said Deaken. "Just like you want your son back."

Azziz smiled, for the first time. "If all it means is stopping a small arms shipment, it'll be easy."

At 2 A.M. the *Bellicose* cleared the Strait of Gibraltar. Edmunson was the officer of the watch. He ordered the freighter's course twenty degrees to port and entered the reading in the rough log. He was conscious of the ship heaving in the more exposed North Atlantic, but knew from the forecast that the swell was moderate. If the weather held, it was going to be an easy, uneventful voyage.

A thousand miles away, from the yacht in Monte Carlo harbour, Grearson put down the telephone from his fifth call.

"France," he announced to the waiting men.

6

They had only bothered with sandwiches and coffee, served and then immediately removed by hovering stewards. In the beginning Azziz and Grearson had talked across him but now they included him in the conversation and listened to his opinions.

"Marseilles is convenient," said the Arab.

"Paris thinks the ship has left already; we shan't know until the port office opens in the morning," said Grearson.

"I thought you said you couldn't ship direct," said Deaken.

Grearson hesitated. "The End-User certificate was arranged through Portugal," he said.

"The what?"

"End-User certificate," repeated the other lawyer. "It's the official documentation, stipulating the destination of any shipment for the benefit of the authorities."

"How does it work for this consignment?"

"They've been sold to a Portuguese arms company, with the Azores given as the port of unloading. During the voyage they will be resold to one of our other companies and the ship advised at sea of a different destination."

"And not more than one or two Portuguese officials know of the transaction?" anticipated Deaken.

"It's a system that works," said Azziz. He looked attentively at Deaken as if expecting criticism. The South African said nothing.

"I'm still not happy about excluding the authorities from the kidnap," said Grearson, picking up the Polaroid photograph which lay between them and staring down at it.

"I didn't consider there was a choice," said Deaken.

"Nor I," said Azziz.

"But I think we could do more," said Deaken, pleased as first one, then a jumble of ideas occurred to him. He reached forward for the picture. "Cornflowers and daisies," he said, indicating the vases of flowers visible on the table and sideboard.

"So what?" said Azziz.

"Underberg's appointment with me was for eleven. He was early, by fifteen minutes. The call came from Karen at about eleven thirty. . . . What time was the boy snatched?"

"About eleven thirty," said Azziz.

Deaken nodded. " 'Just after you left,' " he recited. "That's what Karen said, when she called. By the time they grabbed your son, they'd already had Karen for over an hour."

Grearson shook his head. "I don't understand."

"The distance," said Deaken. "They had to put the boy and Karen together. And Geneva is . . ." He paused, making a quick calculation. ". . . Over a hundred and fifty miles from Zürich." He turned to Azziz. "I want a map. And compasses," he said.

The look of annoyance from Azziz, a man who normally gave orders and never took them, was momentary. He gave the instruction to a steward.

Deaken smiled, happy with the way his mind was working at last—it had been a long time. To Grearson he said, "What's the first thing the authorities would do, told of a kidnap like this?"

The American lawyer didn't reply immediately. Then he said, "Seal the borders."

"Right," said Deaken.

The steward returned with maps and compasses from the navigation room and handed them to Azziz. The Arab passed them immediately to Deaken.

"They wouldn't have taken any chances with the speed limit," guessed Deaken. "That's thirty-seven miles in the cities, sixty-two outside . . ." Deaken found the map and squinted over it. "Basel," he said, looking up.

"Why?" demanded Grearson.

"A good road to the nearest crossing," said Deaken. "Not more than five or six towns where they would have to slow. Let's say they averaged fifty miles per hour. Zürich is fifty-three miles from Basel . . ." To Azziz he said, "How long were the bodyguards unconscious?"

"They estimate an hour."

"Which fits. Just time for them to get across the border."

"There seems to be a lot of supposition," protested Grearson.

"Not too much," insisted Deaken, poring over his maps. "If Tewfik was the important one, then Karen would have been taken north. There's a motorway from Geneva to Lausanne and then again from Bern to Zürich. It would have been an extended route, but worth it for the speed. What time was the photograph delivered at the port office?''

"Six," said Grearson at once. "I checked. It was personally delivered, not part of the normal postal run . . ." Seeing the expectancy on Deaken's face, Grearson said, "No, they couldn't remember what the messenger looked like; there's always a lot of activity in the office at that time of the evening. And there are frequently personal deliveries for Mr Azziz.''

Deaken went back to his maps, of northern France now. "I was specifically told what flight to catch from Geneva. The reservation had already been made when Underberg gave me the ticket," he said. "You had to be expecting me. So you had to have the photograph already. Too long by road . . . too uncertain. So it must have been flown down . . ." He shook his head. "I don't think they'd have risked crossing back into Switzerland. If the alarm had been raised, the photograph would have been disastrous for them . . ." He stabbed the compass point into the map.

"Strasbourg!" he said. "No borders to cross and a good airport . . . Why don't we see if there was a flight from Strasbourg to Nice, say around five o'clock?"

Azziz nodded at once and Grearson went back to the telephone. It took only nine minutes. "KLM 382," he said. "From Strasbourg at 1400. Landed Nice at 1655, on schedule."

"Time even to get to Monte Carlo by public transport and avoid the risk of being remembered by a taxi driver."

"Still supposition," insisted Grearson. "I agree they'd have got out of Switzerland as quickly as possible, but not that they would have gone north. That's pure guesswork."

"Look," said Deaken, gesturing around the room. "What do you see?"

Grearson frowned about him, irritated at not being able to answer the question.

"What?" he said.

"Flowers!" said Deaken. "Every sort of flower, a lot of them subtropical." He picked up the photograph of Karen and Tewfik Azziz. "Cornflowers," he said. "Cornflowers and daisies. Nothing from the south."

"Tenuous," said Grearson.

"Can you do better?" said Deaken.

Grearson looked away without replying.

"The timing was tight." Deaken addressed himself directly to Azziz. "A two P.M. departure from Strasbourg would have meant last-minute boarding by one forty-five. And they would have tried to avoid that, because of the risk of anyone remembering. If it took an hour to get to Basel and maybe another fifteen minutes to cross the border, that takes us to twelve thirty." Deaken stopped, sure of his argument. "That's all they did. Just crossed the border and stopped almost immediately for the photograph to be taken." He scribbled a calculation on the map edge, equating his estimated timing with distance, then setting his compass. He used Zürich as the compass point, sweeping a half circle westwards on the map. It covered Sélestat to the north, Le Locle in the south, with Epinal at the westward bulge of the half circle. Deaken reversed the map for the men opposite, pushed it across the table towards them and said, "Somewhere there."

Azziz stared downwards for several moments and then said, "You've made it sound convincing."

"It's a holiday place," said Deaken. "A farm."

"Why?" said the Arab.

"Look at the picture," said Deaken. "It's a communal room, like a lot of French farms. And the fireplace is a working one, with all the fittings for smoking. But look at the surround. It's white, not blackened by fire or smoke. It hasn't been used for a long time."

"Maybe," agreed Azziz.

"We've only their word that they'll let them go," said Deaken. "You've the resources. Why not inquire specifically around there. We could identify it from a brochure."

Azziz looked at Grearson. "We'll do it," he decided. "Fix it through Paris in the morning." To Deaken he said, "They're making contact at noon?"

"That was the arrangement."

"By then we'll have discovered what's happened in Marseilles. You'll stay aboard tonight." It wasn't a question.

"Thank you," said Deaken, who hadn't considered what he was going to do. "But I haven't got anything," he said.

"That's not a problem," said Azziz.

Deaken was suddenly overwhelmed with fatigue. He looked at his watch and saw it was 3 A.M. But he didn't think he'd sleep.

"It was an intelligent exposition," said Azziz. He had stayed with coffee but Grearson sat with a brandy balloon cupped before him in both hands.

"Unless he's involved, in which case it would have been simple," said the lawyer.

"Then he's directed us to his accomplices, which doesn't make sense," said the Arab. "I believe him. I think his wife has been taken. Just like Tewfik."

"I would have expected a cash demand," said the lawyer, sipping from his glass.

Azziz nodded. "It's definitely a complication."

"A clever one," said Grearson, fingering his spectacles. "If we default on the shipment, the word will get around very quickly. We exist by reputation. And reliability."

"I know," said the Arab. His head was forward on his chest, a familiar attitude of concentration. It was a long time before he spoke. "We can't afford to lose that reputation," he said. There was another pause. "Or Tewfik." His head came up. "I don't want an army," he said positively. "I want a small, compact group. But they've got to be the best. I don't want a bunch of has-beens, fat on beer and boasting about the black women they raped in the Congo."

"Green Beret or British SAS?"

"Just the best."

"Williams was a Green Beret," reminded Grearson.

"He was a mistake," said the Arab. "I don't want any more."

"There won't be," promised Grearson, whose life until now had been a comparatively easy one of creating contracts with people who were always the willing buyers and who enjoyed the comforts with which Azziz surrounded himself. He didn't want anything to change.

"We'll use this man Deaken," said Azziz. "And if necessary his wife—they're our advantage; they're expendable."

One deck above where Azziz sat, but farther to the stern, Deaken stared around a suite only slightly smaller than the apartment he occupied in Geneva, reaching out to touch first the smooth wood of the bulkhead and then letting his hand drop to the silk covering of the bed. He supposed the word was bunk, but it wasn't appropriate: this was a bed, big enough for two. The thought hit him like a blow.

"Oh, my darling," he said aloud. "Poor darling. I'll get you back. I promise I'll get you back."

Tewfik Azziz waited a long time, twice almost drifting off to sleep, only to jerk awake, irritated at himself for the weakness it showed. He was extremely careful, crouching for a long time near the door, tensed for sounds, waiting for the conversation and then the footsteps to cease, for the house to sleep. Even then he waited for the stir of guards placed outside. There was no movement to indicate the precaution.

He had rehearsed the walk, like everything else, so he crossed silently to the window, the worn five franc piece hot where he had held it for so long in his hand. He purposely kept the light off, so it was difficult locating by touch alone the screws which bolted the bars in place. The round edge of the coin fitted only in the centre and there was little leverage on the small disc. Azziz thrust hard down upon it to get the maximum purchase, hands quivering with the effort of making the turn. The coin twisted free, twice, sharp enough to have cut him if he hadn't had the forethought to protect his hands with a handkerchief; his captors might have become curious about such finger cuts. Azziz bit back the groan at the effort, feeling the blood pump through his head. When the screw gave, it was an abrupt, jerking movement which threw the coin wide again. He groped out, feeling for the screw, rubbing his thumb across the head to ensure he hadn't milled the cross-cut sufficiently for them to detect it if they made a check while he wasn't in the room. Then he fitted the coin in yet again, having to put a thumb and forefinger either side to keep the coin in place, and slowly succeeded in unscrewing it completely. Azziz stopped, panting, his clothes glued to him with sweat. For several moments he hunched in the darkness, with the screw held tightly in the palm of his hand like the prize it was. Then, carefully, he reinserted it and tightened it, so it would be undetectable. By the time he became aware of the greyness of dawn edging in through the shutters, Azziz had succeeded in releasing six of the eight screws holding the inner bar into position across one of the windows. When he lay down, he realized his fingers were so numb he could hardly feel them.

7

Karen slept badly, several times waking abruptly, knowing immediately where she was, and tensed for the sound or presence that had startled her. On each occasion there was nothing. She got up finally, before it was properly light, taking a long time to wash and dress. She had been careful to wind her watch, wanting always to be aware of the time. It was seven when she heard movement about the house. It was far away, downstairs in the kitchen or the big room, she supposed. She wished they would come for her. Karen moved impatiently but aimlessly around the bedroom, consciously avoiding that part where the portable lavatory stood. It embarrassed her, so much so that she didn't look at it, which was a stupid reaction but one she couldn't stop.

At the window she reached out, pulling at the bars without any purpose. It *wasn't* with any purpose, she realized, shocked. Until now, this very moment, the idea of escape hadn't occurred to her. She had been too frightened, too confused, to think of it after being tricked from the apartment. And really terrified, during the ride into France, when she realized what had happened and believed that the big man who kept pressing himself against her really would harm her if she didn't do everything she was told. But then she had accepted it. Everything had taken on an air of unreality, like some grown-up game she

had been tricked into joining and didn't want to admit she
was afraid of playing. She *didn't* want to play: she wanted
to get back to Richard. Back to sanity. Back to worrying
about money and why she wasn't pregnant at thirty. She
pulled at the bar, harder this time; it didn't move. She
would have to think of something, make a plan. Not sink
into apathetic acceptance and wait until someone else did
something for her. Wasn't that the attitude that irritated her
so much about Richard, the change from the fervent, ever
moving, change-the-world man into an acquiescent half-
optimist. She felt suddenly ashamed. That had been a
secret thought, until now, hidden always in a corner of her
mind, consciously unformed because to form it would
make it into a criticism of the man she loved. And she *did*
love him, as much as she ever had. She knew how he felt,
because they had talked it through. Richard hadn't sacrificed any ideals. He had just stopped being manipulated,
just as the movements themselves were so often manipulated by the very people or authorities they sought to
correct or improve. He was right then. Honest. Why did
she argue so much with a man who had done the right and
honest thing?

Karen heard them coming and hurried from the window,
not wanting them to find her there. It was Levy who came
into the room.

"You're ready?" The man seemed surprised.

"I didn't sleep much."

"I'm sorry."

There was even an unreality to the conversation, Karen
thought. "I made a list," she said. It had occupied an hour
the previous night, before she had attempted to sleep.

Levy took it without reading it, putting it immediately
into his pocket. "Shall we go down?"

Tewfik Azziz was already in the large downstairs room
when Karen entered. He stood politely, and she smiled.
The Arab waited until she was seated before sitting himself.
He passed her a wicker basket of croissants and bread.

Richard got them yesterday, she thought; she'd behaved like a stupid child, reducing them to crumbs in her petulance. She shook her head, helping herself instead to coffee.

"What happens now?" Azziz demanded.

"We should hear something today," said Levy.

"And we'll be freed?" asked Karen.

"That depends," said Levy.

"Don't you know?" said Azziz sarcastically.

"We'll know soon enough," said Levy.

Karen looked around the room. Two men, who only spoke to Levy in what she presumed to be Hebrew, lounged casually at the door leading out into the garden, and she could see three more moving around in the kitchen. They were making no effort to conceal their identities.

"Mrs Deaken will exercise first," announced Levy.

The men who had brought her from Switzerland emerged from the kitchen. Levy crossed to them and she got the impression that they were arguing. She was aware of Azziz close to her.

"You must run if you get the opportunity," the boy whispered softly. "Forget what he said about one being a hostage for the other."

She had, Karen realized guiltily. "What about you?"

"They won't hurt me."

"They might."

"Run," repeated Azziz urgently as Levy turned.

"May I walk with you?" he said.

"Do I have a choice?"

"Of course."

"I don't mind."

Karen stopped directly outside the door, putting her head back so that she could feel the sun fully on her face, breathing deeply; only outside the farmhouse was she fully aware of how stale her bedroom had been. There was a man positioned on the far side of the garden, at the gate through which they had entered. They moved off to the left where the garden was most extensive. It was L-shaped, with a low barbered hedge down the middle, like a dividing line. Beyond the bordering fence she could see trees and patchwork fields. On the skyline a group of men were gathering crops around a slowly moving machine. Everything looked peaceful.

"What were you and Azziz talking about?" said Levy.

"He told me not to be afraid."

Levy looked at her but said nothing. He was only slightly taller than she was, Karen realized. He wore jeans and a short-sleeved shirt; his arms were matted with hair.

"You haven't got a gun," she said.

"No."

"What would you do if I ran?"

"Catch you."

"What if you didn't?"

"I told you yesterday that you're hostages for one another."

"I don't think you'd hurt him," she challenged.

"Don't put it to the test."

She saw his hands were gripped tightly at his sides, as if he was angry or tense. "Will you speak to Richard?"

"Why?"

"I want him to know I'm all right. That I love him."

"No," he said. "Not me. But he'll be told you're all right."

"Would you hurt me, if Azziz got away?"

"He isn't going to."

"That isn't an answer."

"You'd better hope it is."

They came to a high hedge, as neatly clipped as the dividing line behind them. The lane that led into the village would be on the other side, Karen decided. She tried to remember how far away the village was. From inside the car it had seemed quite close. She strained, listening for any sound that might be coming from it. She heard cooing and looked back towards the farmhouse.

There was a dovecote on the roof of one of the outbuildings.
Pure white birds were preening and parading along the
walkway.

"The books and games I promised will be here this
afternoon," said Levy.

"I don't feel like reading. Or playing games."

"It'll be a way of passing the time."

"Don't be so bloody patronizing!" The helpless anger
burst from her. "Who the fuck do you think you are! What
gives you the right to treat me like this . . . to treat anyone
like this? To tell me when to sleep and when to wake and
when to eat and when I can breathe fresh air instead of air
stinking of my own shit!"

Levy winced at the tirade and at her crudity. "I don't
have to justify myself to you."

"You supercilious sod!" She lashed out, surprising herself as well as him. Her palm slapped across the side of his
face, so hard that he stumbled sideways. It hurt her hand,
the physical pain making her realize what she had done.
She stepped backwards, slack-armed, not trying to protect
herself as he swung in retaliation. Levy pulled back at
the last moment, but his slap still made her ears ring.

"You stupid bitch!"

"Bastard!"

They stood confronting each other, like bantam cocks
waiting to be released for the fight. Karen saw his hand
move, a sideways gesture, and flinched, then recognized
he was waving away the man who had been posted at the
gate and who had started moving towards them. She tried
to prevent it but the tears began to flow down her cheeks.

"Any of the others would have shot you."

"Does that make you any different?"

"Of course it does."

"Shit!" she said. "You're all the same. Thugs."

"We believe in what we're doing."

"Fucking thugs."

"What do you call Azziz?"

"What's it to do with me?"

"Nothing," said Levy. "We're using you. And the boy. Neither of you will suffer . . ." He hesitated, putting his hand to his still-red face. ". . . providing you behave sensibly." He made a shooing motion for her to move ahead of him. "Back to the house."

She didn't move at once, wanting to give the impression of some independence, however futile. He seemed to understand her need, holding back from any further movement until she was ready. She turned eventually, walking shoulders squared in front of him. She wasn't apathetic or acquiescent. She felt proud.

It was clear that the gate guard had relayed an account of what happened in advance of their return. There were five men, grouped inside the room, regarding her blank-faced as she re-entered the farmhouse.

When Levy spoke it was in what she had earlier presumed to be Hebrew. The exchanges were sharp, staccato almost. The Israeli looked beyond her, to Azziz.

"You're a silly boy," said Levy.

"I'm not a boy."

"You blistered your fingers," said the Israeli. "It was obvious at breakfast this morning."

Karen looked towards Azziz's hands but he pulled them instinctively behind his back.

"We've found the screws loosened," continued Levy. "We've put more in—heavier gauge."

Karen was conscious of Azziz stiffening. It was anger, she decided.

"Teach this little bastard a lesson," said Leiberwitz.

Levy walked to the Arab, holding his hand out. "Give it to me," he said.

"I don't know what you mean."

"I want whatever it was you used to undo them," said Levy.

"I didn't touch them."

Levy slapped Azziz, open-handed like he'd struck the

woman earlier, but this time he didn't pull back. Karen
gasped at the crack as the heel of the Israeli's hand caught
Azziz high on the right cheek. Azziz swayed, head jerked
back by the force, but he didn't move. He didn't make a
sound either.

"Give it to me," said Levy.

Azziz said nothing.

"If I have them search you," said Levy nodding behind
him, "they'll hurt you. Maybe badly."

"Let me," said the bearded man, moving forward.

"Give it to him!" said Karen.

"Shut up," said Azziz.

Levy hit him again, palm first against the other side of
his face. Azziz had been looking towards her, so the blow
caught him more in the mouth this time. His lip split in a
burst of blood. The Arab looked fully at Levy, letting it
run unchecked down his chin.

"Very heroic," said Levy. He hit the youth again. This
time Azziz staggered. Quickly he recovered.

"Stop it!" She knew Azziz wasn't being hit for whatever he had done, not entirely: Levy was taking out upon
the Arab the irritation he'd felt at her. She went to them
before anyone else could stop her. "Stop it, I say!"

The Israeli swept her aside, causing her to fall over the
slightly raised edge of a flagstone. She fell backwards, too
quickly and too surprised to put out her hands to save
herself: she landed hard on her coccyx, which was agony,
and then fuller on to her back, driving the wind from her
body. Because of the pain it emerged as a scream. She
rolled over, grabbing her skirt down, knees against her
chest, groaning the breath back into herself, face against
the coldness of the stone. Her cut-off view was of legs.
She was aware of people moving towards her. "Stay
away," she wheezed. "Stay away from me." The legs
stopped moving. She hated them seeing her as defenceless
as this.

"I want it, whatever it is. If you don't give it to me I'll

have them strip you, in front of the woman. We'll turn out your clothes and find it. And beat you.'' She knew it wasn't Levy's voice; it was the man who'd tricked her from the Geneva apartment.

Breathing easier now, Karen raised her head, so that she could see the room again. Azziz was still confronting Levy defiantly but there wasn't the initial stiffness in the way he held himself.

"What's the point?" she said. Her voice wavered, uncertain.

Azziz thrust into his pocket, taking out the coin. Instead of giving it to the Israeli, he threw it on the ground. It clattered against the stone, and rolled away, describing diminishing circles until finally it settled on its side. For a moment Levy looked steadily at Azziz. Then he picked up the coin, studying the edge for the score marks which would confirm it was what Azziz had used. He went back to the Arab and said, "All right, everything else in your pockets out onto the table."

Sullenly Azziz emptied his pockets.

"Now pull all the linings out," said Levy.

Some of the watching men laughed as Azziz obeyed.

"Tonight you'll sleep with your ankle handcuffed to the bed," said Levy. Briefly he looked sideways at Karen. "She was right—there wasn't any point. No point at all."

"Pig," said Azziz. His lips were already swelling, making it difficult for him to enunciate clearly.

"We told you that at the beginning," said Levy. "You should have believed me."

Because it was essential to the operation the man called Rupert Underberg insisted upon a seafront room at the Bristol, with a balcony overlooking the harbour. It was here that he breakfasted off yoghurt and eggs and fruit: he couldn't stand the continental crap. He looked beyond the squared basin, with its clutch of yachts, to where the *Scheherazade* rode at deep-water anchor. As he watched, the rotors of the helicopter suddenly began revolving and then the machine lifted, banked and flew off parallel with the coastline. Westwards, Underberg noted; he wondered how the occupants had entered without his being aware of it.

It must be wonderful to be rich enough to own yachts and helicopters, he thought, returning to his breakfast; to eat like this everyday. Would his wife enjoy it? He wished she was with him, so he could have given her a chance. He had wanted so much for it to be better, during his leave. She didn't think he understood, but he did. He would make it up to her, very soon. In a month or two she would realize that it had all been worthwhile.

8

Deaken emerged from his cabin unable to remember the direction from which the steward had led him the previous night. He went to his right, at once aware of the wind chop of the helicopter take-off. He found a door out onto the deck in time to see it pick up the flight path along the coast. Towards France, he decided, staring directly towards the shore and establishing his directions. Monaco was displayed before him, in pinks and yellows and ochres. The sun was already strong, silvering the water, and he had to squint to pick out the palace, with its flag showing the Prince was in residence, and then the casino. Between him and the shore, yachts squatted at their moorings like nesting seabirds. Deaken strained, trying to locate the telephone kiosk he had to use, but it was too far, merging into an obscure whitish blur.

He heard voices and moved towards them, realizing when he got nearer that he was going to the stern of the vessel. He stopped at the rail, gazing down, isolating first the helicopter pad, with its white-ringed landing pattern. The pool was higher, on the next deck up. Three girls were in the water, giggling and laughing. A fourth was spread on her back, on a lounging chair. The three in the water were topless; the one sunbathing was completely naked.

"If you're joining us you'd better change."

The girl was barefoot, which was why he hadn't heard her approach behind him. Her black hair was short, almost boyish. Her face was deeply tanned, without make-up. She had brown eyes, like Karen. She was wearing a bikini bottom and a diaphanous white gauze top, tied only at the neck; her nipples were dark and full.

"I'm Carole," she said.

There was an accent but he couldn't identify it.

"Deaken," he said. "Richard Deaken." He felt like a schoolboy caught peeping into the girls' dormitory.

"When did you come aboard?"

"Last night."

She nodded. "We knew there was a meeting."

Part of the staff, thought Deaken—harem, in fact.

She smiled, conscious of his discomfort. "How long are you staying."

"I'm not sure."

"Coming down to the pool?"

He shook his head hurriedly. "I heard voices," he said.

"We spend most of the day there, if you change your mind," she said. The smile was professional. "We'd welcome the company."

She walked to the companionway leading down to the pool deck with a fluid, hip-swaying sensuality.

Deaken hurried back into the interior of the ship through the door from which she had emerged, annoyed with himself for having been discovered by the girl, annoyed, even, with wasting his time ogling whores. Almost at once he recognized the alleyway along which Grearson had led him when they had boarded, and then the broad sweep down to the stateroom. At the wide double doors he hesitated, then knocked. Something was said on the other side which Deaken didn't hear but he entered anyway. Azziz was standing as he had been the previous night. He was wearing a sports shirt and slacks.

"I've sent someone for you," said the Arab.

"I lost my way," said Deaken. "Where's Grearson?"

"Marseilles," said Azziz. "I decided a personal visit would be better than a telephone call."

The helicopter, remembered Deaken. The door opened behind him. A bespectacled, dark-haired man began, "I'm afraid . . ." and then stopped when he saw Deaken.

"My personal secretary, Mitri," introduced Azziz. "If you want anything while you're here, ask him."

The man nodded, but did not smile. He carried a leather writing case, with fittings on the outside to hold pens.

"Thank you," said Deaken.

The Palestinian secretary looked inquiringly at Azziz, who shook his head. Mitri backed out, closing the door behind him.

"Will you hear from Grearson before I've got to go ashore?" asked Deaken.

"I hope so," said Azziz. "If we don't, you can say we've located the shipment . . . that we'll do what they want."

"They'll want details."

"So do I."

"What does that mean?"

"I talked to Grearson before he left. We decided we were being too subservient."

"We don't have any choice."

"I want contact with my son," insisted Azziz. "I want to know he's all right."

"Cancel the shipment and you can *have* him back!"

"I can't do that in a day," said Azziz. "I don't even own the arms at the moment."

Deaken stared at the other man, feeling the stir of uncertainty. "You said the sale to Portugal was just a book transaction, a way round officialdom!"

"Contracts had to be drawn up, and money seen to be exchanged, for it to remain legal," said Azziz. "It's not a big problem, but it can't be resolved in a day. Surely you see that?"

"How long?"

"Two or three days," shrugged the man.

"Two or three days!" shouted Deaken. "My wife's with those bastards."

"So's my son," said Azziz quietly.

"Then get them out . . . get them both out."

"I'm going to."

Deaken accepted it was illogical to expect everything to be settled so quickly, but he hadn't thought beyond today. "We daren't take any chances," he said.

"I don't intend to. That's why I want to speak to my son."

Deaken looked at his watch; it was almost a quarter past eleven.

"I've ordered the tender in the water at eleven thirty," said Azziz.

Deaken turned to the telephones. "He must be there by now."

"Over an hour ago," agreed Azziz.

"Why hasn't he called?"

"He's got to trace the shipment. It wasn't handled directly through Paris. They were just the vendors."

"I know they'll expect more," said Deaken again.

"Less than twenty-four hours has elapsed," said Azziz. "There can't *be* more."

Deaken remained looking at the telephones, willing one to sound.

"Here," said Azziz.

Deaken turned to the Arab. Azziz was holding out a small, leatherette-covered box. "What's that?"

"I want the conversation taped," said Azziz. "I want to hear what's said."

"Underberg said I'd be watched, all the time."

"This couldn't be any danger to him."

It was a sensible thing to do, thought Deaken. He reached out and accepted the recorder.

"Do you know how to use it?"

The lawyer nodded, turning it over in his hand and locating the suction-capped receiver to stick onto the telephone.

"You should be going," said Azziz.

"It's not half past yet," said Deaken. Why hadn't the bloody American rung?

"You shouldn't be late."

Deaken moved reluctantly towards the door.

"Don't forget the contact," said Azziz. "I'll accept whatever conditions or arrangements they want, so long as I can speak to him."

"I'll ask," promised Deaken. To speak to Karen as well, he decided. The hollow, disbelieving sound of her voice when she had spoken to him in the Geneva office echoed in his head.

Confident of at least part of the yacht, Deaken found his way easily out onto the deck. The tender was already drawn up at the bottom of the stepway. He went down carefully, glancing back up towards the ship as he reached the platform. Two of the girls were looking over the rail from the pool deck; the sun was behind them, so he couldn't see if either was the girl to whom he had spoken. One waved. Deaken got into the tender without responding.

From the balcony of the Bristol, Underberg focused the binoculars and saw the motorboat pull away from the side of the *Scheherazade*. He smiled and stepped back into the shade of his room.

In the stateroom of the yacht the telephone sounded at the time Azziz had arranged and he picked it up expectantly.

"Sailed nearly forty-eight hours ago," reported Grearson. "Freighter is called the *Bellicose*, Liberian registration, owned by a Greek company called Levcos. General cargo to Madeira, then on with our shipment." The line was extremely clear; it was Paris, not Marseilles.

"Any stated destination?"

"Sailing orders are to refuel at Dakar, then onwards for contact off Benguela. Deaken gone ashore?"

"Yes," said Azziz. "When does the *Bellicose* get to Madeira?"

"Tonight. The weather's good so it should be there on time."

"Who's the Portuguese in the middle?"

"Hernandez Ortega," said the American. "We've dealt with him before. Good man."

"Who's the purchaser?"

"An import company called Okuru Shippers, with an address in the avenue Libération, in Lobito."

"How was the purchase made?"

"They came here, to the office in Paris."

"Any names?"

"Makimber," said the lawyer. "Edward Makimber." The lawyer hesitated. "Do you want me to go to Lisbon, to see Ortega?"

"No," said Azziz at once. "What about the men we want?"

"Paris have got some names."

"American or British?"

"American," said Grearson. "Address for one is Brussels.

"I don't want any Belgian Congo rubbish," repeated Azziz.

"I know."

"Check him, as you're so close," instructed Azziz. "And tell Paris to make a contact with this man Makimber. I want to see if there really is a deadline or whether they'd accept a delay."

"Deaken said they'd thought of that."

"Make the inquiry," said Azziz. "And tell them to arrange a matching shipment. Do we have sufficient stock?"

"More than sufficient," said Grearson.

"Fix it," ordered Azziz.

"It would be an easy way out," agreed Grearson.

"Not for some," said Azziz, more to himself than to the other man.

It was 11:50 when Deaken jumped ashore, before waiting for the crew to tie up. He ran up the steps, looking anxiously towards the telephones. The one in use was not the one which had been identified by Underberg. Deaken hurried into the box, thrusting the door closed behind him. He put the recorder on the ledge and depressed the suction cap against the earpiece of the telephone, tugging it gently to make sure it was attached. Eleven fifty-five, he saw. He looked around. The quayside was crowded, with yachtsmen and sightseers and flower stalls and souvenir sellers. Near the harbour office an artist had erected an easel and was painting the yachts against the background of the palace. A group had formed behind the man. No one was obviously watching him, decided Deaken. But then they wouldn't be obvious. Although he was ready for it, tensed even, Deaken still jumped when the telephone shrilled.

He snatched up the receiver, almost dropping it in his eagerness. "Yes?"

"You're on time. Good," said a voice he recognized as that of the man who had confronted him in Geneva the previous day.

Belatedly Deaken remembered the tape and jabbed the lever down. "How's my wife . . . how's Karen?"

"Perfectly well," said Underberg. "Why the recorder?"

Deaken whirled around. There was no one in any of the other boxes. He turned in the opposite direction. He was overlooked by dozens of windows and at least three hotels; it was like being pinned out, ready for dissection, under some microscope. "We didn't want any mistakes," he said.

"I'm glad you're being careful," said Underberg. "What about the shipment?"

Deaken gripped his hands against the familiar patronizing voice. "Azziz has agreed," said the lawyer.

"That's good, that's very good," said Underberg. "Where is it?"

Deaken hesitated. "Being located," he said.

Now the pause was from the other end. "That doesn't sound very sensible, Mr Deaken."

"It was sold through France," said the lawyer desperately. "Shipment was arranged through Marseilles. Azziz has sent someone there this morning . . ." Remembering the Arab's point, Deaken added, "We've only had a few hours."

Again the man didn't speak immediately. Then he said, "Don't forget why you're involved. Don't forget what happens to your wife depends upon your seeing that everything goes the way we want it to."

Deaken tugged at his collar, loosening his shirt. Sweat soaked him, running down his face and from beneath his arms, into the waistband of his trousers. He tried opening the door but the sound of the quayside was too loud so he closed it again. He could feel the sun burning through the glass. "I'm not forgetting anything," he said. "You didn't give us enough time."

"You'll have enough time," said Underberg. "More than enough."

"Azziz wants to speak to his son. And I want to speak to Karen. To make sure they're all right," blurted Deaken.

"We make the stipulations," said Underberg.

"We'll accept any conditions . . . whatever the arrangement. Let's just speak to them. Hear their voices."

"That's not possible."

"It must be possible."

"I said it wasn't."

"What's happened to them?" Deaken's fear was immediate, his voice unsteady.

"I've told you, they're all right, both of them," said Underberg insistently. "There's no way you can talk to them; it won't work."

"Azziz can make it work."

"All he's got to make work is the rerouting of the arms shipment. Make sure he does that."

The response came at once to Deaken, but he paused, considering it. Then he said, "You've made that impossible."

"What do you mean?" demanded Underberg.

"How can I ensure anybody is doing anything when I'm tied to these telephone calls. Give me some way to contact you."

Underberg laughed. "That wasn't very clever," he said.

"I'm not trying to be clever," said Deaken. "I'm trying to do what you've asked . . . to protect Karen."

"You know how to do that."

"Let us speak to them," repeated Deaken.

"No."

"Make some concession!" pleaded Deaken.

"We're not in the business of making concessions," said Underberg. "We're combatting terrorism, which Azziz feeds upon."

"Bastard!" said Deaken.

"Don't forget it," said Underberg. "Not for a moment. Will Azziz sort everything out by tomorrow?"

"I don't know."

"You're supposed to know." The man paused. Then he said, "I'll give you forty-eight hours."

"I don't understand."

"I won't call you tomorrow. The day after, the same box, the same time."

"No, wait . . ." started Deaken, realizing the man meant to break the contact. The line went dead.

From behind the closed windows of his room, Underberg saw Deaken emerge disconsolately from the telephone kiosk, the recorder clutched tightly beneath his arm. It was fortunate that Deaken had protested about the difficulty of daily calls; if he hadn't, reflected Underberg, then the idea of lengthening their contact time would have had to come from him and he hadn't wanted that. Only another thirty minutes before the call from Mulhouse. Levy wouldn't be as argumentative as the lawyer: Levy imagined they were working for the same thing.

Underberg sighed contentedly. There would still be time before the plane left for him to have a leisurely lunch on the terrace. He enjoyed living well.

On the quay below, Deaken boarded the tender. It was clearly marked as that from the *Scheherazade* and as it moved away from the moorings Deaken looked up at the watching faces. They all envied him, he realized. Stupid sods.

Karen stood stiffly as Levy entered the room. He stopped inside the door and held out the packages to her.

"Everything you asked for," he said. "You didn't say anything about underwear, but I bought some anyway." He hesitated. "Pants at least," he added. "White."

"Thank you," she said. The parcels carried advertisements for shops in the rue de la Bourse, in Mulhouse. She didn't remember that as the name of the last place through which they'd driven before turning off to the farmhouse.

"I've got a message through to your husband, that you're all right," he said.

Karen said nothing.

"You are, aren't you?" said Levy. "You weren't really hurt?"

There was only a small mirror, high on the washstand, so she hadn't been able to see. "Probably just bruised," she said. There was an ache at the bottom of her back.

"He shouldn't have been stupid."

"You said that already."

"I didn't mean to hurt him."

"You did though," she said.

"His father's doing what we want. Everything is going to be all right."

"You will let us free, if he does everything, won't you?" demanded Karen in sudden fear. "You'll let us go?"

Levy smiled, the first time she had seen him do so. His teeth were very white and even. "Of course," he said. "How many more times have I got to tell you I mean you no harm?"

After what he'd done to her and to the boy, she should loathe this man, Karen knew; hate him. She wondered why she didn't.

9

La Grande Place in Brussels, and the café in the corner, is an essential stop for tourists, a place for posing, singly and in groups, for holiday pictures. The café is made entirely of wood, with wooden stalls and wooden benches and an uncovered, wooden floor. It rises through several balconied sections around the central, flaring barbecue pit and is dominated by the complete figure of a stuffed horse. Alive it had been a large, proud animal; dead it gazes through opaque glass eyes onto the square with an expression of vague dismay at having become a sideshow. Almost an entire side of La Grande Place is occupied by the town hall; the exterior is intricately decorated, with criss-crossed beams and fancy brickwork, like the original model for Hansel and Gretel's gingerbread house. It was not the location that Harvey Evans would have chosen for a meeting, but the demand from Paris had been for somewhere easy to find and he was sure that every taxi driver in Belgium knew of the café with the horse.

The American sat in the prearranged stall, both hands around the beer glass from which he only occasionally drank. Twice he had to shake his head against his table being shared, with the explanation that he was awaiting a companion. It was always a polite refusal, because Harvey Evans was invariably polite. He was a still, quiet man, with a trained soldier's neatness. The fair, almost white, hair was close-cropped at the sides far above his ears, and his hard, high-cheek-boned face was closely shaven, so carefully it seemed to be polished. The trousers were freshly pressed and the shoes glistened, reflecting the light from the flickering cooking area. Because he was leaning forward, the windbreaker was pulled back, so that the Rolex watch that had been the Green Beret amulet in Vietnam protruded; on the little finger of the left hand there was a heavy fraternity ring, with a red stone in the centre. Evans revolved it idly, thinking back to the telephone call from Paris. Abrupt and curt and businesslike, the voice confident. American too. So it could be something, he thought. Something worthwhile. He hoped to Christ it was. Since Libya there hadn't been anything sensible. And Libya had been an asshole. Evans sighed. Like everything else had been an asshole, since 'Nam. They hadn't deserved the treatment, when they got back; none of them had. He hadn't wanted to be regarded as a hero, although he probably qualified with the Purple Hearts and the Silver Stars and all the other junk he and the others had collected, too easily in the end, like trinkets for having saved up cardboard tops from breakfast-food packets. All he wanted was to be accepted as the soldier he had become, someone who had shown sufficient aptitude and ability for promotion to one of the youngest majors in the Berets. But he hadn't got it; none of them had. They had gone halfway around the world and risked being maimed or crippled or killed and got back home to find themselves ostracized, treated with contempt even. As if they and not some asshole group of politicians sitting in the warmth and comfort of Washington had started the whole bloody thing and made America look as stupid and as ineffectual as it had appeared in the end. It hadn't occurred to him before, but there was a direct analogy with the military legend: the commanders fuck it up and the poor grunts in the boondocks cop the shit.

Evans had been studying every entrant—he had chosen the seat specifically for the purpose—and looked at Grearson more intently than he had at most others. The man was alone. Had an attitude of authority, which Evans recognized from the army. And the clothes were American, like the voice had been on the telephone. The man looked around, orienting himself, and walked directly up to the stall.

"You're Harvey Evans," he said. It was not a question.

Evans stood, aware of the immediate examination. "Yes," he said. Grearson liked what he saw. The man was in good shape, unneglected. And no beer belly, he thought, remembering Azziz's injunction.

"Sorry I'm late," apologized the lawyer. "Delay at the airport."

The soldier's handshake was firm, without any ridiculous pretence at making it so.

"I didn't mind waiting," said Evans. "You spoke of a job."

"Maybe," said Grearson cautiously. He ordered whisky.

"How did you get my name?"

"Paris."

"That's a city," said Evans. "Who in Paris?"

"People who recommended you as being very good."

"What sort of people?"

"The sort who deal in weaponry."

They had seemed the most obvious contacts when Evans moved into Europe from the Middle East. He supposed he must have contacted about six different arms-dealing organizations.

"Which one?"

"That's not important, not for the moment," said Grearson. "I want to be sure first."

"Of what?"

"Your suitability."

"What do you want to know?"

"Everything about you."

The lawyer's drink arrived. He put it before him untouched and Evans realized it wasn't to drink, merely to entitle him to occupy the seat in the stall. Evans gave a clipped official recital of his career, as if he were reading from the formal documentation which still existed somewhere in Fort Bragg.

"Why did you leave in '78?" Grearson fingered his spectacles.

"I didn't like the atmosphere," said Evans. "Wherever I went . . . said who I was . . . I was made to feel as if I was guilty of something."

Grearson nodded, aware of the attitude that existed in America in the immediate aftermath of the mistaken war.

"Why not a civilian job?"

"Don't have the training," said Evans. "I'm a soldier, that's all I've ever been. Ever wanted to be."

"What then?"

"Heard there was opportunity in Libya. Training their people . . . guerrillas, too, from other countries. Spent

almost two years in a camp near an oasis called Kufra
. . .'' He shook his head at the memory. ''Christ, what a
place!''

''What was wrong with it?''

''Prayers to Mecca God knows how many times a day,
political indoctrination sessions and stupid bastards shooting off guns and throwing grenades and believing they
were immortal so it didn't matter if they got hit.'' Evans
stopped. ''No booze or women either. Like being a god-
damned monk.''

Grearson analysed what the other man said before
speaking. ''You got anything against Arabs?'' he said.

''Do you mean am I Jewish?''

''Are you?''

''No.''

''So what about Arabs?''

Evans shrugged. ''Nothing wrong with Arabs,'' he said.
''That wasn't what pissed me off about Libya.''

''What did then?''

''They're crazy. They really do believe what their priests
tell them, that Gaddafi is leading them into some sort of
holy conflict, they can't be killed.''

''Booze important to you?''

''Booze?'' frowned the man.

''You said there wasn't any booze. Or women.''

Evans smiled apologetically. ''I don't drink or whore
any more than anyone else,'' he said. ''But I was there for
two years!''

Grearson smiled back. ''What have you done since
then?''

''Nothing.''

He had been lucky first time, Grearson decided. He
pushed a sealed manila envelope across the table. ''There's
$1000 retainer, with another $500 for expenses.''

Evans picked the envelope up, felt it and put it into an
inside pocket of his windbreaker. ''What do you want?''

''You formed a deep-penetration unit in Vietnam.''

"Yes."

"How many men?"

"It varied," said Evans. "Usually it was six."

"What sort of opposition could you handle?"

Evans smiled again, proudly this time. "A platoon or company any time," he said. "Frequently happened, in fact. We were well trained."

"Could you assemble six people?"

"How long have I got?"

"Two or three days. And I don't want rubbish. I want men like you, only a year or two out of the services, still trained, still fit."

"I could try."

Grearson respected the man for avoiding the overcommitment. "I'd want to meet them when they're assembled," said the lawyer. "If one isn't right then the whole thing's off."

"I can't recruit unless I know what we've got to do."

"Somebody's got something belonging to us," said Grearson. "We want it back."

"So call the police," said Evans.

"That's not possible, not on this occasion."

"What can I offer?"

"You'll get $2000 a week, as commander. The people you recruit get $1000. All expenses, of course. If the need arises for you to be used . . . if you have to go in to recover what's ours and you do it successfully, there'll be a $30,000 bonus for you and $20,000 for everyone else. Paid in whatever currency you want, to wherever you want."

"So we might not actually be used?"

"Not necessarily," said Grearson. "But you still get the payment and expenses. And a severance bonus: $10,000 for you, $5000 for the others."

Evans nodded. "The terms seem fair enough," he said. "What happens about equipment?"

"Don't bother about anything. Whatever you want will be provided."

"To be effective we've got to train . . . have some idea of what the operation will be."

"I can't tell you that, not yet," said the lawyer. "And I do recognize the difficulty. That's why the people you get together have got to be already well trained; there won't be time for much preparation."

"I don't like that," said Evans.

Grearson was pleased at the professionalism. "It could be something like a surprise assault," he said guardedly.

"Defended?"

"Probably. But you should have some element of surprise."

"How big a building?"

"I don't know."

"We'll have plans . . . layouts?"

"I hope so."

"But you're not certain?"

A waiter returned to the table inquiringly. Both men shook their heads.

"No," said Grearson. "There's no certainty."

"How big is the object to be recovered?" said Evans. "I mean, will it be in a safe . . . under some sort of protection that we'll have to blow?"

Grearson hesitated. "It's not an object," he said.

Evans did not respond for several moments. "I see," he said.

"My client has a permanent need for protection," said Grearson. "Particularly so after this. If everything goes as it must, then there could be permanent employment for you. And for some of the people you recruit."

"What about limitations?" said Evans.

"Limitations?"

"When we recover . . ." he paused and then went on ". . . what it is we have to recover, are there any limitations on the force that's got to be employed?"

"None," said Grearson immediately. "Absolutely none."

"And the authorities will not be involved?"

"No."

"I don't know your name," said Evans. "Or how to make contact."

"My name doesn't matter at the moment," said Grearson. "Let's leave it that I am an attorney." He passed a folded sheet of paper across the table. "There's a name and telephone number," he said. "They'll have immediate contact with me. Call them when you've assembled your people."

This time Evans opened the paper, noting the Paris telephone number against the address of something called the Eklon Corporation. The second place he had approached after Libya, he remembered. A nondescript set of offices on the rue Réamur; the receptionist as haughty as only the French can be, refusing to let him get past to someone in authority. He had been sure she would have thrown his details away. Azziz, he thought in complete recollection. Adnan Azziz. He felt a burn of satisfaction. This could definitely be something worthwhile.

"Is Mr Azziz personally inconvenienced?" said Evans.

This man was a good choice, decided Grearson. "Someone very close to him."

"I understand."

"Understand something more," said Grearson. "There must be absolute discretion. I don't want any of those you recruit to know anything more than the barest minimum. It would be a risk."

"Of course," said Evans. "You'll have no need to worry."

"I want professionals," insisted Grearson. "Absolute professionals. There must be no mistakes."

"There won't be."

Grearson offered his hand and received the firm handshake in return. "Why on earth have that done to a horse?" said Grearson, looking at the rigid animal.

"Everyone gets stuffed," said Evans.

"Jesus!" said the lawyer.

They crowded into the room, appearing to expect him to resist, Levy in front and three others behind. Gradually Azziz was identifying them, always careful that they would be unaware of his eavesdropping on their conversation and remarks. The big, bearded man who had wanted to involve himself in the beating was Leiberwitz; the tall, saturnine man was Kahane—he thought the given name was Sami. The squat man, bull-shouldered and bull-necked, whom Azziz had seen smirking during the beating, was Greening.

"Do you want to undress?" said Levy.

"No," said Azziz. His mouth hurt to talk.

"I don't think he's respectful enough," said Leiberwitz.

"What are you, some sort of sadist?" Levy said to him in Hebrew. In English to Azziz, Levy said, "It's your fault we're having to do this."

Azziz said nothing, aware of the conflict between the two men confronting him.

"Lie on the bed," said Levy.

The Arab did as he was told. The Israeli adjusted the arms of the handcuffs as wide as they would go and, before securing them around Azziz's ankle, he slipped his finger between the boy's flesh and the metal, to ensure it would not chafe. Satisfied, he clicked them shut. He snapped the other armlet around the metal upright of the bed, needlessly tugging to see it was engaged.

"Don't try anything else that's stupid," warned Levy. "If you fall awkwardly from the bed you could break your ankle."

As Levy left the boy's room he looked automatically towards Karen's bedroom door. A thin ruler of light was marked out beneath it. He hesitated and then continued on down the stairs.

Leiberwitz was waiting for him in the large room. "I won't be treated like shit," he said.

"Stop behaving like it," said Levy, unimpressed at the protest. "There's no plan to hurt them."

"He's a spoiled, supercilious little bastard."

"I think he's rather brave," said Levy.

10

The harbour at Funchal is protected by a huge arm, built out across almost half its width to form a protected, inner anchorage. Normally cruise liners are brought inside, to tie up along it and make their passengers run the gauntlet of its length, through the basket salesmen and wickerwork-makers and lace vendors. Tonight there were no liners in port, so the pilot took the *Bellicose* into the favoured place, manoeuvring her close to the cranes.

High above, from the balcony of Reids Hotel, Underberg watched. It was a warm, still night, the lights of the Madeira capital spread out before him like an overturned jewel box; he could hear the blur of the mooring instructions, as far away as he was.

Underberg turned, walking back into the hotel, sorry that he had arrived too late to sit out there in the late afternoon and go through the traditional ritual of Madeira cake and tea. It hadn't been an easy flight, with a transfer at Lisbon, and Underberg felt tired. He wondered if it would be a wasted journey.

It was a short ride down the hill and Underberg stopped the taxi at the seafront road, to walk the rest of the way along the harbour spur, past the café built into the rock face. The jetty was washed in a butter-yellow glow from the nightwork spotlights, the cranes already dipping into the *Bellicose*'s holds by the time Underberg arrived. He held back, perfectly concealed by the containers of some already unloaded wharf cargo. The captain, the rank designated by his cap edging, was on the wing bridge overlooking the quay, staring down at the work. His name was Erlander, Underberg knew. Forty-eight, married, two children, and a home in Strandväuagen, Stockholm.

The freighter was not his predominant interest, so Underberg moved farther away from the water, seeking a more extensive view of the quay. He didn't bother with the immediate bustle of stevedores beside the *Bellicose*, because Underberg guessed the person for whom he was looking would not be that close. Instead he concentrated on previously unshipped, stored cargo, some covered in tarpaulin and net. It was away from the working lights, black and grey outlines, jagged against the night sky. It was a long time before he detected him and when he did Underberg smiled; the man was using the cover as expertly as he was.

Underberg moved from container to container, purposely not trying to disguise his approach, wanting the man to identify him. He was still some way away when he saw the flash of teeth.

"Surprise, surprise," said Edward Makimber. The voice was educated, carefully modulated.

"Not really," said Underberg. At Cambridge the African had anglicized his name to Kimber. Underberg guessed he wouldn't admit to it now.

"Do you normally keep such a close eye on the competition?" said Makimber.

"Quite often," said Underberg. "We're very competitive. Do you normally worry so much about a purchase?"

"About a purchase as important as this," said the African.

"Azziz has a good reputation, hasn't he?"

"Just general caution," said Makimber.

"We could still help."

"We're grateful for everything you've done so far. It's important, if we're going to get independence, for it to be exactly that, independence."

Archetypal intellectual revolutionary, thought Underberg. Makimber could probably quote verbatim whole chunks of Marx and Engels and Lenin; maybe, if he wasn't trying to be fashionable, even Stalin.

"It's good to know we remain friends."

"We always made it clear there was no question of endangering our relationship."

"It's still a good assurance," said Underberg.

"It won't take long," said Makimber, gesturing towards the unloading. "Port office has it scheduled to sail at six."

"Are you going back to Angola?"

"Benguela by tomorrow night. And if that's not possible, then in through Lobito."

The quayside encounter had unsettled Makimber and he decided not to disclose his intention of checking the shipment through Dakar, just as he was ensuring its untroubled passage here in Madeira. It was a precaution; just as it had been a precaution to take photographs and attempt to create a file on Underberg. When Namibia was independent a proper intelligence system would be set up, not oppressive or brutal like all the others seemed to be. Just protective, to ensure there would be no danger to the properly and democratically elected government. "I've told you how important this is," he said. "With what the ship is carrying we're going to wake the world up to what those South African bastards are doing in our country."

Underberg wondered idly if Makimber already had his victory speech drafted; it would be full of rhetoric and artistic inference, he guessed. They always were, from this sort of man. Makimber would expect some reference to be made, he supposed. "We'd like to attend the celebrations," he said.

"You'll be honoured guests," said Makimber. "We don't forget our friends."

Now it was Underberg who motioned towards the freighter. "You did there."

Makimber wearily shook his head at the other man's tenacity. "That conversation goes round in circles," he said. "No hard feelings?"

"Of course not."

Makimber paused uncertainly. Then he said, "Will you and your people be there?"

"I don't know," said Underberg. "Angola certainly."

"It might be better if you weren't."

It was late when the Alouette brought Grearson back to the yacht. Deaken and Azziz had already played the tape recording through twice and the Palestinian secretary. Mitri, made a transcript while the three men ate. They dined properly this time, in the saloon, with laced linen and crystal. Deaken wondered if the women he had seen earlier in the day would join them, but the heavy mahogany table was only set for three places. It was a superb meal, salmon mousse and then duck. What would Karen be eating? thought Deaken. He pushed his plate aside, barely touched.

"I hope Ortega isn't going to be difficult," said Grearson, setting out on the path he had rehearsed with Azziz at a private meeting before they had joined Deaken in the dining room.

"Ortega?" queried Deaken.

"Hernandez Ortega," explained the lawyer. "The Portuguese intermediary."

"It's a book transaction, an arrangement?" Deaken said to Azziz, immediately alarmed.

"Yes," said the Arab.

"So where's the problem?"

"A price had been already agreed for the repurchase,"

said Grearson. "But I haven't been able to contact Ortega all day. I think he wants more."

"How much more?" demanded Deaken.

"We won't know until we get hold of him."

"So the shipment isn't yours!"

"That's why I was late back," said Grearson. "I spent the afternoon trying to trace Ortega down in Lisbon. He wasn't available."

"Purposely avoiding you?" queried Azziz.

"I think so—it's a tedious negotiating ploy."

Deaken looked sharply between the two men. To the Arab he said, "You don't seem very concerned."

"Of course I'm concerned."

"You heard the tape," pressed Deaken. "They're impatient."

"Whatever Ortega wants, I'll pay. You know that," said Azziz.

"But when?"

"We've got forty-eight hours," reminded Azziz. "It'll be resolved by then."

"Everything?" pressed Deaken.

"My son isn't going to die, Mr Deaken," said the Arab. "Neither is your wife."

Mitri came soft-footed into the dining saloon, halting just inside the door. He carried the recorder in one hand and in the other the transcript and several copies.

"The stateroom," decided Azziz, rising from the table.

The two lawyers stood with him and filed behind the Arab into the adjoining room. They took their copies from the secretary and each read, in silence, for several minutes. Grearson finished first. He was nearest the recorder. He pressed the play button, listening to the two voices with his head bent over the typescript, as if he were checking its accuracy.

"Bad," judged Grearson, when the tape stopped. He snapped off the machine and stared at Deaken. "You handled it very badly."

"How else could I have handled it?" said Deaken, immediately knowing a dip in his new-found confidence.

"You were told not to be subservient."

"I had nothing to argue with, no pressure."

"It should have been handled better," insisted Grearson.

"What would you have done?"

"Not pleaded . . . not shown any desperation," said the American at once.

"I *am* desperate. They've had my wife for two days now."

"You won't get her back by showing your weakness."

"Where's the strength, for Christ's sake?"

"Arguing between ourselves is stupid," said Azziz. To Deaken he said, "I think you could have been more forceful. I recognize the difficulty, but there should have been more force."

"What have you achieved?" fought back Deaken. "We're no closer now to meeting their demands than we were twenty-four hours ago. You don't even own the bloody stuff they want stopped. And what about trying to locate wherever it is they're being held . . . what's been done about that?"

"I've briefed Paris," said Grearson.

"So they've had a whole day. What have they found out?"

"We haven't heard."

"Haven't you called them?" said Deaken, outraged.

"There's no point in arguing," repeated Azziz.

"I agree I didn't get anywhere," conceded Deaken. "I wasn't in a position to. But you tell me precisely what *you've* achieved? You're doing the bare minimum and trying to look busy flying around in helicopters. If you couldn't get Ortega to a telephone, why didn't you go personally to Lisbon? You had the facilities."

"You're right," said Azziz. "Coming back here was an error of judgement."

"Why don't I do what he should have done today?" said Deaken. "Let *me* go, with your full authority."

"I don't think that's necessary," said Grearson stiffly.

"I want to know the stuff is back," said Deaken. "I want to get that whole bloody thing over."

Azziz nodded. "Why not?" he said. "If you want involvement, then you can have it."

"I said I don't think that's necessary," protested Grearson.

"It's decided," said Azziz.

As if on cue there was a sound at the door, which immediately opened. At first, because she was dressed, Deaken didn't recognize the girl who had surprised him that morning on deck, staring down at the swimming pool. Carole was wearing white again, a plain white sheath with just a diamond pin on the right shoulder. The other girls waited complacently behind her.

"You said ten," Carole said to Azziz.

"Quite right." To Deaken Azziz said, "We're going ashore, to the casino. Why not join us?"

"Don't be ridiculous," said Deaken.

"Suit yourself," said Azziz.

"Would you like me to stay?" Carole asked him directly.

Deaken felt himself colouring. "No," he said.

She pouted, an expression of professional disappointment. "Sure?"

"Positive."

At the top of the steps leading into the tender, Grearson said to Azziz, "It went the way you wanted. But I'm still not sure it's a good idea letting him see Ortega."

"We'll call Lisbon before he gets there."

"There's a limit to what we can tell Ortega."

"We can tell him enough to make it sound convincing," said Azziz. "And it'll get the damned man out of my way. He irritates me."

From below, one of the girls called something up to them but neither heard. Azziz waved. "You sure about this mercenary fellow?"

"He impressed me," said the lawyer.

"Let's hope he impresses me," said Azziz.

Grearson looked down into the waiting tender. "I like the dark one," he said.

"Carole?"

"If that's her name."

"Then she's yours," said the Arab.

In Brussels Harvey Evans replaced the telephone after almost eight hours of continuous use; because of the time difference, he had left America until last. If they kept their promises and flew in the following day, he had a unit. Not precisely the one he wanted but men he had worked with before and whose capabilities he knew. Evans stretched the cramp from his shoulders, dropped two cubes of ice into the Scotch and then stood at his apartment window, looking out over the rue des Alexiens. Evans believed in instinct and his instinct told him that this was going to be something good, damned good. He took a deep swallow of his drink. It had taken long enough.

11

Deaken felt satisfied, physically to be doing something. Apart from the brief, thirty-minute excursion to the quay-side telephone, he had been aboard the yacht for two days, and until the helicopter lifted him off and whirled away, just off land, he hadn't realized how claustrophobic he had found it.

Beneath him the coastline of the Riviera unrolled, as if on display for his benefit. It was early, just after six, and the Corniche was quiet, just an occasional car and once, near Antibes, what appeared to be an almost unmoving procession of three lorries, the large, trailer-drawing camions with chimneys just behind the cab spouting out black exhaust. The helicopter was low enough for him to make out the inscription on the sides; two road haulage, from different companies, and a chemical container. They seemed intrusive, like a blemish on a pretty face. Out to sea a tanker made its way eastward. Two yachts were moving in the same direction, both under sail, wakes zigzagged behind them as they tacked to catch the wind. It seemed early for such effort.

Through the headset Deaken heard the pilot pick up instructions from Marseilles flight control. Almost at once he took the machine farther out from the land and then swung it to starboard, bringing them in directly from the sea. Deaken had expected to be put down in a separate section but realized as the helicopter made its final descent that he was only a hundred yards from an airliner. A group of people stood waiting, shielding themselves from the machine's downdraft. Deaken got out, ducking low, the rotor blades still clopping above his head. There was an airline representative, a customs official and an immigration officer. The deference was obvious. The formalities were cursory and within minutes Deaken was being led to the waiting aircraft. He was conscious of other passengers already aboard, staring through the windows at his arrival. The first officer was waiting at the top of the steps, leading him immediately into the first-class section with the invitation, once they had taken off, to join them at any time on the flight deck. As Deaken fastened his safety belt, the steward came alongside with the drinks trolley.

"I don't drink at seven thirty in the morning," refused Deaken.

"Anything you want, just call, Mr Deaken," said the man.

They even knew his name, thought Deaken. So this was power. He wanted to despise it but couldn't. He was flattered by it, he admitted to himself. Excited too. He ate a solicitously served breakfast and then, for politeness rather than because he wanted to, went onto the flight deck for the transit landing in Madrid. It enabled him to inquire about timing. They were on schedule, the captain told him: Lisbon arrival was 10:20.

They were ten minutes early and he was ushered off first. Deaken had travelled only with a briefcase, so there was no luggage reclaim delay and he went through customs unchecked. The arrangement with Azziz before Deaken had left the *Scheherazade* was to telephone Ortega's office to learn the result of the Arab's contact while he was en route. If Ortega was there, an appointment would have been arranged; if not, his secretary would pass on an alternative location. The response was quick when he dialled the number, the language conveniently moving into English when he identified himself. Mr Ortega was expecting him at eleven.

After the frustration of the previous forty-eight hours, it was proving remarkably easy, thought Deaken; almost too easy. He hoped it was not a bad omen.

He actually enjoyed the drive from the airport, locating the silver thread of the Tagus River looping out to the Atlantic as the taxi topped one of the enclosing hills of Lisbon. He had never been to the Portuguese capital. It had the slightly declining, faded atmosphere of a once great and important place shunted aside by circumstance, like a dowager of a lost fortune forced to wear the patched clothes of a previous age. Deaken liked it. He thought it was a nicely packaged, easily manageable city, with a lot of churches and black-shawled women, and statues of warriors on horseback looking into the distance for something to capture.

Ortega's office was in an area of tightly packed streets, on the rua da Assunçao. After the opulence of the past two days. Deaken had expected it to be an impressive place, perhaps occupying an entire building, and to be at least as imposing as the smoked-glass, ground-floor suites which he hurried past every day on his way to the garret on the avenue Pictet de Rochemont in Geneva. It wasn't. A second-floor warren of rooms was reached by a not particularly clean set of stairs, to a waiting area, a secretary's annexe leading to Ortega's sanctum at the end of a small corridor. The carpeting began here, dramatically improving in quality beyond Ortega's door. There was a large desk, elaborately carved and brass inlaid, leather furniture, including a matching couch, and a side table supporting the model of a propeller-driven aircraft which Deaken couldn't identify. One wall was occupied by a map of the world and another dominated by the photograph of a man in a grey lounge suit and a lapel full of medals.

Ortega stood but didn't come forward to greet his visitor. The Portuguese was a small, dapper man; the white summer suit immaculate, the pink silk pocket handkerchief complementing the pink silk tie. He smiled when they shook hands and Deaken saw both the man's eye-teeth were gold. It was a peculiar affectation—a rich vampire, thought Deaken.

"You'll be with Grearson's department?" said Ortega.

"In a manner of speaking," said Deaken.

Ortega gestured Deaken to a chair in front of the desk and seated himself. Instead of increasing his stature, which Deaken guessed was the intention, the size of the desk made Ortega look more diminutive.

"There were no difficulties with the shipment leaving France?" Ortega raised an immaculate eyebrow.

"So I understand," said Deaken. The man was presenting his references.

"Or at Madeira."

Deaken concealed his lack of knowledge. "Sailed satisfactorily?"

"Five thirty this morning," said Ortega. "As I knew it would; I've never had trouble there."

"Mr Azziz is grateful; he asked me to tell you that." He hadn't but Deaken had never found flattery a drawback.

Ortega smiled his gold-tipped smile.

"It's an important cargo," he said, still bargaining.

"Aren't they all?" said Deaken. For the first time he was on something like an even footing, although he hadn't known about Madeira and wondered what else there was to learn.

"Africa's a good market," said Ortega. "More money available there than in South America and they're prepared to spend it, for the right material."

"My involvement usually begins after the deals have been struck," lured Deaken. "And, as you said, I'm new."

"Big enough for country agencies to get involved," said Ortega, adopting the lecturer's pose towards which Deaken had hoped he would move. "Great Britain is in there. France. So's America. Russia is particularly active: once there's a big sale, then there's dependence for spares and ammunition and the purchaser becomes a client state."

"With national agencies involved, it must make it all the more difficult for independents," said Deaken.

"That's where Azziz has the advantage over the rest of us," said Ortega. "He's independent but he's understood to have Saudi Arabian backing, real or otherwise—he's got the best of both worlds."

And appears to enjoy it, thought Deaken. He wondered if Carole had slept with Azziz the previous night, and felt immediately irritated by himself. Why should it matter to him? "There should be no difficulty after Madeira," he continued, still searching.

Ortega looked down at the papers in front of him again.

"Dakar by Saturday," he said. The smile flashed again. "But then that's nothing to do with me, is it?"

"As I said, Mr Azziz is extremely grateful."

"Which is why you're here."

"A percentage was agreed, I believe?" said Deaken. Although there was no limit, he didn't want to concede any more than he had to. Azziz had accused him of panic the previous day. Did Azziz's opinion matter, any more than his bedmate? Why the hell couldn't he dispel the inferiority complex?

"Two per cent for the risks involved!" said Ortega.

"You knew the risks before you entered the transaction."

"There's always time for reflection . . . reexamination," said Ortega.

"I would have thought in your business . . . our business," Deaken corrected, "that all the risks and examinations should be decided before commitment."

"Conditions change."

"They didn't here: everything went exactly as planned."

"Oh, no," contradicted Ortega at once. "There were difficulties in Marseilles; people got greedy. I thought at one time the whole thing might get blocked."

"Another two per cent," offered Deaken. Six hundred thousand was a hell of a profit, whatever difficulties Ortega's agent had encountered.

Ortega's expression was smooth with apologetic refusal. 'It's an onward-going thing," he said. "These people are in contact with each other, from port to port. By the time the *Bellicose* got to Madeira, the customs people knew the rate had gone up."

"How much?"

"Five per cent."

Two and a half million dollars for having his name on a piece of paper for four or five days. Bloody ridiculous. "Agreed," said Deaken—the charade had gone on long enough. From his briefcase he took a signed but blank bankers' order, made out against a holding account of a company named as Eklon and lodged in the Swiss Banking Corporation on Zürich's Paradeplatz. He leaned forward against Ortega's elaborate desk, hesitating before he filled it in.

"What currency?" He saw Ortega was fitting documents into an envelope.

"Swiss francs," said the Portuguese arms dealer. "They're always so sound." He saw the lawyer pause and slid a calculator and computer printout of the rates, timed one hour before their meeting began, across the desk.

Deaken made the calculations and offered it to Ortega for agreement. Ortega nodded, but he didn't smile. This was business. Deaken filled in the amount; it was an awful lot of gold teeth, he thought.

When he looked up Ortega was burning a taper beneath some wax, watching the blobs fall on the flap of the envelope. 'What are you doing?"

"Sealing the documentation."

"I haven't seen it yet," said Deaken.

"It's all there, I assure you."

Deaken retrieved the bank draft from the desk. "There can be no payment until I'm satisfied everything's complete." Deaken had no intention of getting all the way back to the *Scheherazade* to discover something was missing; there had been too much delay already.

"I've already spoken to Mr Azziz," said Ortega. It sounded like a reprimand.

"Would you let a representative of yours pay over a million, sight unseen?"

"No."

Ortega picked up an ornate paper knife, fashioned like a miniature two-edged sword, and picked away the still-plastic wax. He offered the envelope to Deaken. The lawyer opened the flap and took out four sheets of paper; two were pinned together. The manifest, Deaken realized. It was in French. Having had sufficient unoccupied time to learn the languages of Switzerland, Deaken read it easily, feeling a lawyer's satisfaction at having tangible evidence to consider.

There were Russian as well as American rockets, Browning machine guns listed with the AK-47 and Armalite, and entry after entry setting out the amount and calibre of the ammunition. There were four gauges of mortar, shells as well as weapons, antipersonnel and antitank mines and five separate listings for shoulder-operated missiles which Deaken assumed were to resist helicopter assault—he remembered the South Africans were fond of using helicopters in the bush.

"Good shipment, isn't it?" said Ortega.

Deaken thought it was an obscene remark. "Very good," he said.

The second was the official bill of sale, from Ortega to Azziz, the purchase price precisely listed at 53,550,000 Swiss francs, the purchaser inscribed as Eklon Corporation. The third, also in French, was what Deaken assumed to be the End-User certificate; it seemed inadequate for all the trouble it had caused. He saw that it had been endorsed, from Ortega to Eklon.

"There's no bill of lading," said Deaken.

"What?"

"Documentary proof that the shipment is aboard the *Bellicose*. There should be one, from your agent in Marseilles."

"I assure you everything is aboard," said the Portuguese.

"It's not for me to believe you or otherwise." Deaken gestured with the papers in his hand. "These mean nothing without the bill of lading." Thank God he'd insisted upon the envelope being opened.

"I can have it delivered to you when I receive it from France. Or you could return, to collect it personally."

More delay, thought Deaken, maybe for days. "I can collect it," he said. "I'm returning through Marseilles."

"You're very conscientious, Mr Deaken," said Ortega.

"I regard it as basic caution." Deaken leaned forward, setting the draft out in front of him. The alteration took seconds.

"What are you doing?"

"Redating the bank authorization," said Deaken. "It's drawable against tomorrow's date, not today's."

Ortega's face stiffened. "That's offensive," he said.

"No," said Deaken. "That's properly considering the risks." He offered the payment. For several moments Ortega looked at it without moving, then reached forward to pick it up. The attitude, which had been patronizing, was now hostile. Deaken didn't give a damn.

"I'll need written authorization for your man in Marseilles. And his name and address," said Deaken.

Ortega's personal notepaper was held in a small brass rack to his left. He took a sheet and scribbled an impatient message, scrawling a signature beneath it. "I had intended suggesting lunch," he said, in a tone indicating he was no longer going to.

"I need to get back to Marseilles as soon as possible," said Deaken; the helicopter was scheduled to collect him from the incoming evening flight. He saw from the second envelope which Ortega gave him that the French agent was named Marcel Lerclerc and that the office was on the boulevard Notre Dame. "Thank you again," he said, rising. Ortega remained seated.

"I'm sure you'll do well with Azziz," said the Portuguese.

"I hope to," said Deaken heavily.

He was back at the airport by 12:30. He started his tour of the airlines at the TAP desk but it was not until he reached Iberia that he found a fast enough routing, a direct flight to Madrid in forty-five minutes, with an immediate transfer connection to an Air France service en route from New York. He reached Marseilles at 4:15.

The evening rush hour was beginning, so it was not until almost five that he reached Lerlerc's office. The arms dealer's agent was a saggy, bulging man with a closed, suspicious face. His attitude changed as soon as Deaken produced the written authorization.

"Has there been a difficulty?" There was the slightest accent; from his colouring, Deaken guessed he was Corsican rather than French.

"Difficulty?"

"When he telephoned from Paris, Mr Grearson said I was to send the bill of lading there."

"Paris?"

"That's where the order came from."

"I know," said Deaken. "You say Mr Grearson called from Paris?"

"Yesterday morning," confirmed the man. "Quite early." Lerclerc got heavily from his chair, bent with difficulty over a safe in the corner and took out the bill of lading. "It's in order," he said, still defensive.

Deaken carefully compared the manifest duplicate with the lading certificate. It took a long time because he was careful. He was conscious of Lerclerc shifting behind the desk. When he looked up Lerclerc said, "All correct?"

"Appears to be."

Lerclerc visibly relaxed. "A little pastis?" he offered, seeming to think a celebration justified.

Deaken nodded and Lerclerc heaved himself out of his chair. As he poured, he said, "We enjoy doing business, even subsidiary business, with your organization."

"So Mr Ortega made clear." Deaken hesitated. "It's a worthwhile intercession."

Lerclerc looked up sharply as he returned with the drinks, still alert for criticism. "There's never been a difficulty from this port, ever," he said. "We've always earned our five per cent. I know where to go, who to see."

Deaken accepted the water decanter and watched the liquid turn milky. "I'm sure you do," he said soothingly.

"To continued business," toasted Lerclerc.

Deaken drank. "So Mr Grearson wasn't personally here yesterday?"

The other man seemed surprised at the repeated question. 'No," he said. "Should he have been?"

"I understood he was."

Lerclerc shook his head. "Been with Azziz long?"

"Just started."

"An impressive organization."

From somewhere just beyond the office Deaken heard a clock strike and confirmed the time from his watch. "I've a pickup scheduled from the airport. I'm going to be late," he said. "Can I use your telephone, to get a message to the pilot?"

Lerclerc grimaced apologetically. "Bloody telephone has been out of order since this morning," he said. "I've had three promises of an engineer's call."

Deaken finished his drink in a heavy gulp. "Then I'll have to leave immediately."

He was forty-five minutes late getting back to Marseilles airport but the helicopter pilot was still waiting obediently. The departure formalities were as easy as they had been earlier in the day and he was airborne within thirty minutes. They left on the same flightpath, directly out over the sea. To Deaken's right the sun was setting in a defiant burst of red and scarlet, half submerged in the distant sea.

There had already been notification from the communications room of the helicopter's return and the two men stood at the expensive panoramic windows of the *Scheherazade* stateroom, gazing westwards in the half light, seeking the identification markings.

"What did you tell Ortega?" asked Grearson.

"That he was new to your staff; that I wanted to try him out. The agreed profit was to remain but I wanted Ortega's assessment of how Deaken bargained up to it."

The American lawyer frowned. "Didn't he find that unusual?"

"I undertook to move the next difficult shipment through him," said Azziz. He spotted the red and green lights of the helicopter. Almost at once they heard the wind-slapping sound and saw the black outline of the machine pass to port. They turned away from the window.

"I'm still unsure about Deaken being unsupervised," said Grearson.

"Don't be," said the Arab dismissively. "He's a fool. What about the second shipment?"

"Everything ready in two or three days."

"Transport?"

"Chartered from Levcos again."

"Anything from Makimber?"

"Not yet," said Grearson. "You know it's often not easy, establishing direct contact at once."

The door opened and Deaken entered. Both men were struck by the new confidence, a bounce in the way he moved. Neither remembered hearing a knock at the door.

Deaken offered Azziz an envelope. "End-User certificate, manifest, official bill of lading and purchase receipt, in the sum of 53,550,000 Swiss francs from Ortega back to you." Deaken realized that he sounded like a schoolboy presenting an end-of-term report to his father.

"You made a good bargain."

"Thank you," said Deaken. "So now there are no more problems? You can turn the *Bellicose* back?"

The Arab nodded.

Deaken looked at him expectantly. Azziz frowned and Deaken said, "Well, why don't you?"

Azziz appeared momentarily surprised at the suggestion. "Of course," he said, moving to the telephones.

Deaken waited until the Arab was sufficiently far away from them and said to Grearson, "I thought you would have brought the bill of lading back from Marseilles."

Grearson looked at him intently. "Why should I have done that?"

"I thought you went there yesterday to see the shipping agent."

"Paris," corrected the American. "I wanted to find out about the original order. And what progress there was in trying to trace where they're being held."

Deaken allowed himself to be deflected. "Any news?" he said.

"Clearly we can't let the people in Paris have the photograph to make their own comparison," said Grearson. "The helicopter is going up at first light tomorrow to bring back all the brochures and information they've managed to assemble on holiday farms."

Azziz came back into the group. "We're contacting Levcos through Athens," he said. "The turn-about instructions will go from Piraeus."

"So maybe the stuff from Paris will be superfluous," said Deaken. "I thought Grearson went to Marseilles, not Paris," he added. He was looking directly at Azziz as he spoke.

Azziz returned the look, his face expressionless. "Paris," he said. "You must have misunderstood."

12

Hinkler and Bartlett, who were the first Evans contacted because he knew they were in Rome and would be together, as they always were, arrived in Brussels on the morning flight, bringing Sneider with them. Sneider was drunk, at that lopsided, unprotesting stage of drunkenness. Evans shook hands with Hinkler and Bartlett; Sneider sniggered.

"Been like it for a week," said Hinkler, who was wide-shouldered and blond and looked more Germanic than Sneider, whose parents were immigrants to Milwaukee. "When he hasn't been drinking he's been getting laid."

"How long has he been out of Libya?" asked Evans.

"Fortnight," said Bartlett.

"I guess he's allowed," said Evans.

"What is it?" said Bartlett.

"We'll wait for the rest," decided Evans.

Hinkler and Bartlett both looked very fit. Despite the drunkenness, Sneider was lean and hard, his face leathered brown from the three years he had spent in the Libyan training camps.

"Sure," accepted Bartlett at once, accepting the soldier's logic against unnecessary repetition. "Why don't we get Sneider bedded down?"

Still smiling, Sneider allowed himself to be taken to the secondary bedroom in the rue des Alexiens apartment. They only bothered to unlace and remove his boots.

With the money he had been given for expenses, Evans had restocked the bar. He nodded towards it when they returned to the living room. Hinkler poured two brandies without asking Bartlett what he wanted. Evans took Scotch.

"How's it been?" asked Evans. He knew Bartlett and Hinkler had quit Libya a year before him.

"Rough," said Hinkler. "There was something going in Iran, training again, but it was a worse disaster than Gaddafi. Didn't get paid for three months and they actually expected us to take notice of their damned religious crap. God keep me from religious revolutionaries."

"We were thinking of San Salvador when you called," said Bartlett. "Good contracts being offered."

"Know anyone there?"

Bartlett shook his head. "Supposed to be some of our guys there, but we haven't heard any names."

"Where's the recruitment?"

"Frankfurt," said Hinkler.

"That's where I found Marinetti," said Evans.

"Is he in with us?" asked Bartlett.

Evans nodded. "He said he'd come."

"Good," said Hinkler.

Marinetti was the explosives expert. They had all expected to be captured by the Vietcong when a deep penetration into the Parrot's Beak in Cambodia fouled up, in 1972, but Marinetti had covered their trail with booby traps and given them the hour they needed to be airlifted out.

"Anybody else?" said Bartlett.

"Hank Melvin," said Evans. "And Nelson Jones."

Hinkler and Bartlett nodded together. "Most of the old team," remembered Hinkler.

"All but Rodgers and Ericson," completed Bartlett.

Rodgers was still in Libya. Ericson was permanently in a vets' hospital in Phoenix, both legs amputated at midthigh where he'd trodden on an antipersonnel mine in Da Nang, three months before Nixon's peace with honour, and mentally unable even to use a wheelchair.

Melvin was the next to arrive. The Texan telephoned from the airport and reached the rue des Alexiens fifteen minutes ahead of Marinetti. The greetings with those already there were subdued, without any theatrical boisterousness, and Evans was glad; they were still a team, he thought gratefully. Melvin had travelled from Madrid where he was negotiating a contract in Mozambique; Marinetti confirmed that until Evans's call, he was considering the San Salvador offer.

"It's always goddam training," said Melvin. "Never combat."

Evans had always suspected that Melvin got pleasure out of fighting, but he had never let them down.

"They'd expected us to take our payment within the country in San Salvador," protested Marinetti. "Can you imagine what a load of crap that would have been, toy-town paper only good for wiping your ass once you're out of the country!''

Because he had had to come from America, Nelson Jones was the last to arrive. The extremely tall black man came quietly but with smooth assurance into the apartment, smiling and nodding in recognition of those already assembled. Without any pretension, he and Evans greeted each other with an open-palmed, slapping handshake.

''Hi,'' said Jones generally. There was a comfortable response, a reaction to someone coming home. Jones was six foot six and completely bald.

''Why don't we get Sneider up?'' suggested Evans.

Hinkler and Bartlett accepted their responsibility, coming from the smaller bedroom within minutes with the third man. Sneider blinked, tried to focus, licked his dry lips, then shook his head. ''Reunion,'' he snorted. ''Mother-fucking reunion.'' He saw the drinks on the side table and moved towards them.

''No!'' Evans spoke softly.

Sneider hesitated, then halted without looking around. 'What?'' he said.

''No.''

The man turned, angling his head to focus upon Evans. ''I want a drink.''

''I said no.''

There was a sense of anticipation in the room, the feeling of spectators witnessing arm wrestling between two evenly matched men. Evans hadn't wanted to put the other man into this position and moved to get him out of it. ''We're working,'' he said. ''It's a job and we're all here. It's time for briefing.'' It was an exaggeration but it allowed Sneider his escape. Another victory with honour, thought Evans; sometimes it was difficult for him to remember he didn't have the inherent authority of the American military to back every command.

Sneider nodded, moving away from the drinks. "Good to be aboard," he said.

Evans realized the man was still not completely sober. Because they were what they were—and because it was all he really knew about—Evans set out the financial details of the contract, intent upon their reaction. Even Sneider looked impressed.

"To do what?" asked Jones.

"Get somebody back," said Evans.

"Kidnap?" queried Hinkler.

"Seemed like it," said Evans. "It was left vague."

Bartlett looked around the room at the assembled men. "Isn't this a little heavy?"

"They don't seem to think so."

"Where is it? What have we got to do?" said Marinetti, always the practical one.

"I don't know yet," confessed Evans. "I had to gather a group together, then report back."

"And we get paid, even if we're not used?" queried Jones, reverting to the financial details.

"In advance," confirmed Evans

"Sure this is straight?" demanded Hinkler.

"Positive."

"How?" demanded Bartlett at once.

"I know who it is."

The seven men gazed at him, waiting.

"It's on a need-to-know basis," said Evans.

One by one they nodded, accepting the refusal. Evans felt a stir of satisfaction that they still trusted him as a commanding officer.

"What about materials?" said Marinetti.

"All being provided."

"Until we know what it is, we won't know what we want," he pointed out objectively.

"It'll be available, whatever we want. Anything."

"How can you be sure?" said Sneider; the effort of concentration was obvious but he was achieving it.

"I'm sure," said Evans.

"Opposition?" said Jones.

"Unknown, as yet."

"It's a lot of money for going around with our pants around our ankles," judged Hinkler.

"No one's going in bare-assed," assured Evans. "There was a preliminary meeting and I was asked to assemble a force. Which I've done. Now I get back and we go on from there."

"You think it's Europe?" persisted Marinetti.

"I said I'm not sure," said Evans. He would be offending their professionalism, he knew.

"Europe's dangerous," said Melvin, entering the discussion. "They're too well organized here."

"You get your money for coming," said Evans. "And your expenses. If you don't like it, when it's set out, then you can back away."

"Seems fair enough to me," said Hinkler. Bartlett nodded in immediate agreement.

"Been a long flight," said Jones. "I might as well hang around to see what the score is."

"Any currency I want, wherever I want it?" queried Marinetti, cautious to the last.

"In advance," assured Evans.

"Then I'm in."

"Me too," said Melvin.

They all looked at Sneider. "That leaves you," said Evans.

Sneider smiled, a straight expression for the first time since he had entered the apartment. "Be a pity to break up a winning team," he said.

Deaken was impatient to leave the yacht. The uncertainties and doubts of the previous evening had been washed away by his awareness that they had met Underberg's demands and that he would soon be with Karen again. He was on deck before the tender was lowered from its davits, tapping his hand irritably against his leg as the boat was manoeuvred into the water and then reversed against the stepway. Deaken was waiting on the platform when it came alongside. There was a shout from the deck, and he waved up to one of the girls.

The tender was halfway across the harbour when he heard the *Scheherazade* helicopter returning. He hadn't realized that it had left the yacht.

There was a tug of nervousness just before he landed, increasing as he climbed the harbour steps. It disappeared the moment he saw that the designated kiosk was empty. The day was close and muggy, and Deaken left the door open to make the most of what little air there was. He positioned the recorder and fixed the listening attachment, staring around him when he finished. It really was beautiful, he thought, properly noticing the harbour and Monaco rising in wedding-cake tiers behind for the first time. Spectacular in fact. Just the place to bring Karen. There would be cheap-enough hotels away from the front. That was all they would need, a clean, comfortable *pension* where he could comfort her and convince her that the nightmare was over and that she didn't have to worry anymore. Just sleep and food and to lie in the sun; not even sex if she didn't want it. Everything at her pace, as she dictated it.

Deaken had turned back inside the box and closed the door against the noise of the harbour when the telephone sounded. There was no nervousness when he lifted the receiver this time, nor forgetfulness in starting the recording.

"Everything's resolved," he announced, as soon as he heard Underberg's voice.

"Tell me how," said Underberg, the voice as patronizing as always.

He had once longed to pulp that arrogant, supercilious face, remembered Deaken. It seemed a juvenile reaction now; all that mattered was getting Karen back.

Succinctly Deaken identified the freighter and gave under Underberg's detailed questioning, the itemized con-

tents of its cargo. He set out its routing and the brief
Madeira docking and insisted, in reply to the repeated
question, "It's already been turned back."

"When?"

"Last night."

"What time?"

"Eight," said Deaken. He should have known more
positively. "About eight."

"Good," said Underberg. "Very good."

"What about Karen? And the boy?"

"I'll need better proof than this," said Underberg. "And
turning the boat around is only half of what I want."

Deaken's euphoria burst, like an overinflated balloon.
"Only half?"

"You surely didn't think we intended letting those arms
go to waste, did you? There's another destination for
them."

"Where?"

"All in good time," said Underberg.

"What do you want me to do?" asked Deaken dully.

"It'll take at least three days, maybe four, for the
freighter to get back," said Underberg. "We'll make it
another forty-eight hours."

"No, wait!" said Deaken urgently. "How is she? How's
Karen?" As an afterthought, he added, "And the boy?"

"Perfectly well," said Underberg. "We're keeping our
side of the bargain."

"And we're keeping ours," said Deaken hurriedly.

"Then everything is going to work out fine, isn't it?"
Underberg replaced the receiver. He was at the window,
binoculars in hand, when Deaken emerged from the kiosk.
Underberg decided he believed the lawyer. Which meant
Azziz and Grearson were deceiving the man, as he had
expected them to do. He moved away from the window
overlooking the harbour, impatient for the call from Levy.

*   *   *

The package had been delivered to the stateroom before the shore-bound tender drew alongside the harbour edge. It contained a list of twenty possible holiday farms, only eight with illustrations. The one at Rixheim was the fifth they came to; the large communal room was considered a feature and was prominently displayed, with two separate colour photographs in the brochure. Azziz and Grearson sat side by side, comparing them to the Polaroid picture showing Deaken's wife and the boy. The sideboard was identical, even to the matching plates and kitchenware and the manner in which it was arranged. The fireplace with its intricate apparatus of cogs and chains was better shown in the brochure. The bench upon which the couple were sitting had been dragged from one side, they could see.

"For once he wasn't foolish," said Grearson.

"It was a good idea," said the Arab. He added: "I'm glad we took the precautions we did."

Immediately Grearson picked up a telephone and was connected at once to Paris. It was a brief conversation.

"The major, Evans, has made contact," he said. "He's got a unit ready."

"Good," said Azziz.

13

Karen was aware of his concern as soon as Levy came into her bedroom.

"What is it?" she said.

"The boy."

"What's wrong?"

"I don't know."

She waited, wanting a small victory. After a moment he said, "Can you help?"

Because of the permanently closed shutters in her room she had grown accustomed to the darkness. As she followed the Israeli along the corridor she realized it was still only half light. The carefully made resolution about winding her watch had been forgotten and it had stopped at one o'clock; she didn't know whether that had been day or night.

Two men were already in Azziz's room. Greening was uncomfortable, not knowing what to do. Leiberwitz turned at their entry and said, "He's shamming. There's nothing wrong."

Karen pushed past him. The boy stared up at her, dull-eyed but aware of what was going on around him. The bruising had developed so that his cheeks and lips were black, fading at the edge into a yellow colour, as if they had been treated with iodine. He was greased in perspiration, hair lank and sticking to his forehead. His bedding was damp from his body and the room was pungent with his smell; periodically, almost at timed intervals, he shuddered convulsively, as if he were cold. Karen reached out hesitantly, touching his wet forehead.

"He's not shamming," she said to Leiberwitz.

"Who asked you?" demanded the bearded man belligerently.

"He did," she said, indicating Levy. What would she have done if it had been her child? A simple answer: get a doctor.

"We can't leave him like this," she said to Levy.

"It's probably only flu."

"You don't know that."

"No doctor," he insisted. "You do something."

"I don't know *what* to do!" she protested. Illness repelled her, made her feel nervous and unclean. Her father had been killed outright in a traffic accident when she was ten, the injuries too severe for anyone to view the body, and by the time her mother became ill she had already left Pretoria and was in her second year at the London School of Economics. None of the family had realized how quick it would be; by the time she got back to South Africa, her mother was dead. It had been her younger sister who had coped with the blanket baths and the bedpans. Secretly—a secret she kept even from Richard because she was ashamed of it—she was glad she had got back too late.

"It's only a fever." Levy was adamant.

"Cold water then," she said doubtfully. Greening went to get it. "Get his clothes off. And fresh bedding."

She stood back while Levy and Leiberwitz took off Azziz's stinking clothing. The boy put up a feeble resistance and they left him with his underpants. They rolled him back and forth to clear the bed-covering and replaced it with some linen from the bottom of the wardrobe. The man who brought the water came with a towel and Karen attempted to dry Azziz's perspiration, trying to prevent her fingers actually coming into contact with the boy's skin,

but at the same time making sure no one else noticed her
squeamishness. She discarded one towel and demanded
another, using it to wipe Azziz after she had sponged him
with cold water. When she was wiping his face their eyes
held briefly, and the boy managed a half-smile. The perspiration broke out afresh the moment she cleaned him.

"I think he should be covered," she said uncertainly.
"Sweat it out."

Greening returned almost at once with more blankets; as
soon as they were put on him, Azziz attempted to thrust
them away.

"And water," Karen said. "He should have a lot of
liquid." She was grateful it was Greening who lifted
Azziz's head and held the cup to the boy's mouth.

Karen pulled back from the bed, wanting to get away as
soon as possible.

"Thank you," said Levy.

"I still think he should see a doctor."

"No."

"What happens if he dies?"

"He won't die. It's a chill, nothing else."

"A little while ago you thought it was flu." She looked
around the room. "I want a bath," she said.

Levy led her to the bathroom and entered ahead of her,
taking the key from inside the lock; there was still a
pushbolt, which secured it from the inside.

"I shall be right outside the door," he said. "If I hear
the bolt go across, I'll break it down."

She noticed that the small window was unbarred, even
lifted, to let in about three inches of early morning light.
The drop to the ground would be about twelve feet, she
guessed, maybe a little more. She said nothing, staring at
Levy and waiting for him to go back into the corridor.

"Right outside," he said, as if fearing she hadn't
understood.

Karen needed to use the toilet but didn't want Levy to
hear. She started to run the bath, turning the taps full so

that the water splashed loudly into it. The heating worked
by an ancient mechanism that operated the gas jets automatically when the hot-water tap was turned. It exploded into
life, frightening her. Everything was loud and echoing and
she was sure Levy wouldn't hear a thing. Afterwards she
crouched at the window, not opening it farther in case he
heard the sash creak; it was like looking through a letter
box.

The window overlooked the front of the house and the
lane beyond. Their exercise area was to the left; dew still
whitened the grass and hung in droplets from the summer
spiders' webs which skeined the bisecting hedge. By
straining, she could pick out the fields and the sloping hill
beyond where she had seen the labourers working. Already
it was touched by the first warm fingers of sun and pockets
of mist were forming, like uncertain smoke. Fairy fires,
she thought; that's how she would describe it to her babies
when they grew old enough to want stories. She often
thought of phrases and simple little plots. When the time
came she wanted them to be her stories, not somebody
else's.

Beyond the bordering hedge the lane ran straight and
black, still shadowed by the clustered hills. She strained
again, in the other direction this time, trying to see some
neighbouring houses or farms; there were a lot of thick-
haired trees and, as she watched, a clock bell struck,
unexpectedly counting off a quarter-hour. She couldn't see
the tower but it hadn't sounded far away.

"You all right?" Levy's voice made her jump.

"Fine," she said.

She undressed and got into the bath, consciously making
plenty of noise. She stood to soap herself completely,
welcoming the feel of the water after so many days. It was
not until she sat down that she looked sideways and saw
the empty keyhole practically level with the edge of the
bath. He wouldn't, she thought at once. And immediately
questioned her certainty. Why not? What justification did

she have for investing him with any sort of decent feeling? But she still didn't think he would have looked. She was careful to dry herself standing to the side, where she would not be visible through the tiny opening, regretting that she had no perfume or cologne. Until that moment she hadn't realized something else that had been taken from her, the right to be feminine.

She released the water and cleaned the bath and at the door paused for a moment, reluctant to leave. Briefly, for a few minutes at least, she had been able to do whatever she liked; it was something approaching a moment of freedom.

Levy was waiting immediately outside.

"Your face is all shiny and pink," he said.

The remark disconcerted her, confused her. "I enjoyed the bath," she said. "Thank you."

"The boy's sleeping. The fever's still the same, but he's sleeping."

"Good."

Neither appeared to know what to do.

"We might as well have breakfast," he said.

"All right."

Initially they ate without speaking, Levy attentive to her needs and passing the coffee pot and the basket of croissants towards her without being asked. Once, as he offered her some butter, their hands touched and he smiled apologetically.

"This seems to be going on forever," she said.

"Yes," he said. "I'm sorry."

"You're not terrorists, are you?" said Karen in sudden challenge.

"We know what we're doing," said Levy defensively.

Karen shook her head. "I was reading politics in London, at the School of Economics, when my mother died. I went to South Africa for the funeral and never bothered to go back and complete the course because I'd met Richard. He was a friend of the family and already involved in politics—

radical politics, for South Africa. He appeared in court for a lot of people, not just there but elsewhere. So I met plenty . . .'' She stopped, knowing that she had made her point clumsily. "You're not like them at all—none of you.''

"We're not trying to be *like* anyone.''

"So what are you?''

"Jews. Doing what Jews have always done. Fighting to survive.''

Karen knew a sudden surge of pity. She *had* encountered terrorists; too many, because although she thought she shared many of their views, she had rarely liked or trusted the people who expressed them. She was also familiar with the men who confronted them: riot police, armoured units, and elite, trained squads, with dogs and gas, and plastic and rubber bullets, and water cannon. This gentle-eyed, crinkle-haired man who worried about breakfast civilities wouldn't stand a chance. He had slapped her, certainly, knocked her down, although that had been more of an accidental trip. And beaten the boy. But that hadn't been the ruthless unthinking cruelty she had known other people capable of; that had been sudden, flaring anger. And nerves. She corrected the thought. More nerves than anger, far more. Poor bugger, she thought.

"What time is it?'' said Karen.

"Eight.''

She set and wound her watch. "Forgot,'' she said. She wouldn't let it happen again—it was important to keep track of the time. Though exactly why, she wasn't quite sure.

"We could walk in the garden if you like.''

"All right.''

He stood back to allow her to go through the door ahead of him. She hadn't been expecting the courtesy and half collided with him. They both smiled, embarrassed.

"You're not going to run away, are you?'' he said.

"No,'' she said. Why give him that assurance so readily? The faraway field was being worked again, bowed men following a machine that appeared to be ploughing a slow, unwavering line. She thought the field was pretty, neatly patterned as if they were knitting the design into the earth. Crows were sounding approval from the high elms and she heard again the clock-chime she had counted in the bathroom. She turned, but couldn't see the tower. There were more trees and more crows, their nests picked out on the upper branches like musical notes for a tune the occupants couldn't get right. It was still wet underfoot. Karen saw her shoes were being stained black. More musical notes.

"How long have you been married?" Levy did not look at her.

"Nine years," she said. "What about you?"

"Three."

"Children?" It was a blurted question.

"Two," he said. "Both boys." He smiled in private recollection. "Shimeon is two . . . named after me. Yatzik is a baby, just four months." The correction came immediately. "Five months. I've been away for a while."

"I haven't got any children."

"Why not?" It was a thoughtless question from a man still enclosed in his own thoughts.

They reached the perimeter edge near the hedge and beyond it the trees with their tuneless birds. He took her elbow, an automatic gesture to guide her around. She was aware of the contact but didn't try to pull away.

"Richard doesn't want to."

"Why not?" he repeated.

She shrugged. "He says he wants to get settled first . . . become established."

She was aware of him stiffening at the words, his hand actually tightening against her arm. "My shoes are getting soaked," she said.

"Why not take them off?"

She was seized at once by the careless, uncomplicated delight of doing something without thought of censure or

explanation or excuse. For now. The coldness of the grass
came as a shock. She shivered, and he tightened his grip
on her arm. Around them birds screeched and guffawed,
as if aware of the awkwardness; the sun finally shouldered
itself up over the barrier of the trees. Karen's feet were
frozen and she felt ridiculous, standing before him with
her shoes in her hand: they weren't even her newest pair
and the insoles were stained with wear. She hadn't thought
she was going anywhere.

"That wasn't a good idea," she said.

"No."

She looked helplessly down at her feet, then at the shoes
in her hand. "It'll be worse if I put them on again."

"We'd better go back."

She gave another involuntary shiver.

"We'd better get you dry. I don't want anyone else
falling sick."

They walked, self-consciously apart, back to the farmhouse. Karen made Man Friday tracks over the flagstones;
they were even colder than the grass.

"I'll use the towel in my room," she said, wondering as
she spoke why an explanation was necessary.

"I'll see how the boy is."

It was a wide staircase and they went up side by side,
careful still not to touch.

"I'll get dry then," she said at the top.

"Yes."

It wasn't until she got back to the room that Karen
realized that she had left so hurriedly, at Levy's summons,
that she hadn't made the bed. She took the towel from its
rail near the washstand and sat down on the thrown-back
covering, crooking her leg in front of her. Her feet had
dried already but walking barefoot had made them dirty.
She put water from the jug into its matching bowl, placed
it beside the bed and immersed both her feet.

She looked up to see Levy in the doorway.

"How is he?" she asked.

"Asleep," said Levy. "Still sweating. No different really."

She dried her feet, taking care to ensure that her skirt didn't ride up over her thighs.

"Your shoes are still wet."

"I'd better wait until they dry; they're the only ones I've got." She tucked her legs beneath her. She wished the bed were made.

"I'll put them outside when the sun gets hotter."

"Thank you."

"That's all right." He remained in the doorway, as if there were a demarcation line he could not cross. "Would you like to try backgammon again?"

He had tried to teach her the previous afternoon, under Azziz's contemptuous stare, and she hadn't wanted to learn. "No thanks."

"Cards?"

"I don't know any card games."

"I want to make love to you."

"Yes," she said. "I know." Why wasn't she outraged? Offended at least? Frightened?

He came into the room and closed the door. Karen knew that if she wanted to she could stop him. But she said nothing. Levy bent down and picked up the bowl. The water was dirty, creating a line around the edge and she wished it hadn't. He put it on the washstand and came back to kneel before her, not touching her but leaning forward, to bring his face against hers and not really kissing; more biting and nipping, trying to get her lips between his teeth. Karen felt a flood between her legs, a flood she hadn't known before and which embarrassed her. They collided in their urgency, his hands moving over her, not groping and pawing but seeking reassurance. She felt his touch beneath her skirt and opened her legs, wanting to help him all she could. He couldn't wait to undress himself, just thrusting aside his trousers and stabbing at her. Karen came to him, the whimper rising into a moaning scream as they burst together and she felt his hardness going on and on as if forever. At first, after the initial coupling, they were wrong, mistiming each other, but then he slid his hands beneath her buttocks and held her, slowing her to his movement until they rode together, each in perfect time with the other. Despite their frenzy and the flow that had already soaked her, it took a long time: they grew comfortable with each other, enjoying the fit. It was Karen who started the race, nails deep into the thickness of his legs, hauling him into her with each thrust.

"Come on," she gasped. "Come on, come on, come on," bucking each time she made the demand.

Levy tried desperately to keep up, like a man running for a disappearing train. He just missed. She was already exploding in a back-arching groan when he made it, hurrying the more to finish at the same time. They ended the journey together, limp and exhausted against each other, conscious of the discomfort of clothes between them.

"Kiss me," she said.

They undressed afterwards, giggling at the reverse order, reaching out to touch and to feel as if afraid that as quickly as it had happened it would end and they would lose each other.

"Your back is bruised," he said. "I'm sorry."

"It doesn't hurt."

Naked they tunnelled into the bed, building their own burrow. Very quickly it became hot.

"I believe this is called the Stockholm Syndrome. Women developing sexual fantasies about men who kidnap them."

"It didn't seem like a fantasy to me."

"It didn't to me, either."

"Sorry?"

"No," she said. "Are you?"

"No."

"It's . . ." She stopped, unable to find the expression

she wanted. ". . . strange though, isn't it?'' she finished badly.

"Yes," said Levy. He was moving his hand over her body, as if he still needed the reassurance of her presence.

"What's your wife's name?"

"Rebecca."

"What's she like?"

Levy thought for a while, as if he needed to remember precise details. "Dark," he said. "Black hair and deep brown eyes. She's tall, slim. She graduated two years before me."

"Graduated?"

"She's a teacher—we both are."

Karen pulled away to scrutinize his face. "It suits you better . . . better than being a man with a gun, I mean." She felt a satisfaction at having been right about him. And at the same time—inexplicably—a disappointment. Was that what had originally attracted her to him, the fervent radicalism Richard had once had but now lost? She pushed the thought away, unwilling to make the comparison.

"Were teachers," he corrected. "Not anymore."

"Why not?"

"Can't be," he said. "Not allowed."

Levy had moved away from her now, his body still close enough to touch but his mind far distant. "We were in Beersheba, in the south. It was a good school; we had a good house. The children hadn't come of course, not Shimeon or Yatzik. Then the war happened in '73. It's strange. I'm a Sabra, born in Israel, but until then I'd never been into Sinai. The Negev but never the Sinai . . ." He reflected for a moment. Karen remained silent beside him, not wanting to intrude. "It was beautiful, so beautiful, even through the eye-slit of a tank. I couldn't get over the stillness and the size and the peace . . ." He laughed at the word. "Peace, even when we were fighting a war." There was another pause. "The Egyptians made it across the canal but we pushed them back . . . right back, right out of the desert. The Sinai was ours . . .''

Karen was conscious that his voice was charged with an intense excitement.

''It became government policy to resettle the areas. Make new homesteads. I persuaded Rebecca to give up our safe home and trust me and to come with me into a wilderness. I felt liberated, like a pioneer, the sort of settlers my parents had been, from Poland. Lots of places were developed . . . Yammit . . . Haruvit . . . that's where we made a town, near Haruvit.'' He laughed, but there was no mirth. ''Not a big town . . . a large village, I suppose. But it existed. We built houses and a school where Rebecca and I taught, and we planted and we made the desert grow. Shimeon was born there. Yatzik too . . . the only home they've ever known . . .'' Levy caressed her, and she settled into the crook of his arm.

''And then came the peace talks,'' he said. ''Camp David, with Carter and Sadat and Begin playing world statesmen. Resettlement land suddenly became occupied territory. Not the Golan, of course. Begin needed to seem strong, so he seized the Golan. But the Sinai was different. It didn't matter about all the people who had put their faith in the government; for the greater good, the occupied territories had to be returned . . .''

''For recognition, surely?''

''What recognition!'' he said. ''Israel is there on all the maps. And always will be. Israel will never gain anything by weakness. What about the Saudi Arabian plan to get official Arab acceptance of the country? They couldn't even start the bloody conference in Morocco because Libya, Syria, Algeria and Iraq treated it as a joke.''

''The Sinai has been cleared,'' reminded Karen.

''Temporarily,'' insisted Levy.

Karen wondered if Levy would accept the analogy that what had happened to the Sinai settlers was almost exactly what had happened to the dispossessed Palestinians. Perhaps a discussion for later, she decided, not now.

"What are you going to do?" she asked softly.

"Fight. Like we've always had to."

Karen felt a great sadness envelop her.

"We fought the Arabs and won. Now, if we have to, we'll fight the Jews," he said.

"You intend to fight your own people!"

"There's a monument in Israel which will always be identified with resistance. It's called Masada."

"I know," Karen said. "The Jews put themselves to the sword rather than be captured by the Romans. They didn't fight other Jews."

"This will be our Masada," he said stubbornly.

"Oh, my darling," she said. "My poor darling."

"You're patronizing me!"

"No I'm not," she said anxiously, feeling up and putting her finger against his lips. "Really I'm not. I'm just frightened for you."

"You needn't be," he said with schoolboy bravura. "We're going to have weapons enough to fight a war." She felt him turn to her. "That's what we're going to get from Azziz. A whole boatload."

"How many are there of you?"

"Enough."

"But you know how good your people are, your army and your security forces," she said. "It won't matter what sort of weaponry you've got; they'll destroy you."

"Maybe, if it was just us . . . only our settlement," conceded Levy. "But it won't be. Once the other settlers see what's happened, the resistance will spread. Throughout the Sinai and onto the West Bank: even Jerusalem. They won't be able to ignore that."

They will, thought Karen; oh, my darling, they will. Just as all strong, determined regimes always crushed any irritating resistance, whatever the morality of their argument. She had studied it, been involved in it for what seemed a lifetime. She knew the arguments, catchphrases, the clichés; and the message was always the same. The smaller sacrifice for the larger good: the justification for every general in every war. David and Goliath was a fairy story, nothing more: in real life the roof only ever fell in upon the weak and the innocent.

"I should see how the boy is," said Levy checking his watch. "And I've got to go to make a telephone call."

"Not yet," said Karen.

This time their lovemaking was slower, without any desperation, and they came together ecstatically. When he kissed her, Levy found her tears and said, "Me too, darling, it was beautiful for me."

"I'm glad," said Karen. She would let him think she cried from pleasure, she decided.

Deaken was comparing the photograph and the brochure like a man unable to accept he had the winning ticket in a fabulous lottery. "No doubt!" he said. "No doubt at all!" His excitement swept away the depression of his conversation with Underberg.

"So we can get them out," said Azziz quietly.

"*We?*" queried Deaken.

"We have some men," said Grearson. "They're already flying to Strasbourg. I made contact with them an hour ago while you were ashore."

"What's wrong with the police?"

"How long do you think that would take?" Azziz spoke dismissively. "Days of dreary explanations, then time to assemble their antiterrorist squads. I want my son back *now*. Like I thought you wanted your wife back."

"Of course I want her back," said Deaken angrily. "But what if anything goes wrong?"

"It won't," said Grearson.

Now that the opportunity had come to take the sort of action he had wanted ever since Karen's kidnap, Deaken felt a curious reluctance to act. He was still frightened, he realized. "What about the negotiations with Underberg?"

Grearson laughed contemptuously. "You heard what he said. All in good time. We're not going to get them back through any negotiation, any payment. . . . You surely didn't think we intended letting those arms go to waste, did you?" he quoted again. "They haven't *made* all their demands yet, it could be weeks before we even get into the position of negotiating."

Deaken couldn't dispute the logic. "What have you arranged?" he said.

"The nearest town of any size to Rixheim is Mulhouse," said Grearson. "There's a hotel there called the Parc. That's the assembly point."

"For whom?"

"I'm flying up."

"I want to come too," said Deaken.

"I expected you to," said Grearson, with weary resignation.

Karen wanted another bath, but she was reluctant to ask permission of anyone except Levy. Instead she got up, naked, from the bed, filled the basin with cold water and washed herself down, gasping at the water's chill. But inside she felt a burning warmth, a completeness she hadn't known for a long time. If ever. She frowned at the qualification, once more refusing the comparison, refusing to consider what she had done and what was happening to her. Only three days ago, or was it four, she had accused Richard of running. Now it was her turn.

Karen was fastening her buttons when the bedroom door burst open. Levy stood there, flushed.

"What's the matter?" she said.

14

They had already registered by the time Deaken and Grearson reached Mulhouse, arriving at the hotel on the rue Sinne singly and in pairs, with the cover story to the management that they were engineers assembling from all over France for an international conference which was due to begin within twenty-four hours across the border in Geneva. It provided a satisfactory reason for their abrupt arrival and what they expected to be an equally abrupt departure. They even paid in advance, and with cash, not credit cards. Because it was the biggest—and his by right as commanding officer—the meeting took place in Evans's room, not technically a suite but with definite aspirations, a larger than normal bedroom with a hollowed-out annexe to the side, with chairs and a table.

Deaken watched, scrutinizing every face, as Grearson explained for the first time what was expected of them. There was no expression from any of them; no shock at the idea of kidnap, no fear or apprehension at confronting unknown opposition or unfamiliar terrain. They didn't even look human. They could almost have been created from some firm flesh-coloured material that would be hard and metallic to the touch, not something that could be bruised or broken.

Grearson showed the Polaroid photograph and the holi-

122

day brochure to Evans. The man made no effort to take it. Grearson shifted impatiently.

"We agreed on terms," said Evans, setting out the priorities.

From one of the two briefcases he carried with him Grearson took sealed envelopes; only Evans' was addressed. He distributed them among the relaxed, composed soldiers who accepted the money as their right, without thanks. Each man opened his envelope and carefully counted the notes. Evans offered Grearson a sheet of paper and said, "Expenses so far."

The American scanned the list, dug into his briefcase then called each man by name, handing over the money. There was a visible relaxation when the transaction was concluded. Evans took the photograph and brochure, spreading them out upon the bed for comparison. The others crowded round.

"Better than nothing," said Marinetti. "But all it gives us is the internal layout."

"We'll need a reconnaissance," agreed Evans.

"I saw a sports shop two blocks up," said Bartlett. "Camping, stuff like that."

"Fine," said Evans. "You go."

Deaken sat silently in his chair, feeling superfluous to the discussion. Karen's life depended on these few men, and he could only watch.

"Any weapons you want will have to come from Paris," warned Grearson. "I'd like to know what they are now."

It was Marinetti who spoke again. "Doors front and back," he said, pointing to the markings on the brochure. "I'll want to blow them simultaneously, outside lock and the hinges as well, in case there are inside bolts." He looked up to Grearson. "*Plastique*," he said. "I don't care what sort. Detonators, obviously. And lead wires. A lot of wire, because I'll want to link back and front charges to go at the same time."

Grearson made neat, careful notations with a gold propelling pencil. Deaken had to concede that the American was handling himself with admirable professionalism and was as cool in this bizarre encounter as the mercenaries.

"Don't like that curve in the stairway," said Jones, sizing up the houseplan. "Be a bastard if they have time to get into position."

"Stun grenades," said Evans. He looked at Grearson. "We'll want the percussion type, developed particularly by Israel: it's better to cause everyone a little discomfort, even the boy and the woman, than for anyone to get really hurt. But we'll need earplugs."

"The Uzi is neat," said Melvin to Evans.

The organizer nodded. "Uzi automatic weapons," he instructed Grearson. "They're Israeli, too. The best."

"We'll need something different for the stand-back," said Hinkler. He was looking at the door, anxious for Bartlett to return from the sports shop.

"One sniper's rifle," Evans stipulated. "Make doesn't matter, although a Mannlicher or an Ingrams would be good. It must have an image intensifier because we'll be going in during darkness and need a night-sight."

"Glasses too," said Jones. "Infrared."

Evans looked to see that Grearson was writing it down. "Dark coveralls," he said. "Black if possible; certainly no leopard suits. Woollen berets. And night-black for our faces."

Deaken wondered if there would be any humorous reference to Jones's natural advantage. There wasn't.

"And a closed van," continued Evans. "To go and come back in."

Grearson looked up. "That all?"

"Ordinary grenades?" suggested Melvin.

"We want to bring people out alive," said Evans.

"What about a stretcher, if the boy or the woman gets hurt?" said Hinkler.

Deaken winced, and immediately composed himself,

embarrassed at revealing any emotion in front of such an impassive group.

Evans shook his head. "No time," he said. "If there's injury, we'll field-carry them away." He looked to Grearson. "You making arrangements for any medical needs?"

"That won't be a problem."

There was a staccato knock at the door. Hinkler moved hurriedly to admit Bartlett. The mercenary arranged his purchases upon the bed: an orange rucksack with a back frame, a yellow anorak, hiking boots, thick socks, and a red hat with a nodding bobble on the end.

"Great," said Evans.

Bartlett stuffed a pillow into the rucksack to give it some convincing bulk, and quickly changed into the hiker's gear.

"Bright, isn't it?" said Grearson.

"Of course it is," said Evans. "People never suspect things that are too obvious." To Bartlett he said "Why not go take a hike?"

Bartlett moved steadily along the lane, adjusting his trained march to the heavy-heeled plod of a tired walker. He had both hands tucked into the support straps of the rucksack and, with head bent, appeared uninterested in his surroundings. The details were, in fact, being recorded in his memory with the accuracy of a movie camera. There was plenty of available concealment—high banks, higher than a man in places, even Jones—topped by hedges which, in the main, were thick and concealing. Confident that he was completely hidden, Bartlett stopped at a gap, and gazed in at the house. Fifty yards of garden, exposed for most of the way unless they could use the cover of that bisecting hedge. Door locked thick and heavy, which he would have to warn Marinetti about. Covered windows, blind against the coming night. From one of the three clustered chimneys a thin curl of white smoke formed like a question mark. Bartlett was alert to everything about him and heard the trundling farm cart long before its occupants were aware of him. There were four of them, spread-eagled along the edges of an open-sided carrier, with beets piled in the middle. It was being pulled by a tractor, the driver of which wore a collar and tie, as if he were proud of the day's harvest and wanted to dress properly for it. Bartlett stood aside and as the cart passed one of the men smiled and said, "*Ça va?*"

Bartlett waved back. It was instinctive caution to shield his face although he was sure that all they would remember would be the colour of his outfit which would be discarded in an hour. He plodded on, looking in at the gate with only the sort of curiosity that a casual passerby might show. There could have been a light at one of the upper rooms, but perhaps it was a trick of the sun penetrating some unseen window at the rear. The lane rose almost immediately beyond the farmhouse boundary, and Bartlett bent into the incline, assessing the distance with each step, wanting to distance himself from any possible observation from the house. Without looking round, he suddenly cut sideways to his left, scrambling up the bank and plunging into the coppice. He sped on until he was deep in the small wood, before turning left again to bring himself out over-looking the house. Before it was visible, he took off the brightly coloured clothing and stacked it against the bole of a tree. Squirming forward on his elbows and knees, he reached the coppice edge. The vantage point gave him a view of both the side and the rear of the farmhouse. The rear door was thick, like the one in front—another reminder for Marinetti. There were no vehicles visible, but there were plenty of outbuildings and barns in which it would have been an elementary precaution to conceal them. As he watched, a man emerged from the back door, strode to the middle of the yard and looked around as if checking for anyone watching. Bartlett didn't move, knowing he was completely concealed. Appearing satisfied, the man went into one of the barns, to emerge almost immediately. He stopped in almost the same place in the yard for another, then reentered the house.

Bartlett wriggled himself backwards until he had penetrated the treeline and then rose to his feet, brushing away the leaf mould. He returned to the discarded clothing, dressed, and regained the lane in minutes. He descended back towards the village, with the same tired, stiff-kneed walk he had adopted when he passed the house the first time. On this occasion he didn't bother to look in at the gate, seemingly uninterested in something he had already looked at.

It was past seven by the time he got back to Mulhouse.

"What's it look like?" demanded Evans at once.

"Well chosen: vision on every side," reported Bartlett. "If we don't surprise them, we could be cut to pieces."

"Shit," said Jones.

It was 1:40 A.M. when the closed van arrived from Paris. It was obviously impractical to bring the contents into the hotel, so Evans went out to inspect them in the vehicle. He only bothered to take Marinetti with him to check the explosives. The two men returned within half an hour.

"Good" said Evans to Grearson. "Everything we wanted. The Uzis are brand new, still with the original grease." To the assembled soldiers he said, looking at his watch, "I've got two ten." There was a simultaneous reaction as they synchronized their watches. "Thirty minutes to Rixheim," continued the man. "Black up and dress on the way. We'll hit the farmhouse at three."

In unison they moved towards the door. Involuntarily Deaken said, "Be careful."

They all looked at him disbelievingly. Melvin said, "Don't be fucking stupid."

Edward Makimber emerged from the Teranga Hotel onto the Place de l'Union, staring around him at the familiar activity of an African township at night. Dakar didn't really resemble an African town, he corrected himself: the French influence was too strong, with its mathematically careful highways and large buildings. He set out towards the waterfront, wanting to orient himself even though it was late and the office of the men he wanted to see would be closed. Perhaps coming here would turn out to be overly cautious, as it had been in Madeira. But he was determined not to take any risk. Which was why the others were flying in the following day, from Angola. Makimber didn't like dealing with such people. But sometimes they were necessary. Just like revolution was necessary, if you wanted freedom.

For a long time Carole lay awake and then finally got up and went out on deck. Despite the lateness, the harbour and the town beyond was still bright with light, cars fireflying along the Corniche and the lower roads. She leaned against the deck rail, and thought about a distracted and seemingly lost man called Richard Deaken. He was obviously vulnerable and she felt sorry for him. Which, she recognized, wasn't professional at all. She would have to be careful.

15

While they had been waiting for the Paris delivery, Bartlett had sketched a series of reconnaissance maps of the lane approach, the side elevation and the front and back assault positions, so now the group moved confidently towards the farmhouse, expertly taking advantage of the high banking and the hedge for cover. The talking, like the map reading, had been done in the Mulhouse hotel room; now the only communication was by hand signals.

Melvin was detached to act as rearguard to warn of anyone approaching from the village, an essential posting after the possible arousing noise of the doors being blown. The inseparable Hinkler and Bartlett were dispatched farther up the lane, to enter by the track that led to the back of the house. Evans, Marinetti, Jones and Sneider hunched by the farm entrance.

Around Marinetti's right shoulder, like a bandolier, was looped the connection wire; the plastic explosives and the detonators—quite harmless when they were unconnected—were in the satchel slung for balance across the other shoulder. Both he, Evans and Sneider carried Uzi rifles. Jones had the night-sighted Ingrams sniper's weapon. The four men crouched, relaxed and unmoving, Evans checking his watch to time the progress of Bartlett and Hinkler to the rear: ten minutes had been allowed. At the count he signalled to Jones. The black man rose and vaulted the gate in one fluid movement. The other three rose too, covering the front of the house; this was the most dangerous moment if a guard had been posted. Jones was in full view of the house even when protected by the shadows of the hedge.

There was no challenge. Marinetti was the next to go over, weighted by the equipment he carried. Evans followed as lithely as Jones had done; Sneider went last. The three men sprinted, bent double, towards the house. Behind them Jones was splayed out on the ground, in firing position, the sniper's rifle to his shoulder, every part of the house clearly visible through the image-intensifier sight.

Evans stopped with his back hard against the farmhouse wall, Uzi at the ready across his body. Sneider halted at the corner, covering the side of the house. Marinetti remained at the door, kneading plugs of the explosive into place around the locks and bolts, fitting the detonator caps and threading the wires to connect the three. He backed away, like a fisherman running out a net. Evans watched until the explosives expert disappeared around the corner of the house towards the second door at the rear.

Evans looked up, frowning at the sky. There were clouds but they were tattered and threadbare, jostled and torn by a bustling wind that swept them in front of a too full-moon; it wasn't as bad as it seemed because he knew where to look, but in several moments of brightness he could see Jones clearly outlined in the garden.

Evans detected the movement as soon as Marinetti reappeared around the corner. The man stopped there, bending to twist the final connection for his wires, making them live. He looked up, giving the signal to Evans and Sneider and in turn Evans jerked the Uzi, a back-and-forth motion across his chest, knowing Jones would have him focused in the night-sight. There was a smooth, shadowy movement and the Jones arrived alongside. There was another sign from Marinetti, and Evans and Jones retreated from the door, hunching down beneath the window. With a minute to go, each man screwed in his earplugs against the percussion grenades. At two minutes to three, Marinetti fired the charges.

Marinetti had balanced it perfectly, using just enough charge to shatter the locks and hinges but no more. The noise came as a crack, the sort of sound that would have carried, like the sound of a poachers' shot, as far away as the village. Evans and Jones were on the move as the door burst in, unrestrained by any inner bolts. They ran over it, darting immediately sideways and out of the framing rectangle of light. They reached the large room simultaneously with Hinkler and Bartlett entering from the rear. Perfectly coordinated, Evans got to the stairs first, halting at the bend with Jones directly behind him: the stun grenades went one after the other, tossed lightly just to clear the upstairs bannister. There was more noise this time, the crump of explosion and then the invisible sonic shiver which they all felt despite their protection. There was hardly any pause as they raced on, no confusion even here, Evans going for the farthest door, with Jones, then Bartlett, then Hinkler taking the bedrooms which had been assigned to them from the brochure details, each door burst in with one experienced kick directed against the lock.

The house was deserted.

They all reassembled at the central corridor. Evans snapped on the light, jerking the plugs from his ears.

"They've gone," he said unnecessarily.

"Fuck it!" said Jones.

"We get paid." Hinkler grinned.

"Three minutes to search every room. Take anything that looks like proof," said Evans.

There was instant, unargued, unqueried obedience, each bedroom and the downstairs area searched hurriedly but well. Marinetti and Sneider remained at the shattered front door, alert for any signal from Melvin. They darted away singly, Evans first to establish guard at the gate, Marinetti staying in position until last at the doorway. Re-formed, they filed back down the lane, moving this time with less caution because they knew there would be no observation. Melvin rose from the ditch when they reached him, looking inquiringly back along the line.

"Too late," said Evans.

They reached the van unchallenged, driving back towards Mulhouse with the rear interior light on so they could rub the night-black from their faces and remove their dark overalls.

"That was like jerking off in a whore house," said Melvin, the man who liked to fight.

"Whoever owns that place is going to be mad as hell," said Marinetti. "We sure made a mess."

"There would have been a lot more, if they'd been there," said Evans.

It was not as big as the first farmhouse, more a cottage this time, but it was much farther away from any neighbouring houses or villages. Karen hadn't really been trying to measure, but she guessed there had been a gap of about ten minutes from the time they had passed through the last sleeping township until they pulled off the road to the new location. Twice, during the hurried departure, Azziz had been sick, ashamed despite his fever at showing weakness in front of a woman. The boy had been her first concern when they had arrived. She had cleaned him again, still careful to avoid any direct physical contact, and had told one of the men to stay with him, mopping him with cold towels. It seemed to be working back at Rixheim. They didn't bother to manacle him to the bed anymore. Despite Levy's attempt to prevent it, there was an inflamed ring of soreness around the boy's ankle.

The house was stocked in readiness. She and Levy ate together off cold meat and wine and fruit. Afterwards, without discussing it, they both went to the same bedroom. They undressed each other with the undiminished excitement of discovery and made love twice in quick succession, as if aware that their relationship had a time limit, not wanting to waste one second allocated to them.

"This place was prepared, just in case," said Karen. The windows were newly barred, like the farmhouse.

"Of course," said Levy. "Everything's been anticipated."

"By schoolmasters and settlers?" She nuzzled against him, arm tight around his waist as if afraid he might try to escape.

"Underberg's no schoolmaster. Just a Zionist who thinks like we do."

"Underberg?"

She felt him tense slightly at disclosing the name. Almost at once he relaxed. "He brought us together," said Levy. "Until then, there'd been no organization, just a lot of people making a lot of noise, but getting nowhere."

"Why did we *have* to leave in such a hurry?"

"Underberg thought it best."

"You mean they'd found out where we were?"

It was several moments before Levy replied. Then he said, "He's not sure, but it was a possibility."

Now it was Karen who remained silent, reminded of what was actually happening to her, that it would have to end; that there *was* a time limit. "Love me again," she said huskily. "Quickly, love me again."

They were trying to conceal the nervousness they had all felt at the abrupt departure, but two empty wine bottles were evidence of the general unease.

"Our leader finds a different way to relax," said Leiberwitz.

"Maybe he's gone to bed," said Kahane loyally.

"He has!" said Leiberwitz. "With the whore."

"He's stupid to get involved," said the smallest man of the group. Mordechai Sela was thin and bespectacled, a schoolmaster like Levy.

"He's treating us like shit," complained Greening. "Tête-à-tête meals which we're expected to serve, like bloody underlings.''

"It's not causing any problem, is it?" said Kahane.

"Not if he's just screwing her," said the fifth man, Levi Katz.

"What does that mean?" said Greening.

"What happens if he becomes fond of her?"

"Rebecca's my cousin," said Leiberwitz. "I'm expected to sit by while a man married to my cousin is rutting upstairs with some gentile whore."

"What can we do about it?" said Morris Habel, the last member of the group.

"Plenty," said Leiberwitz.

16

Deaken had been so sure that he was going to get Karen back: he had rehearsed what he was going to say, how he was going to care for her. Now he felt numbed and emptied.

"It was absolutely clean," said Evans, pouring himself a Scotch. There was no shake to his hand, no indication that he laid his life on the line an hour earlier.

"Maybe . . ." began Deaken, and then stopped, looking at the tie that Evans had taken from his pocket and was offering to Grearson.

"Yes," said the older lawyer at once. "That's the Ecole Gagner colours."

"The boy's name's inside," said Evans. He turned to Deaken. "What about this?"

Nervously, like a man fearing contact with something contaminated, Deaken took the watch. He felt his heart thump wildly and his throat constrict, so that he found it difficult to speak immediately. Then he said, "Yes, that's Karen's watch."

"So they left in a hurry?" said Grearson.

Evans shook his head. "Everything had been tidied, beds made. The whole house. The tie was carefully laid across one bed, the watch in the middle of another."

"You were meant to find it," said Grearson.

Evans sipped his whisky. "That's the way it looked to me."

"Bastards!" said Deaken.

"Certainly seem sure of themselves," said Evans.

"How the hell could they have known?" said Grearson.

"Maybe they figured you'd work it out exactly as you did. They know the resources you've got, after all." The American poured himself another drink; the job was over and he was relaxing. He offered the bottle to the two lawyers. Both shook their heads.

"Where are the others?" said Grearson.

"Away," said Evans, returning to his seat. "By midday tomorrow the inquiries into what happened at the farmhouse will have reached here. We don't want them to find a vanload of weaponry."

"Where are they?" said Grearson.

"Clermont Ferrand."

"Why there?"

"I'd been there before," said Evans. "Knew there was a hotel called Foch. We needed a contact point." The man paused. "We did what we were engaged to do."

"I know," said Grearson. "The terms stand."

"Dollars," said Evans. "Everyone wants to be paid in cash. American."

"Could you come back with us to Monte Carlo?"

"Of course."

Anger flickered through Deaken. They could have been discussing a property deal or buying a car; anything but the botched attempt to recover a woman—his wife!—who was enduring God knows what sort of horror. But the anger seeped away as quickly as it had come. What good would it have done to shout and to rage?

As if aware of Deaken's thoughts, Evans turned to him and said, "I'm sorry it didn't work out."

"Thank you, for what you tried to do," said Deaken. Now he was behaving as rationally as them.

"Yes," said Grearson, rather as an afterthought. "Thank you. Mr Azziz will be grateful."

"Do you want me to disband?" said Evans.

There was a moment's hesitation. "No," said Grearson. "Not yet. Hang on awhile."

Deaken frowned. "Surely you don't think there'll be another opportunity?"

"At this moment," said Grearson, "I don't know what to think."

It took Underberg longer than expected to reach the cottage hidden away in the hills behind Sisteron: he misjudged the holiday traffic and the difficulty of overtaking on the narrow, twisting roads as he climbed up from the coast. Underberg decided the farmhouse assault had been useful because it confirmed his prediction that the Arab would fight. And he doubted that Azziz would capitulate after one failure. Azziz was a proud man, used to unchallenged success; he would be furious at what was happening and at his helplessness to do anything about it.

Levy hurried from the house to meet him, as soon as Underberg turned off the rutted track into the villa. The Israeli was grave-faced.

"Have you heard the newscasts?" he demanded the moment Underberg opened the door.

"Of course," said Underberg. "And seen the television pictures."

"A trained assault force, they said. Soldiers, a trained force of soldiers."

"It's hardly surprising, is it?" said Underberg. "Considering what Azziz does for a living."

"We never considered having to fight trained soldiers."

"You didn't have to," reminded Underberg. "I got you out in good time."

Levy grimaced.

"And don't you intend confronting trained soldiers as soon as you've got the necessary weapons?" said Underberg.

"That's different," said Levy. "Then we'll be ready . . ."

"You make it sound like some biblical confrontation, lining up on either side of a valley."

"In a way that's how we regard it."

Christ, they were stupid, thought Underberg. His carefully prepared role allowed him to give a warning. "Don't," said Underberg. "You should know better than to expect our people to fight by the rules. The Israelis fight to win—they've got to."

"We'll be ready when the time comes," repeated Levy, but without conviction. "It was just that we didn't expect the other business."

"I don't know how they discovered the place," said Underberg. "But they'll never find us here. Even I got lost."

Levy smiled grimly.

"Where are they?" said Underberg.

"I did what you said, locked them in their bedrooms. Both are on the other side of the house."

"I know Azziz is trying to cheat on us," said Underberg. "How?"

"I know," insisted Underberg. "I'm going to give him one more warning . . . to make sure he does what we want. If he doesn't, we'll have to convince him."

"What do you mean?"

"Send him some evidence that's a little more tangible than a photograph."

"No!" said Levy at once.

The rejection surprised Underberg. "What do you mean, no?"

"We're not butchers. The plan was always that they wouldn't be hurt if we could help it."

"Are you prepared to give up your settlement?"

"You know the answer to that."

"You can't fight without guns."

"I won't consider cutting off an ear or a finger. It's repellent. We're not animals."

Underberg looked beyond Levy to the cottage. "There are others who are less squeamish."

"No," said Levy, although he knew Underberg was right. "They'll fight, like I'll fight. But they won't torture."

"Like you, I hope it won't come to that."

As they walked towards the house, Underberg said, "How's the boy's chill today?"

"He doesn't seem any worse." He paused. "Or better, for that matter. I'd still like to get some sort of medical attention."

"You know that's quite impossible," said Underberg. "Let the woman look after him."

"She's doing what she can, but she's not a doctor."

Underberg stopped at the door. "Do you want to risk another commando assault?" he said.

Levy swallowed. "I suppose not."

"Then the boy stays as he is." Underberg went into the house. The Israelis were grouped in the main room, like children awaiting the arrival of a headmaster whose fierceness they had been warned about in advance. Underberg reflected it was fortunate they would never get the chance to mount their ridiculous protest in Israel; they would be annihilated in a matter of hours.

"Everything is going to be fine," he said. "Just fine."

*   *   *

There was an observation room immediately above the larger stateroom where Azziz had listened impassively to every detail of the abortive rescue attempt. Immediately after the meeting broke up, Deaken wandered up there. Padded seats ran in a half-circle below the windows. There was one low, glass-topped table and the inevitable bar. The bar was closed but Deaken didn't want a drink. He stood to starboard, looking out towards Monte Carlo, trying to isolate the blank glimmer of windows in the buildings over half a mile away, wondering if behind one of them was the bastard who kept taunting him in that condescending, mocking voice. Far below he heard the growl of the tender and then saw the craft emerge from the shadow of the yacht; Grearson and Evans were standing side by side, each holding on to the cabin roof, apparently two relaxed guests going ashore from a millionaire's yacht. He supposed that within two hours Evans would be driving northwards to Clermont Ferrand with an attaché case packed with dollar bills. The overwhelming sense of helplessness gripped him once more. Nearly another twenty-four hours before the next tenuous contact. Jesus, he had to do something more!

He turned at the sound of the door opening. Carole was wearing scuff shoes, very short shorts, and a white cotton shirt tied at the waist.

"Hi," she said.

"Hello."

"Can I come in?"

"Why not?"

Her smile faltered momentarily. She came and stood next to him at the window, staring out towards the diminishing launch. "The girls were hoping the guy you came with was going to stay. He looked evil!"

"I think he is," said Deaken mildly. She was close enough for him to be aware of her light, almost imperceptible, perfume. He was also conscious of her gaze but she didn't ask the question he expected. Instead she said, "Everyone's down by the pool."

"They usually are."

"Why are you always so shitty?"

"I didn't know I was."

There was another sad smile. Wearily she said, "Don't sit in judgement on me. We all use what we've got, the best we can. I've got a body which I know how to use. And I'm good to look at."

"Yes," he said.

She made a so-what gesture. "And because I know you can hardly stop yourself asking, I'll tell you. I got myself into the best house in Paris, one where I choose. I haven't been doing it for long and I don't intend going on for much longer. I'm not going to become a raddled old whore, doing ten-franc tricks in back alleys."

"I'm sorry," he said. "Forgive me." She was wearing a light grey eye make-up that he didn't remember from their last meeting. And a more definite lipstick.

"Why not relax?" she said.

"I'm not here to relax."

"We could just talk."

"I'm not sure that it would stop there."

"That's up to you."

This was absurd, thought Deaken. What the hell was he doing, talking like this to a whore?

"No."

Carole walked to the door. "If you change your mind, you know where I'll be."

Three hundred miles to the northwest, in the bedroom of a large cottage set among the encircling green hills of Sisteron, Karen hurriedly stood up as the key moved in the lock.

"What was that all about downstairs?" she asked.

"A visitor," Levy said.

"I thought it might have been . . ." She hesitated. "I'm glad," she said. "Insane, isn't it?"

17

Deaken recognized that the contact had become routine,
almost like leaving home at a regular time to catch the
regular train to the regular nine-to-five job. He didn't even
glance at the approaching shoreline, a commuter and
therefore bored with the landscape, but back over the stern
of the tender, seeing the wake cream behind it. And then
the figure at the rail of the retreating yacht. It was Carole,
he knew; he had seen her as he descended the steps but
pretended not to. And she hadn't called out either, to
attract his attention. Her apparent interest in him had to be
strictly professional, like the solicitous secretary and the
solicitous stewards. And why did it matter anyway? For
her attitude to be important to him under the present
circumstances would be grotesque, unthinkable. So why
was he looking back to catch a glimpse of her?

In no time they were among the outer yachts, able
because of their draught to get in close. All about him
there was the creak and tinkle of mooring ropes and stan-
chions and fantails occupied by people relaxing and laughing and drinking or eating. Safe people. Secure and
untroubled. Lucky people.

The alarm flared the moment Deaken set foot on the
jetty and saw the designated telephone box was occupied:
by a woman, too old for the shorts and the sagging halter
top, eyes cavernous from too much mascara, cheeks ablaze

141

with rouge, lips wounded by scarlet lipstick. He checked his watch: five minutes-time enough. Enormous sunglasses, like screens on stilts, were collapsed alongside her purse, which gaped open at the coin pouch for her to stuff more money into the box. She laughed, turning as she did so. Her teeth were white and even and precise, a graded monument to mathematical dentistry. Her brow wrinkled at his hovering presence and she looked pointedly at the unoccupied booths. Then she turned, hunching her shoulders against him. Her back was deeply tanned, wrinkled by overexposure to too much sun. Two minutes left. Hag, Deaken thought. Ugly bloody hag. He looked worriedly about him, knowing that he was being observed and hoping that Underberg could see what was happening and allow him some leeway. Jesus, why didn't she hurry! From a yacht against the harbour wall there was a burst of laughter followed by shrieks of alarm as a drunken man teetered theatrically, grabbing a stern stanchion to prevent himself falling into the water. Christ, how he hated them, with their comfort and complacency and their wealth! At once his rational mind cut through the panic. That was a ridiculous thought; infantile. They had every right to their money and their privilege, to laugh and drink and flirt and do what they wanted. His anger wasn't at them. The woman had put down the receiver. Deaken thrust forward before she had time to get out.

"There were other kiosks . . ." she began, but Deaken pushed past her. "Bastard," she muttered: her Australian accent made the oath sound more effective. Deaken pulled the door shut. "Bastard," came the muffled repetition through the glass. He kept his back to her. Five past twelve. Please, dear God, don't make me wait another four hours, he thought. The booth reeked of the woman, of her body, of suntan oil and a heavy, cloying perfume. Under the glare of the midday sun the trapped air felt sticky and unpleasant. He put the recorder on the tiny support and realized he had begun to read the English translation of the dialling instructions for overseas calls. He stopped, annoyed with himself and not knowing why. Ten past. He looked out of the kiosk. The woman was stumping away along the walkway on top of one of the embracing arms of the harbour, her fat buttocks wobbling with every gallumphing footstep. Bloody hag, he thought again.

The telephone rang. Deaken looked disbelievingly at it and then grabbed the instrument to his ear.

"I'm glad you waited," said the voice.

I'm glad *you* did, thought Deaken. He remembered the recorder, squeezing the suction cap into place. "Didn't have much choice," he said.

"I told you what would happen to your wife if you weren't careful about what Azziz did," said Underberg. "You let him raise an army."

"I didn't know," lied Deaken.

"You were *supposed* to know. Just as you were supposed to know everything he plans to do."

Deaken felt sick, deep in his stomach. "What else?"

"Two days ago you told me about the *Bellicose* . . . lied to me about it . . ."

"I didn't lie."

"Do you know what Lloyds of London is, Mr Deaken?" Without waiting for the lawyer to reply, Underberg said, "It's the most efficient maritime brokerage and insurance firm throughout the world. Part of that efficiency involves knowing the position of ships insured by them. You told me the *Bellicose* had been turned around . . . gave me timings. I'd already checked with Lloyds. When you told me the freighter was heading northwards it was still going south, down the coast of Africa. It still is, as a matter of fact. Lloyds don't make mistakes in their plotting. They can't afford to—any more than you can. The ship has never been turned."

Azziz was a bastard, thought Deaken. A stupid, lying bastard. "He said . . ." started Deaken but Underberg cut him off, impatient with the excuses. "I told you not to believe what he said . . . I told you to make sure that everything was done exactly as I wanted it, otherwise your wife would suffer."

"Where is she now?"

Underberg laughed. "Miles away from where your Action Men did their number," he said. "I had them out within two hours of realizing you were lying about the ship changing course. I guessed you'd found out where they were . . . and were playing for time."

So that was how it happened, thought Deaken. He said, "Is she all right?"

"Did you get her watch? And Azziz's tie?"

"I asked you if she was all right?"

"For the moment," said Underberg. "But only for the moment. I want you to understand, and more importantly I want Azziz to understand, that I'm becoming more and more irritated by what's happening. If that ship isn't turned back and directed exactly how I want it to be, then next time you and he will get a more unpleasant reminder of what we can do to them. Would you want your wife to lose a finger, Mr Deaken? Or an ear?"

"Wait!" said Deaken desperately. "Don't do that. There's no need to do anything like that. I promise you from now on everything will be done exactly as you want it. Don't . . ." Deaken's mind blocked at the thought.

"Then this time get it right," said Underberg.

"What do you want me to do?"

"Make sure this tedious lying stops," said Underberg. "On Saturday the *Bellicose* docks at Dakar. I want you to be there in person. I want you to board and I want you to be responsible for messages back to the Levcos offices in Greece, giving the precise longitudinal and latitudinal fix. And if I don't think it's right and Lloyds don't think it's right, or if the slightest thing happens to make me suspicious . . . to make me think you intend using your private army again, then your wife loses a finger. And the boy a finger. Then an ear. That's the price, Mr Deaken. A piece of their bodies for every mistake you make. Do you understand that?"

"Yes," said Deaken dully. "I understand."

"Is that recorder working properly?"

"Yes," said Deaken.

"Good. Because I want Azziz to get the proper message. I want him to hear everything I've said. And to believe it."

"Where do you want the freighter to go?"

"With the position, give Levcos the speed, so I can estimate your arrival back in the Mediterranean. Make a refuelling stop in Algiers. You'll be told what to do then in a cable addressed to you on the ship."

Whatever he tried to do he remained a puppet, controlled by the twists and jerks of this man's fingers, thought Deaken. "All right," he said.

"No more attempts to be clever."

"There won't be."

"Your wife's too attractive."

Deaken felt the sickness rise and swallowed against it. "Don't hurt her," he pleaded again.

"Whether she or the boy gets hurt depends upon you and Azziz. Don't forget that for a moment."

"I won't."

"Position and speed," insisted the man.

"Yes," said the lawyer.

"And warn Azziz against trying to trace the contact calls to the Levcos office—they'll be from a public box, so he'll be wasting his time."

"What about this contact?" said Deaken. "Azziz has got a man, Grearson. He could maintain it."

There was a hesitation from the other end of the telephone. "The same time," agreed Underberg. "Every other day."

Deaken felt relief that the link wasn't being severed. "Every other day," he repeated as if Underberg would need the confirmation.

"No more stupidity," said Underberg. "Don't make your wife suffer."

Deaken maintained his control with difficulty while they listened to the recording but, as Grearson leaned forward to stop the tape, he could restrain himself no longer. "You idiotic bastard!" he shouted at Azziz.

The attack seemed to take both the other men by surprise. Azziz recovered first. "No one speaks to me . . ."

"I do," interrupted Deaken. "It's my wife you're putting at risk. And your son. What the hell sort of man are you, willing to risk his child like that? Are you mad? Don't you see what you've done?"

Azziz's face was composed like a mask, but on either cheek tiny patches of white pinched his features. "Having located the farmhouse, we had to take our chance," he said. His voice was flat, expressionless.

"We *didn't* know about the farmhouse when I went ashore to tell him about the boat," said Deaken furiously. "When you promised me it had been turned back. It was a lie and you knew it."

Deaken walked over to Azziz. "We can't take any more chances," he said, his voice calmer. "I don't want to be here on this fucking yacht. I don't want your hospitality. I don't want to have anything to do with you. I want to be home in Geneva. With my wife. Safely." Deaken stopped breathlessly. "I think you're a stupid bastard."

"I think you're forgetting yourself," said Grearson, coming to his employer's defence.

"I'm not forgetting anything," said Deaken. "I'm not forgetting the lies or what it might cost Karen." He indicated the silent tape-recorder. "And I'm particularly not forgetting that if you hadn't behaved like such bloody fools and kept that ship going, they wouldn't have become suspicious and cleared the farmhouse. We'd have them both back by now. Most of all I can't forget that."

"It was a mistake," said Azziz in rare confession.

"It's the last one we're allowed," said Deaken.

The boy lay limp with exhaustion against the pillows, but the constant sheen of perspiration had gone so Karen assumed the fever was over. Tewfik forced himself to reach out for the flannel and then the towel, reluctant to be washed by her. Gratefully Karen surrendered them.

"How are you feeling?" she said.

"Not very strong," he said, slumping against the support and handing back the washing things. "What's been wrong with me?"

"I don't know."

"I ache," said Azziz. "I ache all over."

"You've not eaten anything for a long time," said Karen. "I'll bring you something."

"Thank you," said Azziz. "For what you've done, I mean. I know how you've looked after me. I appreciate it."

He hadn't been aware of her reluctance any more than the others had, realized Karen thankfully. "That's all right," she said.

"Why did we have to move?"

"Your father discovered the first place." She wondered if Richard had been involved. It hadn't occurred to her until now; very little about Richard had occurred to her in the last few days. And she didn't feel any remorse.

Tewfik smiled wanly. "I knew he would," said the boy proudly. "They'll be sorry for what they've done."

"Yes," she said uncomfortably.

"They're bastards, aren't they?" demanded the boy.

This time her hesitation was longer. "Bastards," she agreed at last, knowing she had to.

The response from Africa to their request for a delivery delay arrived thirty minutes after Deaken had left the stateroom. The call was routed through Paris and for better reception Grearson went up to the communications room. It was a short conversation.

"Makimber says no," reported the American lawyer as he reentered the stateroom. "It seems Underberg is right: Makimber insists they're necessary for a specific date. It's got to be the contracted time."

"That's a pity," said Azziz. His anger at the confrontation with Deaken had gone—anger was wasteful and Azziz never wasted anything.

Grearson appeared surprised at the calm reaction. "So we give Deaken all the authority he wants to turn the ship back?"

Azziz didn't reply at once. Then he said, "How about the second shipment?"

"Ready for loading."

The Arab smiled. "What does Underberg want?"

"The *Bellicose* turned back."

"A *ship* apparently turned back," Azziz said. "What if a vessel looking like the *Bellicose* and loaded like the *Bellicose* made the Algeria rendezvous?"

"It won't work," said Grearson. "The instructions are that Deaken sails with the *Bellicose* and reports its position, with independent checks from Lloyds."

"And where do you suppose he'll get the position readings?"

"From the navigating officers and the captain."

"Exactly," said Azziz. "At first light tomorrow we get rid of the damned Deaken for good. I want you to go to Athens . . . see the Levcos people and make whatever deal is necessary. I want the *Bellicose* to sail from Dakar out of sight of land but to continue southwards. But I want calculations given to Deaken showing that it's travelling in the opposite direction. And those are the ones I want the ship and Levcos to transmit to Lloyds."

"But surely even he can work out where the sun comes up," said Grearson. "He'll know he's going the wrong way."

"So what?" said Azziz. "There's nothing he can do. He'll have to go along with it. You're doing the negotiations now, without any involvement from that fool. We'll agree to an exchange. We'll agree on times and places and whatever else they want. When we get Tewfik, they can have the ship and its contents."

"Just like that?" said Grearson doubtfully.

"No," said Azziz, smiling again at his lawyer's surprise. "Not quite. Your excellent soldiers will be on board. If I submit once to terrorism, then it will never stop—that's a worthwhile lesson to be learned from the Israelis."

"What about the woman?" asked Grearson as an afterthought.

"I couldn't care less what happens to her," said Azziz. "Any more than I care what happens to Deaken."

The sun disappeared finally, and reluctantly Underberg moved in from the balcony of the Monaco hotel. He was sure they would move quickly after the threat to hurt the boy and the woman. He would have to warn Makimber, to give him time to get to Dakar and prevent Deaken getting aboard the *Bellicose*. He would have to remember an appropriate time to remind the African of a favour owed.

18

Everything was arranged with the customary efficiency of Azziz's organization: the helicopter connection to the airport, courteous airline officials on standby to escort Deaken to the waiting aircraft, stewards in readiness to show him to his seat. It was a direct flight with no transfer connections and Deaken arrived in the Senegalese capital just after midday. The heat took his breath away, the first reminder of a return to Africa. At once there were others. The forgotten sweet-sour odour; flies which thrive in it; lethargic people accustomed to the sun-slowed pace; colours, seemingly bleached, yellows and ochres, the white of the airport building harsh in comparison.

The airport taxi was a dilapidated Renault, with missing handles and sagging door linings, the dashboard and mirror surrounds a bazaar of dangling amulets and rosaries, as if its very survival depended upon the will of God. The legacy of the city's importance during the French occupation of Africa continued as they entered Dakar. The wide, straight streets were still policed by mottle-trunked plane trees, attendants to the set-back villas, two- and sometimes three-storey, shuttered and square and imposing, monuments to vanished imperial power. Only occasionally were the sculpted, patterned gardens still tended; elsewhere was the tangle of neglect.

Deaken chose a hotel near the harbour, still with almost

twenty-four hours before the *Bellicose* was due to dock, but wanting to be as near as possible. It was terraced, between ground-floor shops and offices above, with wooden fronting verandahs on the first and second floors and wooden steps leading up to the entrance. The street-level verandah had high-backed wicker chairs, glass-topped tables and yellow ashtrays recommending Pernod. Geckos, glued to the walls like ornaments, would suddenly dart at the speed of a blink in pursuit of insects.

Deaken took a room at the front in order to keep the harbour in sight. It was French-built, like everything else, with docks and stiff-fingered jetties and long sheds bracketing the wharves. Beyond, the huge fan of water was flat and polished, cupped in the protective grasp of Cape Verde and Goree Island. Cargo ships and freighters, rusting and middle-aged like cargo ships and freighters always are, were tethered to their berths beneath high-necked, peering cranes. Anchored off were two oil tankers heavy in the water, like logs with straying branches. A working place, thought Deaken: no sparkling, burnished yachts with tinkling rigging and back decks full of topless sunbathers and laughing holidaymakers. After the last few days it was like retreating through the looking glass into the real world.

Deaken was impatient to establish contact with the agent to whom he had letters of introduction and authority, but he knew there would be no work going on at this, the hottest part of the day. To pass the time he descended to the ground floor and located, to the right of the reception area, a zinc-topped bar with stools and beyond it sets of tables with curve-backed chairs. There were five, three of which were occupied. There were more yellow ashtrays which prompted Deaken to order pastis. Remembering he was in Africa, he mixed it with mineral water, refusing the grubby carafe that was offered to him. The Pernod here was weak and already watered. At the far end of the bar, where it abutted the wall, was a gaggle of black whores. They stirred at his arrival and one detached herself from the group, smiling as she sidled towards him. Deaken raised his hand and shook his head. He thought the girl seemed almost grateful to go back to her lunchtime gathering. He wondered what Carole was doing.

He tried to hurry the question from his mind. The idea of Carole was intrusive and distracting: she had no place in his thoughts. He supposed, when everything was over, that he would see Azziz again briefly. But he would not be trapped on board the yacht, not like before. So he wouldn't be seeing her again. Ever. Good, he thought. Very good. That was as it should be. He was still ashamed at how he had felt. Nervous too. There was only room for one thought with no distraction. Karen was all that mattered. Karen and how they were going to start again.

"*Déjeuner?*" inquired the barman hopefully. Even he made the effort to maintain a French ambience, the much-stained shirt originally white, the black trousers threadbare, and a money pouch at the belt. The pouch was flat and empty.

"*Non, merci,*" said Deaken. It was going to be a long wait. Not just until the *Bellicose* arrived but afterwards, days, he guessed, going back up around the fat chest of Africa and into the Mediterranean. And not over even then. There would be Underberg's instructions to comply with. More delay.

He took a second Pernod, conscious of the barmen's flat pouch and leaving a larger tip than before. The girl, encouraged by her friends, made a second desultory attempt. He didn't see her approach, so she had her arm through his and was inquiring in lisping French if he was lonely before he could make the second refusal. He sent her back with a brandy, unsure why he had made the gesture; she would probably despise him for it. There was laughter from along the bar. She raised the glass and he raised his in return. Behind the bar the waiter remained blank-faced and unimpressed.

Deaken telephoned for directions and to ensure that the

agent was back at work and then emerged out onto the harbour-fronting boulevard. The place had that sticky-eyed; just awake feeling. A stretching taxi driver took him along the curve of the sea and then briefly away from the waterfront, into one of the roads that radiated from it like spokes. There was a fleeting impression of *déjà-vu* and then Deaken remembered Ortega's office in Lisbon. Only four days earlier, he thought. Or was it five? It seemed a lifetime.

The Levcos agent was a man named Henri Carré, a mulatto who had clung to his French parentage. He was a thin, fine-featured man with a high forehead of which he appeared constantly aware, running his hand persistently across it and up into his crinkled hair. One wall of the man's office was occupied by an erasable plasticized chart inscribed with the names of the ships for which he was responsible, sectioned so that it showed the departure port, stops en route and estimated time of arrival at Dakar. Deaken saw that the *Bellicose* was scheduled to arrive at dawn on Saturday and that the panel allowed for possible delay was blank. Carré studied Deaken's letter of authority and then, revealing the bureaucratic caution bred into people who had been colonized, asked to see Deaken's passport. Dutifully the lawyer produced it. Carré placed it beside the letter, apparently to compare the name, and then looked up, nodding with satisfaction.

"It is an honour for me to meet you," he said, in stiffly formalized French.

"I am sorry for the intrusion." Deaken was equally polite.

"I'm asked to give you every help," said Carré, pointing to the letter of authority.

"The arrival is still scheduled for Saturday?"

The Senegalese nodded.

"What berth?"

The man made a vague gesture towards the harbour. From the window it was just possible to see a wedge of water. "Undecided yet," he said. As if imagining he were being checked out by a carrier, he added quickly, "It will be a good berth, one of the best."

"I'm sure," said Deaken. "What's the period in port?"

"Just revictualling, fuelling if necessary," said Carré.

Deaken said, "I'm taking passage aboard."

Carré frowned. "It's a freighter," he said.

"There'll be some sort of accommodation," said Deaken. It hadn't occurred to him until now; it didn't matter.

"Do you want me to radio the ship?" asked Carré, eager to show his efficiency.

Deaken shook his head. "All that's being done from Athens," he said. "They'll be expecting me when they dock."

"There's no problem, I hope?" Carré was unable to withhold the question any longer.

"None."

"It's never happened before."

Deaken was concerned at the man's curiosity. Carré had his local position to protect, people in authority to appease. His inquisitiveness could get the bloody cargo impounded. Quickly he said, "It's an important shipment; it was thought best for me to be personally aboard for the last stage of the voyage."

"You've the ongoing orders then?" said Carré.

Damn, thought Deaken. He said, "They're being sent separately from Athens."

"There is a change in routing?"

Damn, Deaken thought again. "No," he said. "It remains according to the original contract."

"I've been the agent for Levcos shipping for a number of years," said Carré pompously.

"And they are most complimentary about your efficiency and ability," improvised Deaken. "In this particular instance they've decided to invest us with the responsibility. It's no reflection upon you. No reflection at all."

Carré relaxed slightly. "I'll need to know victualling and fuelling requirements," he said.

"Maximum," said Deaken. This man did not know what the cargo was nor its original destination so the indication of a long, uninterrupted return passage didn't matter.

"I'll put it in hand," said Carré. "I don't imagine you'll want to be in port longer than necessary."

"No," agreed Deaken. "As quick a turnaround as possible."

"What information should I give the customs authorities?" said the agent.

He's pushing hard, thought Deaken. "It'll be a bonded shipment, travelling in transit."

Carré looked down to a duplicate of the manifest already fixed to a clipboard.

"Machine parts," he read. He looked up. "Machine parts were important enough for you to be sent to accompany them?"

"Yes."

Carré waited, appearing to expect Deaken to elaborate. When he didn't, the agent said, "I'll need to know where you're staying, in case there's any change in the arrival times."

"The Royale."

"There are far better hotels." Carré frowned. "I could have recommended some."

"I chose it by chance," said Deaken. "I didn't want to trouble you more than necessary. It's quite adequate."

"Is there anything else I can do to help?" He offered his card.

"No, really," said Deaken, accepting the square of pasteboard. "I'm most grateful to you." He rose, extending his hand. Carré stood and shook it.

"Anything," assured the agent. "Just call."

*   *   *

Had Deaken inquired from the airport, Carré would have suggested he stay at the Teranga Hotel, although after their meeting he would have considered it inconvenient. The agent allowed the lawyer ten minutes after leaving his office, standing at the window to watch him walk down the spur road back towards the waterfront. Then he dialled the number. Makimber was in his room and agreed immediately to a meeting.

The African was waiting in the reception area when Carré arrived, pulling him at once towards the far corner of the lounge, away from the entrance. Makimber sat forward, arms against his knees, head down, looking at the floor as Carré recounted his meeting with the lawyer, only occasionally halting him with a question.

"Did you get the impression that the destination had been changed?"

"None," said Carré.

The relayed message that morning from Angola about Deaken's arrival had really made his cultivation of this man unnecessary, reflected Makimber. But he still didn't consider it wasted: it provided confirmation and the knowledge of where the man was staying. It had been a sensible precaution, to come to Dakar. And to bring people with him, even if they were thugs. "The authority was definitely from the Eklon Corporation?"

Carré nodded. "As full and complete charterers of the ship. I suppose they've the right."

Perhaps it had been a mistake to attempt independence at this stage, thought Makimber; at least the Angolan message indicated that the friendship was still intact. Azziz was a bastard, attempting to delay the shipment. Makimber supposed there had been a higher offer for what the *Bellicose* carried. He hoped the Arab would rot in hell for what he had tried to do. It was gratifying to be able to defeat him.

"It is a problem?" asked Carré, gauging the other man's concern.

"It could be."

"I'm glad we became friends, if I've helped to resolve it," said the Senegalese.

Makimber smiled. "I shall be properly grateful, believe me," he said. "What time does the *Bellicose* arrive?"

"Five in the morning."

"Maximum provisioning and fuelling?"

"That's what he said."

"He was alone?"

Carré shrugged. "I don't know. He appeared to be."

"If the *Bellicose* arrives as scheduled and the handling starts right away, what time could the ship sail?"

Carré turned down the corners of his mouth, making the calculation. "Around noon, I suppose."

It was a long time, too long. But he would have to do it. Makimber took a sealed envelope from his pocket and handed it across the table to the other man. Carré accepted it, feeling its thickness between his fingers. Knowing that the Senegalese could increase its value by a third again on black-market currency dealing, Makimber said, "I told you I would be properly grateful. There's a thousand dollars in American currency."

There was a moment of shocked surprise before Carré grinned in open excitement. "Thank you," he said. "Thank you very much."

"There's more," said Makimber. He felt like a fisherman landing a catch.

"What must I do?"

"Tell me everything that happens, no matter how small or insignificant it seems."

Carré nodded eagerly.

"And do what I say tomorrow, while the ship's in port. I don't want the captain becoming suspicious . . . thinking anything is unusual, in fact . . . until he sails."

"What about Deaken?"

"He's going to miss the ship," said Makimber.

*   *   *

Andreas Levcos was a man who had spent his life transporting the unquestioned for the questionable and grown rich from his discretion. A portly, shiny man, with oiled hair which gleamed and a silk suit which shone too, from the light shafting in from the window, he showed neither surprise nor curiosity as Grearson outlined what they wanted done. Levcos wore sunglasses, even though they were indoors, not against the glare but simply because he always wore them.

"You want the man given a northerly course, but for the ship to continue southwards?" It was important to extract some logic from the frequent illogicality.

"The false positions must always come from the master."

"What about sunrise and sunset?" said Levcos. "Surely he'll realize what's really happening?"

"Once he's at sea he'll be trapped: it doesn't matter," said Grearson.

"Doesn't he work for you?"

"No," said Grearson positively.

Levcos's office was in Athens's port of Piraeus. It overlooked the ferry terminals and from the window it was possible to see the hydrofoils scurrying to the Greek islands, skittering away like water insects not breaking the surface tension of a pond.

"What's the true destination?"

From his briefcase Grearson took a copy of Makimber's last cable. "Benguela," he said. "The *Bellicose* is to anchor ten miles off and wait for contact on the thirteenth." All information about the delay request and Makimber's refusal had been erased, so Grearson offered the paper across to the Greek shipowner. "Here's the positional fix and the recognition signal."

"Victory?" frowned Levcos, reading the call sign.

"Our clients are frequently given to theatricals."

"Do you want me to inform our people in Dakar?"

"Are they staff?"

Levcos shook his head. "Agents."

"Then I don't think so," said Grearson. "Let's restrict it to the captain."

"It would be best," agreed Levcos. "And the other ship?"

"To remain in Marseilles, until it's necessary to cross to Algiers to coordinate with the supposed arrival there of the *Bellicose*." The lawyer hesitated, coming to the most difficult part of the meeting. "And we would like to sail from Marseilles with some of our people aboard."

Grearson wondered what reaction showed in the man's eyes, hidden behind the glasses. The face remained blank. "What for?" demanded the Greek.

"To protect the cargo."

"There could be trouble?"

"It's possible." The American knew Levcos was too professional to accept anything more than the basic minimum of lying.

"I could not afford difficulties within the Mediterranean," said Levcos.

"It is not illegal," insisted Grearson. "Everything being carried has a valid End-User certificate, issued to a registered dealer in Portugal. Their purpose aboard will be *only* to protect the cargo." As an afterthought, he added, "And the ship, of course."

"This is extremely unusual," said Levcos.

Grearson looked momentarily towards the busy harbour, accepting that negotiations had begun. "We understand that," he said. It was like one of the bicycle races so popular on French television, where the contestants hovered and manoeuvred, reluctant to be the forerunner.

"A ship is a valuable property," said Levcos.

"Of course," said Grearson. At the moment neither wheel was in front of the other.

Levcos made the pretence of looking through the papers before him, as if information on the second freighter was available; Grearson was sure it wasn't. The Greek was an accomplished rider.

"Purchase price was $3,500,000," said Levcos.

Grearson estimated an exaggeration of at least $1,000,000. He didn't have time to check and argue; he'd been wrong to criticize Deaken for his difficulty in confronting the telephone demands. Now he was in exactly the same position, wobbling behind. "For which I'm sure you're insured," he said.

"There are exclusions," said Levcos. "It would be a difficult claim to pursue if my assumptions are right about the problems you might encounter."

"As charterers, we're insured; our indemnity would extend to include any damage to the carrying vehicle," Grearson sought assistance from legality.

Levcos shook his head, a gesture of sadness perfectly rehearsed. "I don't think we've met; that this conversation ever took place," he said.

So Levcos was absolved from any foreknowledge of what might happen, recognized Grearson. There was an intellectual stimulation in dealing with the other man. "What is it you seek, Mr Levcos?"

"A bonded commitment," said the Greek. "Backdated cover, personally liable against Eklon Corporation, from the date of the second charter."

"In what sum?"

Levcos smiled again, that practised expression of regret. "For the full purchase price, of course."

"No charterer would agree to such a commitment."

"Of course not," agreed Levcos. "No normal charterer, that is."

He had just got a puncture, decided Grearson; it was becoming a bumpy ride. "Suppose I could provide such an undertaking."

"Contractually?" pressed Levcos.

"Yes."

"Insurance is against misfortune."

The Greek could smell an advantage like a shark detecting blood in water. "Agreed," Grearson said.

"Which we hope will never befall us."

"Yes."

"I'd like there to be a fuller understanding between us," said the shipowner.

"About what?" The American knew it wasn't even a race anymore.

"Future association."

"I've already made it clear how grateful we are for your understanding," said Grearson. "You'll naturally be a shipper of whom we'll think for a seaborne consignment."

Again there was the sad smile and Grearson decided that, of all the artificiality, that annoyed him most of all.

"There's often a wide gap between thoughts and application," said Levcos.

"What sort of contract would you seek?" said Grearson, in full retreat.

"Three consignments," said Levcos.

"Two," said Grearson.

"Minimum of two-month charter on each."

Grearson sighed. "Agreed," he said.

This time the smile was of complete satisfaction. "I can guarantee that your man aboard the *Bellicose* won't have the slightest idea what's happening—and that the rendezvous will be kept on the thirteenth."

"Thank you," said Grearson. There was little for which he had to be grateful.

"What about this man Deaken?" said Levcos. "He'll realize then that he's been duped."

"We don't give a damn," said Grearson.

Karen hadn't purposely approached quietly, but Levy hadn't heard her. She stood in the doorway, surprised at the slowness with which he wrote, a purposeful, careful formation of letters, with frequent stops to consider the words. Twice he scrubbed out a half-completed idea and started again. She felt consumed with love for him.

"Azziz is going to get up later," she said, not wanting to spy on him.

The Israeli jumped. Instinctively he moved to cover what he was doing, then relaxed back in his chair.

"I'm writing to Rebecca," he said.

"Yes." She had guessed that was what he was doing.

"She worries, by herself with the children."

"Yes," she said again. She had no right to be jealous. "Do you miss her?"

"I miss the children."

"I didn't ask about the children. I asked about Rebecca."

He looked steadily at her. "Yes," he said. "I miss her."

"I'm glad you didn't lie."

"You'd have known, if I'd tried."

"Thank you, just the same."

"I love you," he said.

"I think I love you too," she said.

Levy folded the letter with the care with which he had been writing it and sealed it in an envelope. "I've told her I hope to see her soon."

"Do you?"

"Yes," he said. Then immediately, "No." He shrugged. "I don't know."

"What's going to happen to us?" she said.

"God knows."

19

Deaken was resigned to another long wait, but tonight there wasn't the frustration of the previous days. He was in a position at last to influence things; and by this time tomorrow he would be doing exactly that, aboard the *Bellicose*, already at sea and already heading northwards. How long to get to Algiers? It would depend upon the weather, he supposed. Carré would have had a forecast for the next two or three days at least. Damn! Deaken looked at the antiquated clock behind the bar. Seven thirty. It probably wasn't accurate but even so Carré wouldn't be in his office now. It would have to wait until tomorrow; the *Bellicose* information would be more up to date anyway.

He watched two geckos on the wall near the clock converging upon an unsuspecting insect, with high-elbowed, sticklike legs. They pounced simultaneously, colliding with each other with annoyed, scratching sounds, and the insect escaped. Deaken was glad. The barman brought him a second pastis. The last, he decided. Something to eat and then bed. He wanted to be up before dawn, to be waiting on the quayside when the freighter came alongside. The hopeful whores were still encamped at the far end of the bar. The one for whom he had bought brandy smiled, an acknowledgement rather than a proposition, and Deaken smiled back. She was missing two teeth in the front, he saw. Three of the girls were negotiating with a couple of seamen and a third bespectacled man in a cheap, crumpled suit. Dockyard clerk, Deaken guessed. He looked back to the girls. Couldn't be much of a living; certainly not enough to spend on dentistry. The unfulfilled smile came again, inquiringly this time and Deaken looked away, not wanting her to misunderstand.

From where he sat Deaken could see into the eating area, a bead-curtained annexe of harbour and dock people, all chewing stolidly. None of the bar girls had bothered with an expedition, so Deaken guessed they were all unresponsive regulars. He didn't want to eat there, he decided. But where? There should be good fish in a place like this; something else Carré could have recommended. Deaken settled the bill and walked out through the reception area, pausing at the top of the steps, with the lower balcony to his left. A few of the tables were occupied, the occupants curiously ill defined in the dull illumination from the overhead skein of bulbs which trailed around the outer edge like decorations on a Christmas tree long after the celebrations were over. Deaken paused at the top of the steps, staring out towards the waterfront. Far away, at the very tip of the harbour curve, there was the yellow glow of nightwork and nearer the rusting freighters he had seen earlier, the heavy blackness of their superstructure picked out with an occasional, haphazard light. Deaken gazed around for a taxi; the perimeter road was quiet and dark, sleeping.

In the parked car on the opposite side of the road Makimber smiled and said, "No problem," to the two men with him. There might have been if Deaken had remained in the hotel. The African hadn't really worked out how to resolve it, apart from the luring the man away with some phoney message apparently from Carré. He was glad he hadn't had to bother: he didn't want to involve the Senegalese any more than he had to, although he'd decided the man should be sacrificed if necessary. As Deaken walked down the steps, the two men Makimber had posi-

tioned at separate tables deep in the gloom of the balcony
waved for their bills, paid immediately and got up to
follow.

Deaken had forgotten the heat of Africa, the wrap-
around, blanket warmth even at night. He felt the perspiration prick out on his skin and looked around forlornly
again for a taxi. He went to his right, trying to orient
himself. Sea to his left, city to his right, only the continua-
tion of the dock area immediately ahead. The cathedral
and the Pasteur Institute, he thought, that's where the cafés
and restaurants would be, nearer the centre of town.

There was a stepladder of lanes and alleys climbing
from the docks to the top of the city. Deaken turned right
again, sure of his direction now. This was the daytime part
of the city, a place of warehouses and offices, with only
the occasional surprise of a bar to break the deserted
nighttime loneliness. The street lighting was careless: twice
people were practically upon him before he detected their
presence.

Makimber's car nosed into the alley, two hundred yards
behind. It was only using sidelights, so they couldn't see
the two men who had followed Deaken from the balcony
of the Royale. Makimber knew they would be in place.

"I don't want him killed unless there's no other way,"
said Makimber. It was a frequently repeated warning since
his meeting with Carré. He supposed he should go the
whole way with them to ensure they obeyed. But it was
more important for him to remain in Dakar and ensure the
freighter was safely on its way.

"We know," said the man in the back seat.

"Make sure you remember," Makimber said.

There was a snow line of white teeth in a smile, but the
man said nothing. Makimber hoped too many people hadn't
acquired a taste for killing; it had been an isolated problem
after Zimbabwe's independence, he remembered.

At the end of the road, a long way off, Deaken could
make out the brightness of the city. The light at the end of

the tunnel, he thought, recalling the familiar phrase. The
Vietnam promise of victory, parroted by the commanders
in Saigon and the politicians in Washington. Vietnam had
been the period of his most active radicalism, the breaking
point with his family. He had told Karen it didn't matter,
being disowned by them, but it wasn't true. It made him
feel rootless, belonging nowhere. He felt the anger build
up at the memory of South Africa. The convoluted logic
was typical of the fascist bastards, employing terrorism to
combat what they regarded as even worse terrorism; but he
believed Underberg, that his father wasn't involved. His
father might be a Nationalist and support apartheid as well
as embracing every concept and policy which was anath-
ema to Deaken, but he wouldn't have resorted to this.
Deaken had known operations like this before—and repre-
sented people caught up in them—covert schemes dreamed
up by the Bureau of State Security, renamed the Department of National Security after BOSS had earned the
reputation of being as repressive as the security organizations of Russia and the South American banana republics.
He wouldn't let them get away with it. He would go along
with everything they said now; he had no choice. But
when he got Karen back he would expose the whole
business. He was strong enough now to face the publicity,
to put himself back in the limelight from which he had
temporarily fled. Now the running was over. Before this
ended, people would be fleeing from him.

Deaken was never fully to know what happened. His
memory was simply of a flurry of sounds, not really
distinguishable as running feet, a confused imagery of
people—he didn't know how many—and then a blinding,
aching pain as he was struck repeatedly, first along the
side of the head when he instinctively drew back and then
somewhere at the base of his skull, causing a hurt that
made him feel sick before almost immediate black unconsciousness. It was too deep for him to feel the last
needless blow across his shoulders.

Makimber's car was alongside when it happened. He saw the man pull up to bring the baton down for another crushing blow, and shouted for him to stop.

There was a hesitation and for a moment Makimber didn't think the man was going to obey. "I said stop."

The club was lowered reluctantly.

"Get him into the car," said the African.

The man who had travelled with him in the rear got out to help the other two hump Deaken's flopping body inside. Near the door sill they dropped him hard against the road and two of them giggled.

"Get him in!" hissed Makimber.

One went round the other side of the vehicle to lean across to pull Deaken from the other two. They were careless of bumping him against the car, stretching his body lengthwise across the floor in the back, over the transmission tunnel. They scrambled in after him, sitting with their feet resting on his back and legs. It had seemed a long time, but the car accelerated away down the gloomy road within two minutes of Deaken being clubbed down. Having reached the brighter part of town, the driver turned right, then right again, to disappear into the darkness of the waterfront. Makimber remained screwed around in his seat, alert for any pursuit: if he were to be detained and implicated in the assault, then everything would be ruined.

There were vehicles behind but none taking any particular interest in them. Makimber exhaled slowly, not wanting the others in the car to be aware of his concern. He was the *bwana mkubwa*, the big man; he was not supposed to be frightened.

They had been in the Senegalese capital for a week, with the opportunity to learn its basic layout, and the driver steered the car carefully into the delivery bay alongside one of the waterfront warehouses. It was a dark, secluded place, bordered on three sides by blank, empty buildings. Makimber still raised his hand to caution against any movement, staring around the car to ensure they weren't observed. Then he gestured for them to turn Deaken over. The lawyer groaned, an involuntary sound as the air was forced out of his body by the manhandling.

Makimber leaned over the seat. He found the South African passport in the left-hand inside pocket, operating the interior light to examine it briefly, snorting contemptuously. He replaced it, going to the other inside pocket. It was there he found the envelope addressed to Captain Erlander. He broke it open and turned in the seat, with the paper held close beneath the light, wanting to read every word.

In his anger Makimber slapped the face of the unconscious man. Deaken's head twisted away under the force of the blow and Makimber regretted it at once. He wasn't a savage.

Makimber had found what he wanted, obtained his confirmation, but he went carefully through Deaken's pockets for anything further about the *Bellicose* and its cargo. But that was it. He snapped the inside light off, not wanting to attract attention to the vehicle.

"Tell me what you've got to do," he demanded from the men in the car, anxious there should be no mistakes.

Haltingly, one prompting the other, they went through the disposal procedure that Makimber had patiently rehearsed with them throughout the afternoon.

"Far beyond Kaolack," insisted Makimber.

"Far beyond Kaolack," recited the driver first, closely followed by one of the men in the rear.

Makimber felt the tug of unease at their getting it completely right.

"Is he a bad man?"

"Very bad," said Makimber. Swine, he thought again. "Take me back," he said to the driver. It was only a short journey to the Place de l'Union and the Hotel Teranga. Makimber stopped the car before they reached it and got out; there was a possibility of a road check.

"Nearly all the way to Tambacounda." He leaned in

through the window. From inside the car came movements and grunts of understanding.

Makimber stood in the road and watched the taillights out of sight. On his way to the hotel he tightened his arm against his chest, feeling inside his jacket for the bulk of the envelope he intended shortly to destroy. There were times, as a Moslem, that he regretted the teachings of the Koran. Makimber had spent most of his adult life in the West and would liked to have celebrated the odd special occasion with alcohol. Tonight was certainly a special occasion—he had averted a catastrophe.

The *Bellicose* had picked up a following current and the headwind had dropped, so they reached the shelter of Goree Island four hours before they were scheduled to dock. Knowing that no port facilities would be available until their arranged arrival, Captain Erlander anchored off, using the shore lee for protection in case the calm weather changed during the remainder of the night. He let Edmunson complete the final anchoring, because the cable from Athens was a long one and he didn't want to misunderstand it.

He had been reading steadily for fifteen minutes when the first officer came into his room. They had sailed together for four years, but Edmunson never took advantage; he waited until Erlander suggested a drink, then poured for both of them.

As the first officer brought the vodka to him, Erlander proffered the Athens cable and said, "What do you think of that?"

Erlander had almost completed his drink before the first officer finished reading.

"What sort of bloody stupidity is that?" demanded Edmunson.

Erlander shrugged. "I've queried it hours ago. There was a repeat, identical to the first. We're to take on a man and make him believe we're taking a northerly course and all the while go south, to Benguela. And anchor ten miles off on the thirteenth.''

"Which means this trip could end nastily.''

This time it was Erlander who filled the glasses. "That's what I think.'' He looked through the porthole towards the yellow and orange smoulder of Dakar on the shoreline. "I wonder who the poor bugger is?''

Ashore, the car carrying Deaken had already made its northerly diversion and passed through Thiès and was on its way towards Diourbel.

One of the men tried to kick at Deaken. The space was too restricted in the back of the vehicle, so he jabbed down viciously with his heel, feeling the body jerk with the impact.

"What shall we do with him?'' asked the driver, intent upon the unlighted road ahead.

"Kill him,'' came the reply.

20

The pain pierced Deaken's unconsciousness, then agonizingly engulfed his whole body. He didn't move—couldn't move—because of the hurt. There was something hard—raised—beneath his stomach, bending him. Dust. A lot of dust. More than dust; road dirt, gritting into his face and nose, a stale, dried odour. The smell grew. Of people and oil and petrol. Like the earlier pain, the realization came in a rush. A car. He was on the floor of a car, face down, nose and mouth ground into the carpet. People had their feet on him, several people; one place worse than the rest, a foot jabbing at him in some sort of relentless pattern, again and again in the same spot.

The control came, he didn't know how, through the whirl of impressions. The first thought was against movement to alert them, made easy because his body was afire against the slightest jar. He tried to remember but couldn't; just the darkness of the alley, something about Vietnam and then sounds. Sounds and then the awfulness of something clubbing into his head. Terrible pain. Not as terrible as now though. Not an ordinary backstreet mugging, otherwise he wouldn't be face down in a car, being taken to God knows where; he'd have woken up in the same alley, everything gone, even his clothes. What then? The pain coiled around him, band after band, preventing coherent thought.

From above, seeming sometimes far away and sometimes close, came the blur of conversation and Deaken forced himself to concentrate, straining for the words. He had breached the segregation, even as a child, when his mind had been most receptive to languages and he had managed a smattering of a lot of African tongues: none perfect or even extensive, but sufficient for day-to-day communication. They weren't speaking Bantu. Or Zulu either. Or Shona. Swahili! The recognition settled without any satisfaction, because it was not one of the Swahili dialects he understood. He was picking up isolated words, even those flattened against positive identification. The speed with which they were talking made it more difficult, because they were arguing. Deaken recognized *mtu mkorofi*, bad man, repeated several times: nearly always it seemed answered by reference to *bwana mkubwa*. Their leader, the *bwana mkubwa*, had told them something, given an order, *taratibu*, but they couldn't agree over it. Every time *mtu mkorofi* came there was the repeated, relentless kick and Deaken was in no doubt he was the one they were referring to. Several times there was the word Kaolack and then Deaken remembered the airline map he had studied during the flight from Nice, recalling the Senegal place-name: his memory was of it being somewhere far inland. Dust and fumes crowded into his nose and throat and he wanted to cough against them. He managed to suppress the need, guessing there would be a renewed attack if they suspected he was recovering. Why was he *mtu mkorofi*? Why had he been attacked at all? It didn't make sense. If only the pain would go away, lessen at least, so that he could think straight. *Mtu mkorofi* came again, like a taunt. Then another kick. Abruptly, so suddenly that he was rolled forward against the rear of the front seats, the vehicle stopped; he felt it skid as the brakes locked and then, because he was against it, he felt the driver twist in his seat, to continue the dispute without the distraction of navigating.

Gradually Deaken picked up one particular word, uncertainly at first and then positively. It came from the man who kept kicking him, he was sure. Just as he was sure what the word was, despite the variation of dialect. In Swahili *kuua* meant to kill. The pain was pushed aside by a new feeling, the numbness of terror. Deaken tasted the vomit, acid in his throat. He thought he had shuddered, a physical movement they might have felt, but couldn't be certain; he waited for the sounds above to lessen with their awareness of his recovery. They shouted on, almost as if they were unaware he was in the car with them.

As immediate as the terror the calmness came, a bizarre sensation of serenity which he knew wasn't serenity at all but the approach of some sort of hysteria. Deaken still tried to hold the feeling, wanting the detachment whatever its cause. There was nothing he could do, not thrust face down, underfoot and boxed within a car. It was a logical, calculating thought, not one of despair. He had one small advantage: they didn't know he was conscious, listening to everything.

The shouting frenzy above subsided into a repetitive

exchange of words. There was only a solitary voice saying *bwana mkubwa* now: met by a chorus of *mtu mkorofi*. And a new expression, one he missed at first and belatedly snatched for, recognizing the phonetic similarity and then fitting it into the context of what they were saying. The *mtu mkorofi*, which was him, was guilty of *kupunja*. Which meant to cheat. He had cheated the big man, the *bwana mkubwa*. And no one should be allowed to do that. What in the name of God or Hell or whatever Holy did it mean?

The fury all round him was subsiding now, the lone protesting voice overwhelmed by the weight of the others. Surprisingly, he felt no fear.

There was a sudden silence in the car, each waiting for the other to move. It was very hot in the enclosed space, thick with body smell. Abruptly, decisively, the rear door near which his head was wedged thrust open. A foot scraped against his cheek as the man got out. They were getting ready to kill him. Still no fear. Instead he began to become aware of minuscule inconsequential things. Fresher air; cicadas chattering from the underbush; absolute darkness.

The movement of one man released the others. He heard the front door open and then there was a shudder as it slammed shut. Suddenly he felt his feet and ankles seized as they began hauling him from the vehicle, turning him over for better access to his clothes. Before any attack they were going to go through his pockets. His shoulders and then his head bumped off the transmission arch, jarring fresh pain through him as they hauled him out. He kept his eyes closed, head turned against the seats to cover any expression he couldn't control; the interior light didn't seem to extend to the rear. Fetid food-fouled breath sprayed over him. Deaken let his body flop, without resistance.

One chance, thought Deaken, that's all he'd have. Two men pulled him by his legs from the car and, when he was almost clear, the third grabbed his arms. The eager ones—those who want to kill him. With the reluctant one a spectator. And if he were reluctant it was unlikely he would have any weapon in his hands. A guess, Deaken knew, but a reasonable guess. Everything was going to be a guess. One chance, he thought again.

The scream, as he moved, was involuntary, a mixture of tension and instinct, but it startled them. At the same time Deaken made a coordinated, body-arching eruption, lashing out against them with his hands and feet, twisting from them as he did so. They dropped him awkwardly, one leg, then the other. Deaken had yanked at the man holding his arms, and felt him begin to topple. As Deaken struggled to keep his balance, he was suddenly conscious of the ground dipping beneath his left foot. He guessed they were by a storm ditch. With desperate ferocity, he lashed out again. One of the men toppled with a groan into the darkness. Deaken was free. And his one thought was to run.

The pitch-black night helped him; the driver had only left the sidelights on, which did little more than mark out the shape of the car. An advantage. Like his breaking the pattern, confusing them. And he was better oriented, knowing the way the car was pointing, and from it the line of the road. Which gave him the positioning of the storm ditch, parallel to it.

The pain surged back immediately he tried to run. He concentrated against it, trying to force it aside just as a swimmer on a freezing day tries to ignore the icy coldness of the water. The darkness, his help a moment before, became an immediate liability. There was no marker to guide him. A soft crack broke the still night. Deaken realized that somebody had fired a gun: he had no impression of a bullet passing anywhere near him. He felt out delicately with his foot, waiting for the dip of the ditch. As he found it he was aware of groping, scuffling sounds as they came for him. Deaken stepped back, counting, trying to measure his run-up; never more than one opportunity, he thought. If he missed, they would get him. The beating had slowed him so that it was more of a stagger than a run. He had miscounted the backward steps, so the ground was already falling beneath his feet, making his jump across the ditch a clumsy, awkward plunge.

He didn't clear the ditch. Instead he crashed into the opposite bank, gushing the breath from his body. He clung there as if he were impaled, chest and arms over the rim, the lower part of his body dangling into the emptiness below. From above and behind there was a shout as they realized what he had done. He heard the sound of collapsing earth and stones as one of them scurried after him into the ditch. He strained to get some air into his lungs.

They were close enough now for him to feel the vibration of their running feet through the earth against which he was pressed. There were more shots, two this time, perhaps three, fired in close succession. Deaken's right foot found purchase and he pushed upwards, hauling his body over the edge. A rock was dislodged under his weight. It clattered invisibly into the ditch, and there were more shouts. He could hear the panting of the man in the storm ditch. Deaken dragged himself out of the gully seconds before the man reached him. Deaken held his breath, straining not to give away his position. He felt the man plunge beneath, close enough for him to have reached down and touched him. Deaken was shuddering with the physical effort. Puffs of dust rose directly beneath his nose and mouth which were jammed against the earth. The footsteps had gone past, away from him. He ached to stay where he was, to rest, but knew he couldn't afford the luxury.

Deaken tensed, concentrating his strength, then, using the ditch as another marker, he scurried away at right angles to it, bent low, stumbling and tripping over the dragging undergrowth, hands stretched out in front to protect himself if he fell. There were fresh yells from behind, seeming far away now. He heard another shot, so faint it might not have been a shot at all but the cracking of a stick underfoot.

Where the hell were the trees? He had been sure they

were close. Instead he found himself on one of those vast
African plains, low, stunted scrub with the occasional
isolated bush sticking up like some sort of lookout. Don't
let it be endless; please God don't let it be endless, he
thought. He was staggering, his sense of direction gone,
snatched and grabbed at by the twigs and grasses and
undergrowth.

Snakes, Deaken thought, in sudden horror. There were
bound to be snakes. Mambas certainly. Puff adders too.
He stopped, hearing himself whimper. He thought puff
adders were slow-moving, more likely to strike than to get
out of his way, but he couldn't be sure. He started off
again, no longer a headlong plunge, instead scuffing slowly
forward, feeling his way with his feet, hands stretched out
like a blind man in unfamiliar surroundings. They were
still shouting, but he had lost them.

There was a scurrying movement to his right and he
jerked to a stop. Not a snake, he decided. Too much noise.
Maybe a bird, startled out of his path.

There was no warning of the treeline. One moment
Deaken was walking through scrub, the next a branch
whipped across his face, slapping him backwards. He felt
a fleeting sense of relief that he had found somewhere to
hide. But snakes could also be in trees. Were they black or
green mambas? Green, he remembered. Able to strike
from overhanging branches. That's why unladen African
women often balanced a rock or brick on their heads as
they walked, to provide an alternative target. Involuntarily,
Deaken ducked. He couldn't hear them shouting anymore.
Just night sounds, screeches and cries, occasionally a nerve-
jumping crash of pursued and pursuer through the bush.
Sweat began to dry on him and he shivered, wondering
why it seemed colder here than it had in the city. Deaken
tried to crouch against the bole of a thick tree. As the
panic began to subside, the pain returned, isolated at first
and then taking hold of him in a solid, dull ache. His head

was throbbing. Gently he began to explore with his fingers, trying to detect any cuts. He couldn't.

At first he didn't recognize the grinding cough of the engine but then he realized with a surge of hope that they had started the car. He heard it pull away. He had beaten them, not bravely or cleverly, but beaten them nevertheless.

And now he was stranded, in the middle of nowhere, and couldn't consider leaving until the morning because he didn't have any idea of the direction of the highway he had to find if he was to get back to Dakar. And by daylight he would only have seven hours to do that if he were to catch the *Bellicose* and ensure that it altered course.

"Christ," Deaken moaned to himself.

Say as little as possible, remembered Carré. That was Makimber's repeated instruction, through the long night of rehearsals for this encounter with the *Bellicose*'s captain. Say as little as possible, always take the lead from Erlander. If he got it right, there would be another $5000 in American currency.

"I was told to expect someone aboard," said Erlander.

"The man came to my office yesterday. Told me about it," said Carré unhelpfully. Through the porthole of the captain's cabin he could see the bowser lines being manoeuvred to connect to the freighter's fuel tanks. Because only a comparatively small amount was involved, they were loading stores with the ship's derrick rather than a shore crane.

"It's still early," said the captain.

"He's staying at the Royale," said Carré. "I'll send a car for him."

"Who is he?" inquired the captain.

"An employee of the consignee, as I understand it," said Carré.

"What's he like?"

Carré hesitated. "He seemed pleasant enough," he said.

"I hope you're right," said Erlander. "This ship isn't designed for passengers."

And wasn't going to be put to the test, thought the Senegalese.

21

Grearson stood self-consciously before the telephone kiosk, aware from Deaken's experience that the conversations were conducted under observation and wondering where the man was. Activity swirled around him, on the jetties and in the harbour, people at play in the sunshine. It increased the discomfort; for one of the few times he could recall, Grearson felt overdressed in a business suit. It wasn't the thought of being watched, not entirely; any more than it was wearing a suit while everyone else wore the bare minimum. It was the thought of what was going to happen in a few minutes. Another negotiation, and nothing to bargain with. The lawyer knew Azziz was unimpressed by the concessions he had had to make in Greece. Azziz's judgement—"the cost is too great"—had sounded ominous to a man who had sacrificed a corporate career to work exclusively for one employer, was fifty years old, and knew it would be a bastard trying to earn a quarter of what he pulled in now if Azziz fired him. Which he might. Grearson was frightened of losing it all, the luxury of an always available helicopter and hotel, and an airline staff on permanent, personal standby. And that wasn't counting the other privileges, like the penthouse in New York and the yacht here in the Mediterranean. Not just the yacht. The women too. Carole was a very desirable new addition, the best there had ever been. Grearson stirred, excited by the thought of her. He had never known anyone screw like her; she was fabulous.

Grearson entered the phone booth and fixed the recorder, gazing around again in a fresh surge of discomfort. The suit was definitely wrong in this heat. The whole thing was wrong—a stupid, melodramatic charade. He attached the recorder, ensured it was properly connected, then stared blankly at the receiver, waiting. It sounded precisely on time. Grearson depressed the record button and lifted the telephone delicately between his extended thumb and finger.

"So you're the other lawyer," said the voice.

"And you're Underberg."

"Yes."

"Deaken's gone to Africa, as you instructed. He's going to make sure the ship comes back."

"The instructions were clear enough the first time round."

"It was a mistake."

"If my people make a mistake, your boy dies," said Underberg. "You'd better hope we're more careful than you are."

"We have to talk to Tewfik," said Grearson.

"I've already been through this with Deaken."

"The yacht has every sort of communication device," said the lawyer. "We can manage any sort of linkup that you want."

"The answer's no," said Underberg.

"There won't be any trickery," said Grearson. "Mr Azziz just wants to hear his voice . . . make sure he's okay."

"I've told you he's okay."

"We want to hear it from him."

"Get that ship back and you can hear it soon enough."

"That's going to take days," said Grearson. "It's been more than a week already."

"It would have been over by now if you'd done what you were told."

"We've admitted the mistake," said Grearson. "Let's start from a new base." The American was sweating, the receiver slippery beneath his fingers. This wasn't going any better than Greece.

"There was only one base. You screwed it up."

"We want proof the boy is okay." At least, decided Grearson, he was controlling his voice better than Deaken; he was surprised at his need for comparison.

"I told Deaken in the last conversation the sort of proof you'd get if you didn't follow our instructions."

Grearson swallowed, feeling a sudden chill, despite the ovenlike heat of the kiosk. "If Mr Azziz receives any part of his son's body, he'll know he's dead," he said. "He'll know the negotiations are over."

It was a desperate gamble, more desperate than he realized as he spoke the words. From the other end of the line there was a silence which seemed to go on and on. Grearson clamped his lips between his teeth, physically biting back the anxiety to know if he was still connected.

"The first will come from the girl," said Underberg at last.

A concession! Grearson recognized it at once, snatching at the advantage. "We've no interest whatsoever in the woman," he said. "She's Deaken's pressure, not ours. You can do what you like with her."

"You're bluffing," said Underberg. He was at the window gazing down at the indistinct figure enclosed in the kiosk, knowing he had been unexpectedly outmanoeuvred.

"I've admitted an error on our part," said Grearson, savouring his new-found strength. "And told you there won't be another. We're doing exactly what you asked and in return we want proof that the boy is all right. I repeat, as far as Mr Azziz is concerned, Tewfik will be dead the moment we receive part of his body.''

''Do you want to put that to the test?'' demanded Underberg.

''Do you?'' said Grearson.

There was another long silence. Then Underberg said, ''No telephone linkup; we won't be tricked.''

''Proof,'' insisted Grearson.

''When I get confirmation that the *Bellicose* is returning.''

Grearson recognized the further concession. ''Levcos will have a position by tonight,'' he said. ''So will Lloyds. Tomorrow at the latest.''

''We'll talk about it during the next contact,'' said Underberg.

Grearson had listened several times to all the earlier recordings and detected the change in the man's voice between the previous conversations and this one: Underberg was anxious for the first time to conclude a conversation. ''When will that be?'' he said.

''Two days.''

''Why not tomorrow?''

''Two days,'' repeated Underberg. ''I want the ship more than halfway back by then.''

''The boy's not to be harmed,'' said Grearson.

''Make sure the ship's on the proper course.''

Grearson decided it was degenerating into something like a schoolboy shouting match. And he didn't want that.

He put the telephone down.

The lawyer's hand was shaking and he was soaked with sweat. He wasn't quite sure what he had achieved. Remembering the observation, he unclipped the recorder, moved purposefully from the kiosk, and strode directly to the tender, looking neither left nor right. He retained this pose of indifference when he got aboard, remaining conspicuously in view against the midships cabin and gazing out over the stern, towards the *Scheherazade*. Carole, who had come ashore with him, smiled from inside the tiny cabin and Grearson smiled back. Christ, he thought, I hope I've got it right.

High above, Underberg stood rigidly at the hotel window, hands white with anger gripped by his side. He had been beaten, outbluffed and outmanoeuvred. During all the rehearsals and preparation, this sort of opposition hadn't been allowed for. A sudden nervousness shivered through him. It was fortunate he had taken such elaborate precautions.

The boy insisted he felt well enough to exercise in the garden but he returned to the cottage within minutes, coming unsteadily to the table at which Karen was already sitting. He eased himself gratefully into a seat and Karen saw that he was shaking with the effort. The squat guard, Greening, who had escorted Tewfik remained for a few moments at the door and then went outside again.

"You all right?" she said.

"Just weak, that's all." For once there wasn't the usual embarrassment. Instead he looked around to ensure they weren't being overheard and then said, "And I want them to think I'm worse than I am."

Karen had looked with him towards the door, impatient for Levy's return; he had said he would only be away for an hour and it had already been almost twice as long as that.

"We're definitely farther south," continued Tewfik. "I can tell by the temperature and the things that are growing in the garden."

"Yes," she said. "I suppose we are." She wasn't interested where they were, only that she could stay here and that it wouldn't end quickly.

"Have you heard anything . . . something that might give us an idea where this is?"

"No," said Karen. "Nothing."

"It'll still be France," he said. "They wouldn't have risked a border crossing. And beyond central France, I guess. There's quite a lot of pine and fir around. Have you noticed that?''

"No," replied Karen honestly. "I haven't."

Tewfik was too involved in his own thoughts to notice her lack of interest. "I tested them today," he said. "They don't think there's any risk."

"Risk?"

"Of my getting away. They still think I'm ill." He smiled at her encouragingly. "Don't worry," he said. "I won't go without you."

22

Deaken hadn't rested at all. He remained nervously apprehensive at the sudden, hidden sounds around him. Towards first light, he was attacked by swarms of mosquitoes which stung so badly that he had tried to cover his face with his jacket and sat, cowering, beneath its inadequate protection.

Dawn came at 4:50 in the morning, an almost imperceptible darkening of the tree and shrub outlines against the increasing greyness and then abruptly dissolving into glowing reds and apricots. Deaken rose to his feet, cramped and aching, shook out his jacket and carefully ran his hands over his stubbled face; his skin was lumpy and throbbing from the insect attack.

He moved slowly out to the edge of the coppice, crouched against overhanging branches and staring down at the coarse grass and bracken underfoot. Each footstep precipitated an eruption of dust and fresh squads of flying things which buzzed angrily around him. Deaken fanned them away furiously. The chill of the night had not been melted by the morning sun, and Deaken shivered, realizing he was damp from the dew. He stopped at the treeline and stared out over the barren plain.

There was no sign of the road.

His coppice was like a furred wart against the smooth, unbroken face of the plain, without the slightest elevation or undulation which might have provided a vantage point to pinpoint the broken, metalled line of the highway.

He was lost, even in daylight.

He tried desperately to orient himself. He could pick out the tree against which he had spent the cramped night. He thought he had come upon it directly at right angles. Which meant that if he walked away from it in a straight line, he would hit the road. But what if it hadn't been at right angles?

"Shit!" he said aloud. "Shit! Shit! Shit!"

He shouted, but his voice was swallowed by the vast emptiness. To his left, maybe not more than four hundred yards away, a dancing class of high-stepping gazelles paused in their foraging, gazing around with ear-pointed tenseness. After a moment their heads dropped back to their feeding.

"Shit!" Deaken shouted again. This time they didn't even look up.

The sun appeared yellow over the rim of the horizon, but it was not high enough yet to dispel the chill in Deaken's body. Christ, he felt awful: tired and dirty and itchy. Awful. Thirsty too. But not hungry. He didn't feel as if he wanted to eat again. When had he last eaten? Not since the plane, bringing him here. Only yesterday—less than twenty-four hours, to be precise. It seemed much longer; why did everything seem so much longer than it actually was? He checked his watch again. Six.

Where was this bloody road? Like a novice swimmer

venturing out of his depth, Deaken moved away from the trees, halting after only a few yards; to his right, close enough to make him jump, a disturbed squabble of birds winged suddenly into the brightening sky. This time the gazelle herd scattered in their high-floating, slow-motion run. The sun was strong enough to affect the nighttime dampness now, hollows he would not normally have recognized puddling with a white gauze of mist. Deaken frowned towards the rising sun, trying to gauge its strength. Metalled roads overheated in the African glare send up a miragelike shimmer; would he get the marker that way, from a shiver of heated air? No good, thought Deaken. That would take hours. High above, so high and so far away that there was no sound, a silver flicker of an aircraft trailed by with agonizing slowness. Washed and shaved and perfumed and pressed, passengers and crew would be confident, even careless, of their timetable and destination.

All around the mist thatches were being dried out by the heat. Knowing at least the direction from which he had approached the outcrop of trees, Deaken turned a full 180 degrees, seeking the telltale quiver of air which might indicate the road. Nothing. Just the gazelle grazing again. An occasional hovering bird poised over some unseen prey. Miles and miles of flat, tobacco-coloured ground, with the occasional upthrust thumb of an anthill.

Very soon Deaken was too hot, and made for the shelter of the trees, consumed by a bitter sense of continued impotence. He was certain Kaolack had been mentioned during the stifling car ride. A major town, he remembered from the aircraft map. If he was right about Kaolack, then the road had to be one of the main routes through the scorched and arid country, an artery in constant dawn-to-dusk use. So where were the cars and lorries and buses?

Another fifteen minutes, Deaken decided. If there was no identifying movement by then he would take a chance and strike out directly from the coppice. It would remain a marker anyway, so if he got too far away without locating the highway, he could always return and try another route.

Why fifteen minutes? Why not right away, without wasting any more time?

Occasionally scurrying things—only rats or field mice, he hoped—darted noisily through the underbrush in front of him as he edged hesitantly forward. He jerked back at a sting worse than the others, high over his eye. At once a puffiness formed, soft under his fingers, the swelling quickly closing his left eye.

The bus was already firmly on the plain by the time he noticed it. There was a surprised moment of total immobility, impressions kaleidoscoping through Deaken's mind—he was going in the wrong direction, parallel rather than towards the road.

He started to run, waving his arms wildly and yelling to attract the driver's attention, careless now of any danger underfoot or of the pain pumping through him.

There was a horrifying surrealism about it all. The bus seemed to be travelling slowly, as the aircraft had earlier, and his progress through the snagging scrub seemed equally slow. Realizing that he would never reach the road in time to stop the bus, Deaken halted, snatching off his jacket and waving it above his head. The speed of the bus didn't alter and he began running again. He ran with his head bent sideways, able to see the shape of the occupants through the slatted side windows and their luggage bundled on the rimmed rack of the roof.

Deaken stopped again, cupping his hands to his mouth and shouting, "Stop! Help! Stop!" The vehicle continued on, speed unchanged.

Deaken couldn't run any more. His breath was wheezing and his body ached and throbbed. He stood, aware he was a long way from the road, vainly waving, and then stopped bothering even with this, to watch the bus become smaller and smaller until it finally vanished from the plain. It took a long time for his breathing to become normal and the pain to diminish. Deaken remained slump-shouldered, feeling the sun burn into him. Then, head bowed, he began to trudge towards the road. Sweat rivered his face, making the bites irritate even more. He was still some way from the road when he saw the air quiver for which he'd been looking while far back among the trees. He was surprised how far from the road the coppice was: it looked very small from where he stood. He must have been very frightened to have travelled that far the previous night. Deaken moved on, coming finally to the storm ditch. It was wide and deep, filled at the bottom with the junk of passing travellers, wrappers and boxes and rotting fruit and the inevitable Coca-Cola can. The bank upon which Deaken stood was sheer but the opposing one was sloped up towards the road. It was wide, but he thought he could jump it. He moved back several paces and then attempted a stumbling run-up. At the last moment he missed his footing, and launched himself into the air with hardly any pace. Arms and legs flailing, Deaken thumped down on the other side, but felt himself sliding backwards into the filthy ditch. His fingers scrabbled to catch a grip, and groaning with the effort, he hauled himself upwards, until he could feel the macadam hot and sticky under his fingers.

Deaken levered himself upright. The road ran black and ruler-straight from horizon to horizon, the cooked air dancing crazily above it. There was no shade in either direction. The sun seemed to be burning into him at the very crown of his head. He took his jacket off again to create a protective canopy and crouched down in the dust at the side of the road. Flicking his tongue against the dryness, Deaken felt his lips were already hard and scaling. Down there among the bottle and the cans there would be trapped water. But it would be stagnant and stale, diseased. His throat felt swollen and gritty. Deaken dropped his jacket to look at his watch. Nine thirty. Still time, if someone were to come along soon. He screwed around, looking back and forth along the road. Nothing. It seemed to be getting more difficult to swallow, as if his throat were closing. He coughed and it hurt. Deaken stood to ease the cramp from his legs.

At first he imagined that it was a trick of the distorted light against the heat of the road. He squinted, squeezing his eyes tightly shut to clear his vision and when he opened them he saw that there was definite movement, a black shape materializing down the highway. Deaken struggled back into his jacket and stepped out onto the road, feeling the heat scorch at once through the soles of his feet. He stood in the very centre, arms raised in front of him. It was a lorry, open-backed with slatted sides to hold its cargo, bulbous wings and a dust-covered cab; the wipers had cleared two semi-circular eyes in the windscreen, which made it look like a vast, metallic insect.

Then he heard the horn sound, strident and impatient. It hadn't occurred to him that people wouldn't stop, coming upon him stranded in this deserted savannah.

"Dear God, no!" Deaken moaned.

He waved his arms faster. The engine note didn't change and the horn blast was more prolonged. He wouldn't move, Deaken decided. He would stay right where he was. The man would have to halt or run him down. Deaken glanced desperately to left and right, trying to estimate if there were room for the man to swerve around him at the last minute. A hundred yards now, maybe less. The insect face was bearing down, horn screeching, and then suddenly the headlights flared on in a warning flash. Deaken moved sideways, bringing himself more directly into the path of the vehicle. There was a puff of burning smoke from the squealing rear wheels as they locked. The back slid in the soft tar, slewing the lorry towards the ditch. The driver released the brakes, correcting the skid, then braked again. There were fresh spurts of smoke. Cold with fear, Deaken remained where he was, staring up at the lorry, so close now that it towered above him. He could see the driver's face, black, eyes pebbled with fear. Behind the ballooned wings were rusting running boards, Deaken noticed. He had slowed the lorry sufficiently to leap aboard if he had to dodge at the last minute. He *wouldn't* lose the lorry. *Couldn't*. It slewed again, slow and controllable. Deaken had to move, but backwards, not sideways, so that he still blocked the road.

There was a moment of dust-settling silence. Deaken recovered first. He went immediately to the passenger side, hauling at the door, not thinking until he was framed at the opening that the man might have a weapon. He didn't. From his startled expression it was obvious he expected Deaken to have one. The lawyer smiled, splaying his hands.

"I need help", he said in English. "Transport."

The driver looked blankly at him but there was a discernible relaxation in his attitude.

"Assistance," he said, attempting French. "Aid." There was still no comprehension. What was help in Swahili? Fervently Deaken tried to recall the long-unused words, remembering at last. *"Saidia,"* he said. Still nothing.

Deaken pointed to the road. "Dakar?" he said.

The man's face cleared. He said something Deaken could not understand, nodding and smiling agreement. Deaken indicated that he wanted to sit in the adjoining seat, repeatedly pointing ahead and repeating "Dakar." Smiling, clearly relieved, the man met the request with a further nod of agreement. As an afterthought, Deaken indicated the way from which the lorry had been travelling and said, "Dakar?" again. Once more there was a nod of agreement.

"Shit!" said Deaken.

The driver nodded and smiled, apparently now enjoying the encounter, a relief from the boring, lonely drive.

"Dakar?" said Deaken again, not offering an opinion this time. He was given another smiling, acquiescent nod.

"Which . . . ?" started Deaken and then stopped, realizing the hopelessness. "Shit!" he repeated. Another nod.

He got in, slamming the door. It was movement, whatever the direction. At the first township or hamlet he would inquire again, get it right. Maybe find a taxi. Ten fifteen, he noted. The driver ground the gears into mesh with a shudder of cogs, snagging up through the gate in a ritual flourish which Deaken realized he was supposed to appreciate. When the speedometer needle registered seventy-five kilometres, the man hunched forward over the wheel, arms encompassing the rim.

Surely this hadn't been the speed at which he had approached, horn blaring, fast enough to burn the tread off the tyres when he braked? Deaken stared at him and the Senegalese answered the look, smirking at what he believed to be admiration. There was nothing he could do, Deaken accepted. At least he was moving, he tried again to reassure himself, not stuck in some wasteland, being gradually dried in the sun.

The oblong of the rust-framed window gaped behind him; dust drifted in, fashioned in weaving snakes. Beyond he saw the load, a haphazard pile of vegetables and fruit. Deaken groped for an orange. It was green and unripened, hard under his hands. He gestured for permission to the driver, who shrugged and nodded. The fruit was as hard as its outer skin. Deaken bit into it, face twisting at the sourness, his mouth stung by it. He gulped at the orange, devouring the flesh almost without awareness, snatching back through the hole for another orange as soon as the first went. The rear window was not the only entry point for the dust. It seeped in wedges through the floor and ill-fitting doors and Deaken became aware of the vehicle's age. The cab, he realized, was more than the driver's workplace, it was his home, as well. Two jackets jostled from a peg immediately behind the man and, level with the back of his head, there was a shelf containing two shirts and a pair of shoes. Deaken looked down and saw that the driver was barefoot, skeletal legs jutting from the frayed ends of greased trousers. The plastic bench seat upon which he was sitting was covered with a plaid blanket which Deaken assumed was the man's nighttime sleeping protection. Deaken eased forward uncomfortably.

Deaken followed the driver's example, and wound down the side window to get some air. He tried resting his arm on the sill but hurriedly pulled back, the underside of his elbow burned by the heat of the metal. The plain stretched unbroken and unending, proof that the world was flat. They passed more gazelle and then a group of stunted piglike animals, which gazed back without fear but with ear-cocked curiosity. Around a distant anthill black birds wheeled in maypolelike flight; crows, Deaken thought, and maybe vultures. He wondered what the unseen carrion was. It could easily have been him.

Anxious to please, the driver groped beneath his feet with one hand for a small battered portable radio. One dial was missing and the plastic frame was supported by strips of tape and sticking plaster. The man extended an aerial and looked carelessly from the road while he selected a station. There was a blurred fuzz of interference from the unsuppressed engine, beneath which it was just possible to detect the monotonous ululating of what Deaken presumed was some local pop song.

The man said something in identification, nodding to the radio, and it was Deaken's turn to smile and nod with a complete lack of understanding. The dashboard clock was smashed, robbed of its hour hand, and Deaken travelled with his left arm twisted across his lap so he could count away the time. It was exactly thirty minutes from the moment of his pickup to their arrival at the top of an incline above a small township huddled in a protective valley not more than a mile away. Deaken sat forward eagerly as they descended, taking note of the outlying fields and the irrigation stream and the needle spires of more than one church.

The French influence remained, with the place-name

visible despite the chipped paint, secure on its rusting pole.

"Kaolack!" shouted Deaken in despair.

The driver smiled and nodded.

Carré had gone ashore from the *Bellicose*, ostensibly to pick up Deaken from the Royale, but really to limit the time with the captain, prolonging his absence as long as possible before returning. When he made his way onto the ship from the quayside, he saw the bowser cables being lifted away on their umbilical lines. Erlander was on the bridge wing.

"Where the hell's our passenger?" he said.

"I sent a car," said Carré. "He wasn't there."

"We're refuelled and revictualled," said the captain.

"Should I check with Athens?" Carré welcomed the opportunity of getting away from the ship again.

Erlander shook his head. "I've already done so by radio. I've been told to make it an on-the-spot decision."

There was a shout from the deck signalling the final freeing of the fuel lines, and Erlander led the way into his day cabin. He poured two glasses of gin, topping both lightly with water. Carré picked up the jug, adding another inch.

"What are you going to do?" said Carré. He had never before earned as much on the side as he had from Makimber. He was unsure whether to hoard the dollars, in the expectation of the conversion rate going up, or change them at once. It was a lot of money to move at one time and risk alerting the currency controllers. And if that happened he would have to bribe his way out of trouble. He would shift just a little at first, he decided. It was a warm feeling, to be rich. It justified the present unease.

Erlander walked to the starboard side of his cabin, looking out over the quay. The early morning activity was slowing in the full heat of the day, the shore cranes bowed with inactivity, stevedores and harbour workers grouped in the warehouse shade or trailed to the liquor stalls. "Did this fellow tell you what he had to do?" he asked.

"Just sail with you."

The captain turned back into the room. "What authorization did you see?"

"I told you."

Erlander was a man who knew he sailed on the shaded side of every route, never properly believing the manifest listing on any voyage. It was a risk he took consciously, for the money which Levcos paid. Despite which, he was a careful man, running a clean, efficient ship with a reliable professional crew, never exposing himself to unnecessary danger. The preposterous sailing instructions and the presence of a man who had constantly to be duped with false positions and speeds constituted precisely the sort of conditions which Erlander had until now succeeded in avoiding. Which was why he was pleased the man had not turned up. And why he had lied to the agent about making contact with Athens. There would be contact, but not yet.

"We sail at noon," said Erlander. "I'll wait until then. But no longer."

One hundred and twenty miles away Deaken was agreeing to double the price if the taxi driver could get him from Kaolack to Dakar in time.

Greening and Leiberwitz stood watching Levy and Karen walking in the garden and Leiberwitz said, "Look at them! Mooning like youngsters."

Greening looked sympathetically at the bearded man. "It must be difficult for you, involved in the family," he said.

"That's not my first consideration."

"What then?"

"I don't think Levy is capable of leading us anymore."

"He's not let his relationship with the woman interfere so far," said Greening.

"I don't think he can be trusted anymore to make dispassionate decisions," said Leiberwitz.

"What are you saying?"

"That it's time someone else took over."

23

Deaken chose a Peugeot with the best bodywork and least tattered upholstery, hoping that the engine would be in matching condition. The taxi driver was a mulatto, so there was a bridge with French. Fighting against the impatience and despair that swept through him when the man told him how far they were from Dakar, Deaken still insisted the car be checked at a service station for oil and water, and to fill the petrol tanks. Having escaped once from the wilderness, he didn't want to be trapped there again.

The Kaolack market was at its busiest, the streets crowded with unhurried people and obstructing animals. The driver forced his way through with his hand constantly on the horn. It took ten minutes to clear the township, but the car was moving easily with no sound of strain from the engine, and Deaken felt a prick of hope. They actually accelerated on the gradient from the town, and by the time they had reached the played-out ribbon of the Dakar road, the speedometer was flickering at 130 kilometres.

Deaken anxiously scanned the dashboard, ensuring that all the temperatures and levels were reading properly.

Between the driver's hands the steering column jarred from imbalanced wheels, but it did not seem to worry him.

Deaken eased back against the sticky upholstery, recognizing the surrounding countryside and then what he believed to be the tree outcrop where he had hidden. Freed from the stomach-tightening anxiety and with nothing to do except sit, Deaken examined the events of the previous night. It certainly hadn't been a simple backstreet mugging. There had been no attempt at robbery, not until those last few moments when they hauled him from the car. *Bwana mkubwa*, he remembered. Who was the big man they had kept talking about? Underberg possibly, but Underberg wouldn't have attempted to keep him off the *Bellicose*. It was Underberg's idea that he sail, to ensure the freighter's return. Azziz then? No. There was no logic in that, because Azziz wanted him aboard as well. And he had seen the thugs Azziz employed. Evans and his trained mercenaries wouldn't have allowed such an amateur, panic-ridden escape. Had Azziz ordered him stopped, he would have been stopped. So it was another unanswered question, to be filed away with all the rest.

The plain ended at last, the landscape becoming stubbled with isolated trees and then thicker vegetation. Occasionally there were villages, clusters of mud-walled huts with corrugated metal roofs set out along the highway, staffed by scattering chickens and round-eyed, pot-bellied children. Deaken noticed that the fuel was already half gone and that the water-temperature gauge was twitching up towards the amber-coloured danger area. He gestured towards it and the driver nodded. "Diourbel in fifteen kilometres," he promised.

Halfway, guessed Deaken, maybe slightly less. Sixty miles then. He checked his watch again. Could he hope to do sixty miles in an hour and ten minutes?

"How's the road, beyond Diourbel?" he demanded.

"Good," said the driver, shrugging in what appeared to be immediate contradiction.

Deaken realized the man didn't know. "Noon," he said. "I must be in Dakar by noon."

"No problem."

But there was, Deaken knew. No road in Africa, certainly not this part of Africa, was good enough to allow the sort of speed necessary to cover sixty or more miles in just over an hour, even if the overstrained, overheated engine could maintain a good average. The idea came abruptly to Deaken, his first reaction one of excitement, quickly followed by that of annoyance because it was so obvious and hadn't occurred to him earlier in Kaolack. When the taxi pulled into the service station, he leaped out before they came to a halt, and ran into the office, Carré's card in his hand, shouting in French for the telephone. A surprised attendant pointed to his right where the instrument was clamped to the wall. Deaken obtained the price of the call to the capital from the operator and then asked him to wait while he dashed to the cashier for change. He pumped the money in, repeated Carré's number and then stood, shuffling his feet with growing frustration, while the ringing tone purred out at him. Through the cracked window out on the forecourt he saw the driver make sure that the fuel cap was fully tightened and then look inquiringly into the office. The tone purred on with no reply. Angrily Deaken slammed down the receiver and ran from the building without bothering to reclaim his unused coins. It was as difficult getting through Diourbel as it had been to leave Kaolack and Deaken was unable to sit still, impatiently tapping his hands against the front seat. He should have tried to call from Kaolack, he thought in bitter self-recrimination. Obvious, downright bloody obvious and it hadn't occurred to him until it was too late!

Under an hour to go, he saw. "Hurry," he said. "Please hurry!"

There was more traffic as they approached the coast, most of it moving at the customary, sedate African pace, and so much coming the opposite way that overtaking was almost impossible. Several times the driver pulled out to risk head-on collision, blaring his horn, to be met by matching blasts as the oncoming vehicles had to swerve to avoid him. It was 11:45 when they reached Thiès and almost noon by the time they got through it. The petrol tank was half empty again and the driver started to indicate pulling into a station, but Deaken urged him on, willing to take the risk rather than sacrifice any more time. They got to Rufisque by 12:20, the temperature needle already halfway through the amber colouring, the heat from the engine, combined with the scorching sun, making the atmosphere in the car almost unbearable.

They entered the outskirts of Dakar at 12:30. Deaken waved the man on in the signposted direction to the harbour, stopping only for directions to Carré's office when they were among the dockyard warehouses. As they moved parallel to the water, Deaken strained to make out the *Bellicose*. There seemed to be a lot of freighters and coasters in port but none with the name he sought. Deaken had the money ready as soon as they reached Carré's office, throwing it onto the seat beside the driver and dashing from the vehicle and up the stairs to the second floor, bursting into the agent's office without knocking. Carré jumped at the intrusion, half rising from his seat and then settling again.

"Where have you been?" he said.

"It doesn't matter," said Deaken urgently. "Where's the *Bellicose*?"

"Sailed," said Carré.

Deaken's shoulders caved and he slumped into a chair. Trying to recover, he said, "Can I get a fast cutter to overtake it and board?"

Carré shook his head, "The pilot vessel has already come back. It's been gone more than an hour now. It'll have cleared our waters."

"Why didn't it wait?"

"I sent a car for you . . . even went to the hotel myself. No one knew where you were. There were no messages."

"Did anyone know I was here . . . inquire about me?" Deaken asked.

Carré's face remained expressionless. "No," he said. "Should they have done?"

The Senegalese had been his only contact, the only person who could have guided the attackers to him. Intent on the man's reaction, Deaken told him what had happened the previous night and of his desperate efforts to get back to Dakar before the *Bellicose* sailed. Carré managed a look of incredulity but Deaken guessed it was forced.

"We should tell the police," said Carré. Makimber's rehearsal had seemed to work perfectly well with the *Bellicose* captain so he saw no reason why it shouldn't with this man.

"Who notifies Athens of the sailing, you or the *Bellicose*?" said Deaken.

"Both." Carré wasn't prepared for this question.

"When will there be a position report?"

"Probably in twenty-four hours." Carré didn't seem very sure.

Everything would be all right if Azziz had instructed Athens. He had twenty-four hours, decided Deaken; maybe thirty-six, if he included the remainder of this day. Thirty-six hours to do what he should have done before, instead of slavishly attempting to follow the kidnap directions. He accepted the decision that Karen might die. But that would happen anyway if he didn't act. Deaken was surprised at his detachment.

Azziz snapped off the recording but didn't speak. Grearson waited opposite, trying to conceal his apprehension.

"I wanted contact," reminded the Arab. "You didn't get it."

"I got concessions." Grearson fingered his spectacles like worry beads.

"What if he doesn't believe you and maims my son?"

Azziz was a bastard, thought Grearson. When there was conciliatory acquiescence he demanded forcefulness and when there was forcefulness he wanted subservience. "You heard the tape," insisted Grearson. "For the first time there was a balance, something from our side."

"But what did it achieve?"

"Maybe proof that your son is still alive," said Grearson, wishing he could disturb Azziz's calmness. "It's been more than a week now."

Azziz nodded. "It's something I suppose," he said. "Thank you."

Grearson's concern subsided and he fitted the spectacles back into place.

"Don't you have something else to do?"

Grearson stood up. "We're meeting in two hours."

"Make sure they know what to do."

He wasn't secure, decided Grearson, not secure at all. Before he left to meet the mercenaries, he would find Carole and let her know he would be back late that evening. Christ, she was exciting!

"You did well," said Makimber, counting out Carré's money. "Extremely well. Thank you."

"It wasn't easy," lied Carré, wanting to give the impression that he had earned his bribe.

"I'm positive it wasn't," said Makimber. "Sure you don't know the reason for his asking you about notification of sailing?" It was the only thing they were still uncertain about.

Carré shook his head.

"There's no way he could intercept the ship, now it's sailed from here?"

"It's fully victualled and fuelled," said Carré. "There's no need to make land for at least two weeks, possibly three."

"What about changed sailing instructions from the owners?"

"I'd be telexed a copy of that, automatically, from Athens. There's been nothing."

"You'd tell me at once?"

"Of course."

Makimber added another $5000 to the pile of notes. "You'll find me grateful in the future," he said.

Carré smiled.

"You say he seemed anxious to get away, once he knew he'd missed the ship?" repeated Makimber.

"Extremely so. He didn't stay more than about thirty minutes, forty-five at the outside."

"I wonder what he'll do," said Makimber, more a question to himself than the other man.

24

Evans arrived first from Clermont Ferrand, having accepted Grearson's suggestion to take a villa on the outskirts of Marseilles, on the Aubagne road. The rest travelled individually and booked into separate hotels in the town, except for Hinkler and Bartlett, who went everywhere together and registered at the same hotel. The meeting with the American lawyer at the villa was the first time they had assembled as a group since Mulhouse.

Grearson concentrated first on money. "Same terms as

last time," he said. "Payable in any currency; I presume that will be dollars."

There were nods all round. Marinetti said, "Last time there was a bonus."

"Which will apply again," said Grearson. "Twenty thousand each upon successful conclusion."

"What do we have to do?" asked Sneider.

It took Grearson almost thirty minutes to outline what Azziz wanted done. Throughout the briefing the men showed no surprise and no one interrupted. When the lawyer finished, Evans said, "Do we have the opportunity to examine the ship?"

"Today," said Grearson. "The captain is expecting us; I said about three."

"No need for any particular explosives," said Marinetti.

Jones stirred, stretching his long legs. "It'll be simple enough if they're by themselves," he said. "What happens if they bring the boy and the woman for exchange on the spot?"

"There'll need to be a contingency plan," said Grearson.

"So we'll have to wait until we're sure?" said Melvin.

"Unless it's made clear in the exchange terms," agreed Grearson. "They'll imagine you're crew, of course. You'll be sailing from Marseilles."

"What if they're watching the port?" said Hinkler.

"They won't be," said Grearson. "As far as they're concerned, the *Bellicose* is on its way back from Dakar for the Algiers rendezvous."

"Wonder what they want the arms for?" said Bartlett.

"It's immaterial," said Grearson. "We don't intend they should have them."

"No idea how many there'll be?" queried Evans.

"None," said Grearson.

"Presumably they'll be armed?" said Hinkler.

"Presumably," said Grearson.

"We've still got some stun grenades," said Marinetti.

"They're not as effective outside a confined space, but they might be useful."

"Remember that Mr Azziz wants an example made," said Grearson. "He doesn't want to be a victim of terrorism again."

"Not after we're through," promised Evans, getting to his feet. "There's no need for us all to go to the ship. I'll make the reconnaissance and come back to brief the rest of you here."

Grearson followed the former major out to the car and got in the passenger seat beside him. Evans took the car out onto the main Marseilles highway but kept in the slow lane, letting even heavy lorries pass.

"There was a differential in the bonus last time," said Evans, intent upon the road.

"You get $30,000 against the others' $20,000," said Grearson. "I didn't think you'd want me to set it out in front of everybody."

"Thank you," said Evans. "In Brussels you spoke of other employment."

"Permanent protection appeal to you?"

Evans allowed himself to shrug. "Never done it," he said. "It's getting more and more difficult to get proper paid soldiering."

"Why don't we talk about it afterwards?"

Evans entered the city, turning almost immediately towards the harbour. "Isn't there a possibility they'll anticipate your doing something like this?" said Evans.

"As far as they're concerned," said Grearson, "the ship's been at sea since this whole thing began, with no opportunity of our getting anyone aboard. It'll be a nice surprise for them."

They were driving parallel to the sea now. There were several French warships in the naval section, grey and pompous at anchor, with a group of corvettes trailed one behind the other like a family of ducks. Nearer, the civil docks were crowded with vessels, from coastal fishing ships to ocean freighters.

At the dock gates Grearson produced the Levcos authority and was directed on to a peripheral road inside the walled area. The *Hydra Star* was alongside a jetty, already loaded, so there was little stevedore activity around her. Grearson led the way aboard and was directed by the gangway crewman to an outer ladder to reach the bridge. The metal felt oiled and greasy to the touch and Grearson thought being a sailor in a ship like this would be a distinctly unpleasant way to earn a living. There must have been some communication from the deck because by the time the two men reached the bridge the Greek captain had emerged to greet them.

"Nicholas Papas," he said. The captain was younger than Grearson had expected, olive-skinned and dark-haired. Because of the heat he wore the insignia of rank on his shirt, so he could dispense with a uniform jacket.

Grearson took the proffered hand, introduced Evans and then produced his letter from Andreas Levcos. The captain read it and said, "There's been a lot of communication from Athens about you." He looked at Evans. "How many men have you?"

"Seven."

"Accommodation will be a problem," said Papas. "I've a full crew."

"We're used to difficult conditions," said Evans.

To Grearson Papas said, "Everything is loaded. When do we sail?"

"Two days," said the lawyer. "Maybe three. It depends upon the sailing conditions from Dakar to Algiers."

Papas led them back into his cabin. Grearson saw there were several family photographs showing a pretty, dark-haired woman and two children. The captain offered drinks but Grearson and Evans declined. Papas poured himself ouzo.

"I am responsible for the safety of my ship," he said.

"We understand that," said Grearson. He put his hand on Evans's shoulder and felt it tense. "These people are going simply to protect a cargo."

"Where will I be sailing, after Algiers?"

"I don't know," said Grearson.

To Evans the Greek said, "I control this ship at all times."

"Naturally," said Evans.

"Nothing is to happen without prior consultation with me."

"Of course."

Papas studied the mercenary as if he doubted the quickness of the replies. Then he said, "Do you want to look over the ship?"

"Please," said Evans, politely.

Papas took them down an inner stairway to the deck. The forward hold was still uncovered and Grearson and Evans stared down at the containers and crates.

"Could the ship's derrick lift them out without the need for a heavier shore crane?" asked Grearson. Although there was no intention of parting with the weaponry, he had to be prepared for any question that might arise during their telephone contact.

"If necessary," said Papas.

Evans was examining the decking, expertly assessing the cover available from the raised lip of the cargo hold and the other deck fittings.

"Just this hold?" queried Grearson.

"There's a small overflow in number two hold," said Papas. "Only about six tons."

He led them back inside the freighter, towards the crew accommodations. The two cabins allocated for Evans's men were small, normally only occupied by two people. "That's all we've got," said the Greek.

"That will be all right," said Evans.

"How many crew do you carry?" said Grearson.

"Twenty-five," said Papas. "Twenty-five good men."

By a series of internal ladders and walkways, they got into both holds through the bulkhead doors, enabling Evans to inspect the cargo crates, and then returned to the bridge. Papas offered them drinks and again they refused. It was almost four o'clock when Grearson and Evans went back down the ladderway onto the quayside.

Evans paused, turning back to the *Hydra Star;* Papas was watching them from the bridge wing.

"He won't be easy," said Grearson. "And the crew is larger than I imagined it would be."

"Numbers aren't a problem," said Evans. "We can take care of ourselves." He went over to the car. "There's plenty of cover. Particularly down in the hold."

"No worries then?"

Evans stopped with the driver's door open and looked hard at the lawyer. "Mr Azziz will get his money's worth," he said.

The garden of the house curved in a gentle arc down to a high bank. Levy scrambled up and then leaned down to help Karen. He sat with his back against a fir and she leaned against him, head on his chest. Here they were shielded from the house and their elevation gave them a panoramic view out over the distant Durance River.

"It's beautiful," said Karen.

"Yes."

"I'd like to stay here forever."

He kissed the top of her head. His hand was around her waist and he shifted it slightly, moving it gently against her breast. She covered his hand with hers.

"Something should have happened and it hasn't," she said.

"What?" he said, not understanding.

"I'm late."

Levy stopped moving his hand against her. "How late?"

"Two or three days" said Karen. "Which is unusual. I'm very regular."

"It's probably because of all that's happened," he said.
"I think I'm pregnant."
Levy moved her around so that he could see her face.
"I'm sorry," he said.
She stretched up to kiss him. "I'm not," she said.

25

Deaken, who had rehearsed everything he had to do and was trying to rest in his window seat, stirred at the landing announcement, pushing aside the inadequate blanket to gaze out into the velvet African night.

Home—the home he hadn't known for so long. And which had not wanted to know him. A different arrival from the last time, he thought, deep in reflection. It had been a week after his tenth victory in as many hearings, he remembered, this time before the Human Rights Court in Strasbourg. He had already been well known—too well known for the comfort of his family—but the Strasbourg decision had been against Britain over their treatment of detainees in Ulster and made him an international media figure. Reporters had flown to South Africa with him, even an American television crew for a documentary they later called "Spokesman for the Oppressed." He had cooperated, not through the vanity of which his father subsequently accused him, but because he saw practical benefit from it. He had changed his opinion about many things but not about publicity. It was a useful weapon—the best—against governments or regimes or ruling parties or juntas that wanted something hidden. And could be again.

There was the sound of the undercarriage groaning down, a sparkle of the spread-out lights of Johannesburg once more and then the snatch of the landing. As the aircraft waited for direction towards the disembarkation finger, stewards and stewardesses made their final tour, offering immigration forms to holders of non-South African passports. Deaken refused, wondering what his status was. Not prohibited. If that had been the case, his passport would have been withdrawn. But certainly listed. Entered in the central indexes and computer banks and in the immigration records at ports and airports along with the subversives, the doubtfuls and those who should be detained or questioned or just refused entry. Underberg had been right in his threat that the Department of National Security would know the moment he tried to contact his father. Which made his plan all the more desperate but the only one that had a chance of keeping Karen alive.

Deaken squeezed into the disembarkation queue and funnelled out into the airport building, immediately alert for the signs. The line for South African nationals was long but moving more quickly than the others through the immigration checks. The officer at the desk was young and blond and fresh-faced, smiling and polite. When he reached him, Deaken thrust his passport across the desk and said, "My name is Richard Deaken."

He indicated the large, loose-leafed book on his left and said, "You'll find me listed in your check register. My father is Piet Deaken. I would like you to call a senior officer. It's very urgent."

The young face clouded and the immigration officer swallowed, a pleasant shift of duty suddenly a problem. The interest rippled from the attentive family immediately behind Deaken and travelled all down the line.

The man at the desk looked from Deaken to his picture,

back again and then shuffled through the book alongside him. His finger stopped a third of the way down the page.

"I told you it would be there," said Deaken. Despite his anxiety, he was curious what the listing read.

The officer waved the rest of the queue towards an adjacent desk, apologetically indicated the register and then Deaken to his suddenly overburdened colleague as he lifted the desk phone.

"It's urgent," repeated Deaken.

"I heard you," said the young man officiously.

The conversation was brief, in mumbled Afrikaans, and Deaken wondered if the man speaking it believed he wouldn't understand. But he quickly learned that his register listing was "subversive." To the right of the arrival hall was what appeared to be an insubstantial, temporary wall made from plasterboard or some processed material. It was from here, through an unmarked door, that the senior immigration official appeared. He wore a darker uniform than the desk officer, with shoulder crowns of superior rank and a peaked cap firmly in place. He was a small, fat man, with pink cheeks and pudgy hands. With obvious irritation he looked at Deaken's passport, then checked the register.

"What do you want?" he said at last.

"To speak with you. Privately," said Deaken. Before the man could respond, the lawyer added, "It's a matter of security."

The pink face broke into a frown. "Come with me," he said. Deaken followed, aware of the junior officer falling into step slightly behind him. Every face in the waiting queue was turned towards him.

The office appeared as temporary as its outer wall, furnished with only the basic necessities—desk, filing cabinet, two phones, and a picture of the Prime Minister. The officer in charge kept his hat on when he sat down. He didn't invite Deaken to sit but he did so anyway.

"I want to contact my father," he said. "Inform him

that I am here on a matter of some urgency and that I want
to see him immediately. Tonight. And that I want a senior
official of the Department of National Security to be
present.''

By the door the junior officer shuffled his feet. ''Is that
all?'' said his superior, attempting sarcasm.

''You know who I am,'' said Deaken. ''Who my father
is. Please do as I ask.''

''You talked about security,'' said the man.

He was going to be obstructive, thought Deaken. He
said, ''It is. Of vital security. Far beyond the jurisdiction
or control of this department.''

''That is for me to decide.''

''No,'' said Deaken firmly. ''It is for me. I want to see
my father and an official from security . . . . If you ob-
struct me or refuse to help, and expel me without the
opportunity of seeing someone higher in authority, then
this country is going to be involved in an incident of
international proportions, as embarrassing as any that has
happened in the past. And I shall ensure that your identity
is fully disclosed as the officer who took it upon himself to
interfere.'' Deaken was aware how pompous he sounded
but he marked the man as a bully who would respond most
quickly to bullying.

The man glanced over at the junior officer, and Deaken
knew he regretted now bringing him into the room. ''I
don't think you're in a position to dictate what I shall and
shall not do,'' he said to Deaken.

The opening was ideal. ''That's for you to decide, of
course,'' agreed the lawyer. ''Just make sure you don't get
it wrong.''

There was a burst of Afrikaans to the young man at the
door, ordering Deaken to be taken to a detention room.
''Thank you for doing what I ask,'' said Deaken, also in
Afrikaans.

The younger immigration man was unsure how to treat
him now. He gestured for Deaken to precede him, but

hurried to open the door for him. They walked smartly down a narrow corridor to a smaller office with no furniture except for a desk and a chair. The only light came from an overhead lamp, recessed flat into the ceiling. Deaken tried to remember how many annexes and cells he had visited just like this, to talk to beaten and bruised detainees. He gave up. There had been too many. He sat down at the table, feeling the undersize seat stop halfway along his thighs, as they always seemed to do, for maximum discomfort and disorientation. Nothing had changed, he thought.

"I've been away a long time," he said to the young officer, who remained with his eyes fixed over Deaken's head at some point upon the blank wall.

To the northeast, in the South African capital of Pretoria, Piet Deaken emerged from the premier's private suite of offices in the government building, stopping for a moment in the corridor. He had suspected the reason for the summons after the late-night cabinet meeting. Hoped and prayed for it, after all the rumours and discreet approaches. But the confirmation still numbed him, the excitement making his legs feel weak. He put his hand out against the wall, a tall, angular man of muted greys, his white hair tightly clipped high against his scalp. He was going to be Minister of the Interior! One of the most important portfolios in the entire government; perhaps *the* most important, in a country with the internal misalignments that South Africa had. Which meant trust, absolute trust, not just from the other members of the cabinet and the party, but from the backers, the blurred-image businessmen and sponsors who had such power. More, even, than trust. Full acceptance by them. So the embarrassments of the past were forgotten, finally and properly determined to be neither his fault nor capable of correction. And there was a deeper meaning. It meant that Interior Minister needn't be the only government office available to him. He could still get the premiership that had once been denied him because of Richard. Hannah would be pleased. And proud. His wife had waited a long time for this.

He heard the footsteps and pushed himself away from the wall, smiling as he recognized his private secretary. He wanted to break the news but knew he couldn't, not before the official announcement the following day. Piet Deaken had nothing to learn about discretion.

"A telephone call," said the man. "From the airport at Johannesburg. Your wife told them they could reach you here."

When Deaken picked up the telephone in his office he felt his brief elation draining away; it was as if a hand had plunged deep into his stomach, a cold, cruel hand, and was wrenching at his innards.

"I do not have a son called Richard Deaken," said the old man, rigid-voiced.

At the other end the immigration man winced at the pedantic disclaimer. "I called the security headquarters in Skinner Street when I couldn't get you immediately. They've already got a deputy director on the way."

So he couldn't avoid it, couldn't block it out, thought the older man.

"Sir?" said the official at the airport, uncertain at the silence.

"I'm still here," said the politician. For how long? he wondered.

Around the pool there had been a lot of talk about Grearson and Carole knew from the girls who had been on the yacht before her arrival that he was always a flop, a grunting, mechanical man who had to be coaxed and praised and encouraged and with whom it was always over practically before it started. But Carole was superbly accomplished, completely concealing any reaction but the one he wanted.

"That was fantastic—you're amazing," she said.

"It's always fantastic with you," said Grearson, reassured that he had pleased her. He was breathing heavily.

"What's happened to that man who was here?" she said. "Deaken?"

"He wasn't necessary anymore," said Grearson, who liked to boast to her.

"Is he coming back?"

"No."

Carole had detected Deaken's attraction to her even though he had done his best to conceal it. She wondered if he would have succumbed if there had been more time. She looked at the hump beside her in the darkness; it would have been a bloody sight more exciting than this had just been.

"I thought we were going to be cruising," she complained. "We've been stuck here for days."

"We'll get away soon," promised Grearson. "Just as soon as Mr Azziz's son gets aboard."

"When's that going to be?"

"Only a day or two now."

"Just the boy or will there be a bigger party?" she asked hopefully.

"Just us," said Grearson. He kissed her clumsily. "You don't want anybody else, do you?"

"You know the answer to that," she said. Christ, how she wished it could soon be over.

26

Deaken hoped his father would be the first to arrive so that immediate pressure could be imposed upon the security service, but it didn't happen that way and he knew he was going to have to be very cautious, to prevent any message getting through to Underberg in Monaco.

The security official was as short and squat as the senior immigration man, but it was a muscled body, not an overindulged one. He came stern-faced into the room, the immigration man behind him, stopping at the doorway to look Deaken over. He was in plain clothes, without any insignia of rank.

"You wanted to see me?" The accent was thickly Afrikaans.

"I wanted to see somebody from security."

"My name is Swart."

"You know my name. And who I am," said Deaken.

"So what do you want?"

"So far I only know your name," said Deaken.

The man reached inside his jacket pocket and showed Deaken his identification wallet. There was a photograph and the shield of the security service that Deaken remembered so well, imprinted above the name. The rank of colonel! Higher than he had expected; the man could be a deputy even. Certainly with sufficient authority to have contacted Underberg before coming here.

"Satisfied?" demanded Swart.

Deaken attacked at once. "You've got my wife. If anything happens to her, I guarantee it won't just be the publicity. I'll see that my father takes your whole fucking service apart!"

"What the *hell* are you talking about?" said Swart, amazed.

"I asked to see my father," said Deaken. He realized gratefully that his voice didn't show his anxiety.

"He's coming," said the fat man.

Swart lowered himself into the one chair.

"If it weren't for who you are," he said, "your record . . . and your father . . . you'd have been seen by one of the airport staff. As it is, I have driven all the way from Pretoria and I'm beginning to think I've wasted my time. I want to know now . . . right now . . . what you're doing here. And not in gibberish. In words I can understand."

The arrival of Deaken's father saved him. There was movement from the doorway, and he looked up to see the tall, upright old man. Five years, he thought; nearer six. The final screaming row in the study of the Parkstown mansion, the accusations of disgracing the family, of being disowned, took on a Victorian, almost humorous, unreality. Except that it had been painfully real. Deaken smiled, wanting to reach out and touch his father, make now the apologies he had never been able to make before, but realized that would be as inappropriate as the smile. Piet Deaken came hesitantly into the room, looking not to his son but to the other men in the room for guidance. Swart stood up smartly, the demeanour of respect obvious, introducing himself and offering his hand. The old man took it with indifference, looking fully at his son for the first time. His appearance in the doorway had been misleading, Deaken decided. The initial impression had been that his father was upright and forceful as ever, but it wasn't so: there was a bend to his body, an uncertainty, like a once strong tree under pressure from a sudden wind.

"Why have you come back?" he said. The voice, like the stance, was hesitant.

"For help," said Deaken simply.

The ingenuous honesty of the reply surprised his father. He blinked, looking to Swart again, then back to his son.

"I want to save Karen's life."

"What!"

To Swart Deaken said, looking at the immigration officials, "I'm happy for them to stay if you are."

The colonel's reaction was immediate, a head jerk of dismissal.

Deaken realized he had penetrated the barriers his father had erected but Swart was still regarding him doubtfully. Politely he offered the chair to his father, preferring to stand, as he had stood a hundred times in a hundred courts, to make his case. Except that this case was the most important of his life. He started from the morning in the Geneva apartment, not referring to the argument with Karen but mentioning the arrangement to meet during the day, because he considered the timing important. And then of the encounter with Underberg, Karen's frightened telephone call, the photograph with Azziz and his meeting aboard the *Scheherazade* with the boy's millionaire father. Deaken had always prided himself on his ability to read the expression on the juries' or judges' faces. His father sat frowning, uncertain; Swart's expression was one of bewilderment, deepening when Deaken concluded with the attack in Dakar.

The old man responded first. "Do you know anything about this?" he said to Swart.

"There have been rumours of some campaign underway in Namibia, but nothing definite."

"I mean about my daughter-in-law?"

"Absolutely nothing," insisted Swart.

"What about Underberg then?" said Deaken.

There was a wall-mounted telephone near the door. Swart went to it, standing with his back to them and speaking quietly, so that neither could hear the conversation. When he hung up, Swart said simply, "Our service is in no way involved."

"Have I your word?"

"I've spoken to the Director," said Swart. He looked at Deaken. "He said the suggestion was as preposterous as the story."

"What about the name?" demanded Deaken.

"There are two men named Underberg in the service," agreed Swart. "Marius Underberg in central records. Jan Underberg is in the transport section."

"What does it mean?" asked Piet Deaken.

There was a pause and then Swart said, "Perhaps, sir, your son is unwell?"

As he had when he planned his first escape, Tewfik Azziz waited until the house quieted and he was sure that everyone was asleep. Carefully he got out of the bed and for thirty minutes practised every noiseless exercise that he could recall from the gymnastic and calisthenic instruction at the Ecole Gagner, wanting to test his strength as fully as possible. He ached at the end but knew that it was from the exertion, not from any lingering effect of the illness. So he was fit again; fit enough to get away. He got back into bed, cupping his hands behind his head and staring up towards the ceiling. It had been instinctive to promise the woman that he wouldn't go without her. No, not instinctive: politeness. Automatic, polite gratitude, for what she had done for him when he had been ill. By himself, he stood a chance. They would never make it together. He felt a flicker of guilt. But he had nothing to feel guilty about. It was him they wanted, not her. She was just a pawn. They wouldn't harm her, if he got away. He was sure they wouldn't . . .

There had been no argument from Swart about letting the father stand guarantor for his son, but during the drive from Johannesburg to Pretoria there wasn't the reconciliation that Deaken had imagined in the detention room. Instead his father retreated behind the usual barriers, deep in his own thoughts.

Deaken was thoroughly confused. If the South African security service was not involved, then Karen was in no immediate danger from his being in the country. And the rerouting instructions for the *Bellicose* had been sent independently. So for the next four or five days Underberg—or whatever his name was—would receive information that was going to keep her safe. But who was holding Karen and Azziz? It was a maze. Deaken had turned the first corner and all he could see was another blank and impenetrable wall.

As they approached the Parkstown suburb, Deaken looked out at the jacaranda trees which were black against the night sky. In the morning they would be showing violet and purple; Deaken wondered if the arbour in the grounds of the house would be as spectacular as he remembered it.

When they telephoned from Johannesburg airport, Deaken's mother was in bed. They arrived to find her fully dressed, carefully made up and immaculately coiffed, waiting for them in the larger of the garden drawing rooms, the one which overlooked the tennis court and the stepped terraces.

"Hello, Mother," said Deaken.

She acknowledged him with a curt nod, the sort of gesture she would have accorded a stranger. He supposed he should go across to kiss her, but didn't think she would want him to. He decided to sit down on one of the deep, green velvet settees.

"What is this all about?" His mother was as rigid and formal as her carefully waved white hair. It came as something of a surprise to Deaken to realize that she was a stronger person than his father. But it was he who elected to tell the story, more concisely than Deaken had done, missing none of the details, and showing the ability that had taken him from the advocates' floor to the judges' bench before exchanging a legal career for one in politics. But he didn't stop at the account of missing the *Bellicose* in Dakar.

"There's something else," he said to his wife.

"What?"

"I've got the Interior Ministry. I was told tonight officially."

She looked at her son. "And then he had to arrive!"

"I need your help," said Deaken, understanding now the reason for his father's silence in the car.

"What do the authorities say?" asked his mother.

"They deny all knowledge or involvement," said her husband.

"They think I'm insane," added Deaken.

She looked at him. "*Are* you?"

"Of course not."

"You don't look well."

"Karen's been kidnapped. I've been tricked, cheated and left for dead in the middle of nowhere. I've just flown four thousand miles. How do you expect me to look?"

"We've a meeting with the Director in the morning." As always the old man tried to come between them. "They're making more inquiries."

The woman didn't look at him, eyes fixed on her son. "You almost ruined your father's career once," she said. "I won't have you do it again."

"I've no intention of ruining anything," said Deaken wearily. "I just want Karen back."

She didn't speak for several moments and when she did Deaken realized she hadn't listened to him.

"I'd have you committed rather than let it happen again," she said.

Deaken knew that she meant it.

27

The appointment with the Director of the Department of National Security had been arranged for ten, but just as Deaken and his father were preparing to leave the Parkstown house there was a telephone call from Skinner Street, postponing it until midday.

"Why?" asked Deaken.

"I don't know. They didn't say," replied his father.

Deaken was still at the breakfast table, set out on the wide, sweeping verandah overlooking the gardens. The water sprinklers were already revolving over the grasses and shrubbery to beat the cooking heat of midday. Deaken noted that the arbour was still as colourful and as carefully kept as he remembered it. He could see four Africans working in the grounds but knew there would be more. The maintenance staff had been twenty strong when he had lived there. His mother had always insisted on neatness and efficiency. He was glad he didn't look such a mess this morning. Whoever had cleaned, pressed and mended his suit had made an excellent job of it.

His father, who had remained standing after returning to report the telephone call, sat down again and gestured for the waiting houseboy to clear the breakfast debris. Deaken saw that the serving staff still wore white gloves.

"I'm sorry about last night," said the older man unexpectedly.

Deaken shrugged. "I suppose she'd reason enough."

"It was still rude . . . unnecessary. She was very hurt by what happened last time."

"I'm sorry."

"Your mother was always ambitious. She thinks if I'd got the original appointment, I could be premier now."

"Couldn't you still?"

"I've got to make a success of the Interior Ministry first."

Deaken looked back at the garden and the working Africans. His father epitomized the Boer: member of the Broederbond, the closed, secret society of ruling class, always a participant in the Voortrekker marches, which commemorated the occupation of the country and their subsequent fight against the British. There was everything he hated in the man he loved so much.

"Do you believe Swart . . . that this country wasn't involved?"

"My appointment has been rumoured for some time," said the older man. "They wouldn't lie to me, knowing that I can find out easily enough."

"Then I won't do anything to embarrass you," promised Deaken. "I intended to. The threat of publicity was the only weapon I had to protect Karen. But not now."

The old man nodded.

"Do you believe me?"

"It's difficult to."

"I'm not mad."

"I don't think you are."

"What do you think then?" demanded Deaken.

"That it's going to be difficult to convince anyone else."

Deaken caught a movement from the French windows. It was one of the house servants. Seeing his expectation, his father said, "She won't be coming out."

"Oh," said Deaken. He supposed half a reconciliation was better than none. Was this really a reconciliation with his father? Or the action of a man who had lost one opportunity and was trying to minimize the risk of losing another? It really wasn't important. Deciding what to do next was important and he realized, emptily, that he didn't know.

"We'd better go," said his father. "They said noon."

The limousine which had brought them from Johannesburg was waiting, with the uniformed driver at the wheel; it had been washed and polished and gleamed in the sun. They moved off along the broad residential roads, between landscaped gardens jewelled by mansions and villas and beneath the purple and violet jacaranda trees. Deaken was surprised to feel a certain nostalgia.

The Department of National Security was a modern, tall, tinted-glass building and the office of its Director, Brigadier Heinrich Muller, was on the top floor, occupying a corner with a panoramic view over Pretoria. Deaken followed his father into the room and closed the door behind them. Muller was a large, heavy-bodied man, full-featured and with thick, heavy hands. Like Swart, who stood alongside and was the only other man in the room, he wore plain clothes. In fact Swart didn't appear to have changed since the previous night. Deaken saw that the expressions weren't as sceptical as he had expected, just blank. His father made the introductions and Muller offered his hand. Deaken took it, surprised.

"I'm sorry for the delay," said Muller, gesturing to chairs. "Things took longer than we thought."

"What things?" said Deaken.

"Checking that a yacht owned by a man called Adnan Azziz, who has a son in a Swiss school, was in harbour at Monte Carlo," elaborated Muller. "That there was an unexplained and so far unsolved assault upon a holiday villa near a small French town called Rixheim. And that a freighter named the *Bellicose*, owned by the Levcos shipping company, sailed from Marseilles over a week ago and made a call within the last two days at Dakar."

Deaken experienced the sensation of being in a lift that suddenly descends faster than expected.

"Thank you," he said, soft-voiced. "For believing me . . . for bothering to make the inquiries."

"It wasn't altruism," said Muller. "We've an interest in stopping major campaigns in Namibia." He hesitated. "Which remains a problem."

"What do you mean?" demanded Deaken's father.

Muller looked at Swart. The stocky man cleared his throat and said, "According to what you told me last night, Azziz has ordered the *Bellicose* to return for a rendezvous off Algiers."

The falling sensation hit Deaken again, but this time it was a result of fear—fear and blinding anger. "Don't say the bastard has—!"

"Lloyds report a northerly course," said Swart. "The last report put the freighter forty miles off the Mauritanian coast, making twelve knots in a medium swell."

Deaken frowned at the man. "So he is doing what he said?"

"We've long-range reconnaissance aircraft," interrupted Muller. "We ordered a check, initially little more than a precaution. At dawn this morning a freighter, later identified from aerial photographs to be the *Bellicose,* was proceeding southwards towards Angola."

There was a protracted silence in the room. Deaken's father broke it. "That doesn't make sense," he said.

"Only if there are two ships," said the security chief. "And we know there aren't. That's why we delayed this meeting. We overflew the Mauritanian position two hours ago—a supposed Air Force training flight to the Azores. We've swept the area. There are ships certainly. But none of them is the *Bellicose*."

"So Underberg . . ." said Deaken, beginning to understand, "or whoever he is will think we're keeping to the arrangement," he said. "He is getting his information from Lloyds."

It made sense of what had happened in Dakar. Azziz was the *bwana mkubwa*, the big man who had wanted to keep him off the *Bellicose*, so that he wouldn't discover that a change of course was never intended for the freighter.

"I understand your reaction," said Muller. "Of more concern to us is that whoever bought all the weaponry appears to be getting delivery as planned."

"It has to be SWAPO surely?" said Deaken.

"That's the obvious conclusion," said Muller. "But there are still too many uncertainties about this business."

He looked at Swart again. The man took from Muller's desk two photographs and showed them to Deaken. "Do you recognize either of these two men?"

They were official pictures, both men staring directly and self-consciously at the camera. "No" said Deaken. "I've never seen either of them before."

"I'm glad," said Muller.

"Who are they?" said Deaken.

"Marius Underberg and Jan Underberg," said the Director.

"So who's the man I saw in Geneva?"

"Will you do something for us?" asked Muller.

"Of course," said Deaken. As he spoke, he realized the final irony. He was cooperating, even seeking the assistance, of an organization which he had criticized and fought all his life. But there was no choice. "What do you want?" he said.

"For you to work with our artists. Identikit and photofit specialists. We need a picture of the man you met in Geneva."

Two men were waiting in the office next door, one with paper pinned across an artist's drawing board, the other standing at a table before assorted boxes. Deaken worked first with the photofit expert, picking his way through the containers holding every feature of the human face, from basic outline to warts, moles and strawberry birthmarks. Deaken worked with total concentration, occasionally closing his eyes mentally to picture again the smug, self-assured countenance that had confronted him over his cheap office desk in Switzerland. It took a long time and at the end he ached with the effort.

"It's as good as I can get it," he said.

"Then let me improve it," said the artist.

While the photograph was being taken off the composite image, Deaken went over the photofit features with which he was not completely satisfied. He remained at the man's shoulder while he worked, with fine-haired brushes and then an air brush, tinting and paring until at last Deaken was staring down at the man who called himself Underberg. The retouched version was photographed again and then the three of them went back to the Director's office.

"Comparisons?" asked Muller.

"Begun from the original photofit," said the man who had created it. "This version is put through a physiognomy computer."

Deaken looked curiously between the intelligence director and his technicians. "So what happens now?" he said.

"More checking," said Muller.

It took ten minutes. A third, white-coated man came in with a folder and handed it to Muller. The Director detached a snapshot-size photograph and handed it to Deaken. "Is this the man?" he said.

It was clearly a photograph that had been taken without the subject's knowledge. It showed him striding down a wide highway, bordered by modern buildings, and from the number of blacks Deaken guessed it was somewhere in Africa.

"Who is he?" said Deaken.

"His name is Vladimir Suslev," replied Muller.

Mitri brought the message from the radio room, padding respectfully into the stateroom and handing it to Azziz. The Arab read it, his face clouding. He studied it a second time to ensure that he had properly understood. Then he looked up to Grearson and said, "It's from Levcos. They've had a signal from the *Bellicose* that Deaken didn't board in Dakar."

"What!"

"He apparently made contact with the agent there the day before the docking. But that was the last they saw of him."

"So where the hell is he?"

"God knows."

"What about the messages?"

"They're being sent as arranged. They were never dependent upon Deaken's presence anyway."

"If he tries something on his own, he could ruin everything." Grearson brought his fist down hard on the chair arm.

"Your people in Marseilles—Evans and the others—they know Deaken, don't they?" asked Azziz.

"Sure," said Grearson.

"If they see him, poking around the docks . . . doing anything . . . I want him killed."

It was a long, frustrating discussion, with frequent cul-de-sacs from which none of them could find an exit. It had long since grown dark, and Pretoria was still and quiet. The Director's office was littered with debris of long occupation, discarded coffee cups and half-eaten sandwiches.

"Why should Vladimir Suslev, whom we know to have acted as a military adviser to Angola and again with SWAPO guerrillas in Namibia, represent himself as South African? Why should he kidnap a Saudi Arabian arms dealer's son—and the wife of a South African of some notoriety—and stipulate the ransom to be the rerouting of an arms shipment for an organization which the Soviet Union supports against us?" demanded Muller.

It was the recurring question, the maypole around which they had all danced until the strings had become tangled.

"And what the hell is Azziz doing?" said Deaken.

"That at least we may be able to find out," said Muller.

"I'll have people with me?" said Deaken.

Muller indicated Swart. "He'll be in charge. There will be as many men as are needed. We'll get your wife back."

It took a couple of hours to make all the arrangements and assemble an immediate advance group to join Deaken and Swart. When the time came to leave, his father asked if he could drive him to the airport at Johannesburg.

"If the guerrillas are planning an offensive in July, the government have got a lot to thank you for."

"Will you tell mother what happened?" said Deaken, unsure why it was so important for him to impress her.

"Of course," said the older man. "As far as I'm allowed to." He smiled ruefully.

"I'd like her to know."

The man stretched across the car, putting his hand upon his son's arm. "Come back," he said.

"I will," promised Deaken.

"And bring Karen."

"Yes," said Deaken after a pause. "I'll bring Karen."

28

Eight men flew from South Africa with Deaken and Swart, in two separate aircraft. Two more went directly to Paris to the South African embassy to collect the weapons that had been shipped over in the diplomatic bag to bypass customs interference. There were contingency plans for more men to follow if Swart decided it was necessary. The first priority was to locate the Russian and, even before the conference in Muller's office had ended, everyone had recognized the problem facing them in Monte Carlo and the risk of Deaken's accidental recognition. They chose Nice, taking a series of rooms in the Hotel Negresco; Swart's suite overlooked the Promenade des Anglais, and it was here the group assembled early on the first morning.

Deaken sat beside Swart but took no part in the briefing, admiring the military precision with which the security man deployed his men, dispatching six to Monte Carlo but reserving two for Marseilles, the departure port of the *Bellicose*. Despite the speed with which they had left South Africa, Deaken saw Swart had managed to bring a family photograph with him: a woman, as small and stocky as her husband, and two children, a boy and a girl, both fair-haired, smiling into the camera from what appeared to be a picnic scene. It disclosed a personal side of a man whom Deaken had regarded as a hardened professional.

As the men filed from the room Swart said, "And now we wait."

"And think," added Deaken.

"About what?"

"The Lloyds reports give the speed of what's supposed to be the *Bellicose* sailing back?"

"Yes."

"So it's a simple calculation to work out when it should arrive off Algiers."

"But we know it isn't going to," said Swart. "How can Suslev contact a ship that isn't going to be there?"

Another dead end, thought Deaken.

"I'd like to know what we're working *against*," said Swart.

Deaken looked up sharply. For these unexpected new allies it was a matter of vital security to discover Russia's part in the arms shipment and if possible to prevent a major battle in a disputed area. For him it was simply a matter of getting Karen back.

The telephone sounded insistently. Swart lapsed into Afrikaans as soon as the caller identified himself, smiling at Deaken. As he replaced the receiver, he said, "Why is it that so often the most complex problem is really the most simple?"

"What's happened?" said Deaken.

"One of the people I sent to Marseilles did the obvious thing as soon as he arrived there and checked the ships in port. There's a Levcos-owned freighter named the *Hydra Star,* loaded and waiting sailing instructions."

"So that's how Azziz is going to do it!"

Swart held up his hand. "It looks promising," he said. "But it could also be a coincidence—Levcos is a big company, with lots of ships. We shouldn't jump to conclusions."

"You don't have to," said Deaken.

Deaken made good time along the coast road and arrived in Marseilles before midday. He parked the car and approached the boulevard Nôtre Dame on foot, deciding against telephoning ahead in case Marcel Lerclerc checked either with Ortega or with Grearson direct. The confidence he had felt in the Nice hotel room had evaporated slightly during the drive. There was no certainty that Azziz would have obtained his End-User certificate through Portugal and Ortega again. And if he hadn't, then the encounter with Lerclerc was going to be ridiculous; worse, it would be suspicious, practically guaranteeing that Lerclerc would check back and that Azziz would come to know about it. It was still worth the risk, though.

Outside the office of the arms dealer's shipping agent Deaken hesitated, rehearsing his strategy in his head, and then pushed his way through the narrow door and along the cluttered, dirty passage. When he entered the office,

Lerclerc looked up without recognition, his face as closed and suspicious as on their first encounter.

"I've come without an appointment—forgive me," said Deaken. When the man didn't move, Deaken added, "The last shipment, remember? Mr Azziz?"

The huge man heaved himself upwards, extending his hand. "Good to see you again, good to see you," he said, overeffusive to compensate for his earlier reserve. Almost at once the smile faltered. "No problem this time, is there?"

Deaken pretended to cough, putting his hand to his face to cover any expression of satisfaction. "None at all," he said. "I was passing on my way back to the yacht and it seemed like a good idea to call to see if everything was all right this end."

"Pastis?"

"Thank you."

With his back to Deaken, Lerclerc said, "I told you last time things don't go wrong here. The certificate has been accepted, as I advised Mr Grearson, and the export licence has been issued." He turned back and gave Deaken his glass. They drank. "All we're waiting for now is the sailing instructions from you," said Lerclerc.

"It will be a day or two." Having taken one chance, Deaken decided upon another. "There might be some additions. Could they be added onto the export agreement?"

Lerclerc made a doubtful rocking gesture with his hand. "Might be a chance of something small," he said. "Nothing big."

"There's room though, isn't there?"

"For a tank at least," agreed Lerclerc.

"I've been away for almost a week," said Deaken. "Have you sent on the bill of lading?"

Lerclerc nodded and then said, "Do you want to check the duplicate?"

It was going almost too well, thought Deaken exultantly. "To remind myself," he accepted.

The other man took a folder from a filing cabinet and handed it to him. Beneath a copy of the latest manifest was a duplicate of the *Bellicose* shipment. They were identical.

"Everything okay?" said Lerclerc.

Deaken nodded. "I think I'll advise against trying to add to the shipment."

"It might be best." The agent paused. "Having got the clearance, I don't like the stuff hanging around on the docks too long."

"We'll move it very soon," said Deaken. He decided he would be straining his luck if he hung around much longer. As he stood to leave, Lerclerc beamed and said, "Things seem to be very satisfactory all round."

"Very," said Deaken.

As he walked back along the boulevard Nôtre Dame he suddenly thought back to his initial visit, after the bargaining with Ortega in Lisbon. He had argued Ortega into a commission of 5 per cent. Which was the figure Lerclerc had stipulated when he had arrived within hours, a figure the agent couldn't have learned from Lisbon because Lerclerc's telephone hadn't been working. So the Lisbon visit had been a setup, a ruse to get him out of the way, just as the attack in Dakar had been arranged to get him out of the way, permanently this time, after another fool's errand. Only this time he wasn't the fool.

Grearson snapped off the recording of that morning's interchange from the quayside telephone and said, "He seems satisfied that the *Bellicose* is on its way back."

Azziz nodded.

"And we're going to get a picture showing that Tewfik is all right." Grearson wanted to make sure his employer was in no doubt about his successful negotiation.

"I'm grateful to you," said Azziz. "You've handled everything extremely well."

Ashore, the patient South African search team reached the Bristol Hotel which had been given to Deaken as a

backup contact point. From the head porter, whom they
tipped 100 francs, Suslev was identified as the guest in the
harbour-front room on the sixth floor. He was registered as
R. Underberg. They omitted to make a note of the supposed
passport number, which was a considerable mistake.

29

At one stage the intention had been for the conference to
be chaired by the Prime Minister and to include responsible ministers from the cabinet, but it was finally decided to
restrict it to service chiefs and their respective intelligence
heads, for a fuller report to be compiled before positive
and direct government involvement.

Muller conducted it, from a raised dais in the conference
room of the Skinner Street building. Easels and black-
boards were arranged behind him to accommodate the
maps and photographs available; the centrepiece was a
detailed chart of the west coast of Angola, Namibia and
South Africa, marked with a model of a ship and a dotted
line showing the progress of the *Bellicose*. Against the
line, at timed and dated intervals, were positions obtained
from the aerial reconnaissance. The last inscription was
three hours earlier and the naval chief-of-staff, an admiral
named Hertzog, said, "What's the latest position?"

Muller looked instinctively at his watch. "As of half an
hour ago, forty miles off Luanda." He used a pointer,
indicating the distances between timings. "From these

we've been able to make an estimate of the speed: she seems to be making about eight knots."

"Still heading south?" queried the army chief, Brigadier General Althorpe.

"Still heading south," confirmed Muller.

"What's the information from Namibia?" said Althorpe. He hesitated, looking at his own intelligence officer. "We've isolated reports but no indication of any concerted mobilization."

"I ordered the highest priority the moment the risk seemed genuine," said Muller. "There's certainly indication of assembly at Tses, Gibeon and Maltahöhe. A lot of movement farther north, in the Caprivi Strip, too."

"We're not limiting reconnaissance to the ocean," said the Air Force chief, a man named Youngblood. "Within twenty-four hours I hope to have some definite information."

After his meeting with Lerclerc, Deaken had itemized everything he could remember from the cargo manifest of the *Bellicose*. Muller had duplicated it and made a copy available to everyone in the room. Hertzog raised his sheet and said, "There's too much here for any seaborne unloading; it'll have to dock."

"Benguela is the most obvious place, if she doesn't turn east towards Luanda," said Muller. "There's Moçâmedes, but that's far too close to our border. I don't think they'd risk it."

Althorpe gestured towards the enlarged map. "There are thousands of inlets and bays."

Now Muller lifted his copy of the cargo list. "Even if the ship's derrick was capable of offloading them, the freighter's draught would keep her offshore. She'd need to be alongside."

Youngblood looked sideways, towards the army contingent. "Any indication of a Soviet buildup?"

Althorpe nodded for his intelligence chief to reply. He was a thin man named Harper, whose Adam's apple bobbed nervously up and down when he spoke. "It's always difficult to estimate. As you know, Moscow usually avoids direct involvement by working through Cubans or East Germans. We don't estimate they've more than a hundred Soviet personnel on the ground.''

Youngblood turned to Muller. ''Do you agree?''

Muller hesitated, not wanting to contradict a colleague. ''About a hundred military advisers,'' he said. ''But I think in Angola and probably Namibia too, there are more straight intelligence operatives who aren't bothering with any sort of advisory cover.''

''What about Suslev?''

The photograph located after Deaken's photofit re-creation had been enlarged and occupied almost all of one blackboard. Muller said, ''We don't know a lot. The indications are that he isn't KGB but an officer in the military division of Russian intelligence, the GRU. Certainly a long-serving officer. Positively identified in Angola in 1978 and then 1980, when this photograph was taken. No sightings for over a year and then a brief appearance, about four or five months ago. After that, nothing.''

''Anything yet from Europe?'' demanded Hertzog.

Muller shook his head. ''They haven't had a lot of time. Swart's a good man, one of the best in my service. And he's got a good team.''

''I'm concerned about the involvement of Deaken,'' said Youngblood. ''Not a good history.''

''I'm quite aware of it,'' said Muller. ''He's not acting as a provocateur, I'm sure. So's his father.''

''Who's been named today as Minister for Interior,'' reminded Althorpe. ''It's a delicate situation.''

''Which I'm also aware of,'' assured Muller. ''And so are the people I've got with him in France. Swart has got two briefs. The first is to find out what the hell the Russians are doing. The second is to avoid any embarrassment that might affect a member of our government. Our involvement with Deaken will be kept to the minimum.''

"Seems to me that the apple splits almost perfectly in half," said Hertzog. "The freighter is one problem. Europe another."

"I don't want that weaponry ashore," said Althorpe positively. He patted the list on the table before him. "If there is mobilization and if this stuff is distributed, then we'll have the biggest conflict yet on our hands. Maybe not just one battle; probably several. Which means more international attention and more UN criticism."

"There'd be a damned sight more international attention if I intercept it at sea," said Hertzog. "The *Bellicose* is miles out of our territorial waters. It would be piracy."

"Who's going to know about it?" demanded Althorpe. "Are the arms suppliers going to protest and be shown to have been starting a war? Or the shippers, to have been carrying the weapons to it? And any SWAPO publicity isn't going to worry us."

"That's not going to be our decision," pointed out Muller. "That's a political conclusion, which is why we're having this meeting today. We've all got to make recommendation."

"Prevention is always better than cure," insisted Althorpe. "Mine is that it should be stopped."

"Mine too," concurred Youngblood. "With the advantage we've got, we'd be mad to let one round of ammunition ashore."

"What about Europe?" said Hertzog. "I don't think we can be definite about anything until we know what's happening there."

"True," agreed Muller. "But I think we should make contingency plans."

"Mine are already in operation," said Hertzog. "We've sailed."

Vladimir Suslev emerged onto Monaco's boulevard Albert and on the corner bought a copy of that day's *Nice Matin*, glancing idly at the headlines as he walked to the car.

The Russian drove slowly along the coast road, going eastwards initially, before branching up on the inland road that would give him his route to Sisteron. From the latest report from Lloyds and from Levcos in Athens, the *Bellicose* was supposed to be making twelve knots. Which meant Algiers in two days; three at the outside if the weather worsened. And that was unlikely; he had taken the trouble to get the long-range weather forecast. Suslev smiled, settling himself back into the seat; three days and it would all be over. He would be on his way back to Moscow for the promotion and the honours he had been promised. And which he had earned.

And for which his wife had suffered. He knew that was how she regarded it, from his leave in Moscow. It would take a long time for them to reestablish the relationship they once had had. But he would do it, he determined; she was so beautiful, so loyal. Maybe he had been wrong expecting her to make the sacrifice for his career. He didn't think she would feel that way for long when she saw what it meant for them.

The route was crowded, as he had found it the first time, but today he drove without impatience, actually admiring the scenery. It was prettier than anything around Moscow; even the hills in springtime, after the snow went. He had heard that Sochi, on the Black Sea, had a climate like this. Perhaps he would be permitted to go there as part of the reward. She would enjoy that.

Levy was expecting him, coming from the house as soon as he saw the car.

"We'll talk afterwards," said Suslev.

"All right," said the Israeli. "Why the newspaper?"

"It proves the date."

"I'm glad it's being done this way."

"I decided it was better," said the Russian easily. He remained in the car, hunched down in his seat, as Karen and Azziz were brought out into the garden at the side of the house and posed with the copy of *Nice Matin* held before them. Levy took two Polaroid pictures, plucking them one after the other from the camera and watching them develop.

The South Africans had a more elaborate camera, with a telescopic lens, and they managed four exposures before the driver, frightened of discovery, said, "OK, that's enough," and drove on.

30

There was a communal table, as there had been in the farmhouse at Rixheim, and the Israelis gathered around it for the final briefing from the man they knew as Underberg.

"Everything is going as planned," he said. "It's going to be a perfect operation."

There were smiles and nods of satisfaction. Leiberwitz said, "How soon?"

"Two days, three at the outside," said the Russian. "That's why I wanted this meeting. We've got to move to the next stage now."

"Getting the stuff into Israel?" said Levy.

Suslev nodded. "Which normally would be impossible," he said. "But I've found a way."

There were more smiles.

"I'm calculating that the freighter will get back on the thirteenth; the excuse for returning, officially, will be engine trouble," he said. "All its documentation is in order so there'll be no need for customs examination. I've hired two lorries. The ship's crane is sufficient to offload what we want. I want it put into the lorries, to convey the impression that we're going to try to move the stuff by road.''

"How *is* it going to be moved?" asked Greening.

"I've chartered a smaller freighter," said Suslev. "The *Marriv*. It's docking on the twelfth. We just use the lorries as carriers to transfer from one vessel to another and then sail up the Mediterranean to Haifa. I'm calculating five days for the voyage, but it's not important because there will be contact ashore. In the customs department at Haifa there's a friend, Hanan Cohen—his parents were among the first to be thrown out of Hammit. Now they've no business, no home, just some paltry compensation. When he hears the *Marriv* is approaching, he'll arrange to be on duty. Everything will get straight in.''

"Do we all sail?" asked Levy.

Suslev nodded. "It's the obvious way to get back," he said. "When you disembark in Haifa, I'll be waiting."

"It sounds remarkably simple," said Kahane admiringly.

"It is," said Suslev with a grin. "Like I said, it's going to be a perfect operation."

"How about the exchange, the boy and the woman?" said Levy, immediately aware of the concentrated attention upon himself.

"Nothing can go wrong here either," said Suslev. Succinctly he explained how the return was to be made, in a way to protect all of them, conscious as he talked of the tension forming among the men.

"That entrusts everything to Levy," complained Leiberwitz.

The Russian frowned. "Levy's in command; that was the arrangement we made before we left Israel."

"I don't think he should be any longer," said Leiberwitz, making an open challenge.

There was no place in any contingency plan for these

people to argue among themselves and Suslev felt a spurt of uncertainty. "Why not?" he said.

"I don't think he's impartial any more," said Leiberwitz.

"Nothing is going to endanger our mission," said Levy. "We'll get the weapons as we intended—and we'll stage the protest as we intended."

"What about the woman?" demanded Leiberwitz.

Suslev saw Levy flush, and began to understand.

"You've heard the arrangements," said Levy tightly. "She's returned, like the boy."

"Why shouldn't she be?" said Suslev to Leiberwitz.

The huge man sneered towards Levy and said, "I'm not sure he'll be able to part with her."

Suslev made a quick assessment and decided that the situation didn't present a danger to his plans—as a distraction for them, it could even work to his advantage.

"Well?" He looked questioningly at Levy.

"It needn't concern anyone in this room," came the reply. "It's not going to cause any problems."

"Was it wise?" Suslev said, feeling he should be seen to take some position.

"I don't have to account to you or anybody else," said Levy, tight-lipped.

"What about your wife?" said Leiberwitz.

"That's my business," snapped Levy. The flush had gone; now the man was pale with anger.

The Russian looked round him trying to gauge the feeling of the other men. To Levy he said, "Do I have your promise this won't end stupidly?"

"You don't have to ask me that!"

"I think I do."

Levy hesitated, then said, "Yes, my promise."

To the rest of them Suslev said, "Shimeon has been involved in this since the beginning; it's as much his action as it is mine. I'm not interested, morally, in what's happened—only that nothing interferes with the success of the operation. I'm prepared to accept his assurance."

Levy relaxed slightly.

Only Leiberwitz had spoken in open criticism, realized Suslev. Deciding to take the risk, he said, "Should there be a vote on it?"

"Yes," said Leiberwitz at once.

"In favour of Shimeon remaining in command?" proposed Suslev. He raised his hand as he spoke. Kahane and Sela responded immediately. Katz hesitated and then he came out in favour. Seeing the direction of the feeling, Habel finally raised his hand in support.

"Against?" said Suslev.

Leiberwitz and Greening voted simultaneously.

"Shimeon remains in charge," said Suslev.

"It's a mistake," insisted Leiberwitz.

"The matter is closed," said Suslev.

But the tension between them increased when Suslev asked to be left alone with Levy for the handover briefing. The Russian produced a map to ensure that Levy knew the identity of the place, then passed over the keys and a photograph of the villa where the boy was to be left.

"It's miles from anywhere" said the Russian. "No one will find him accidentally."

"I don't like the idea of abandoning him like this," protested the Israeli.

"There's a good reason."

"I understand that," said Levy. "And it's good. I just don't like the idea of leaving him."

"If Azziz is sensible, it'll only be for an hour or two," assured the Russian. He left the Sisteron villa thirty minutes later, the developed proof in his pocket. The internecine squabbling was a definite advantage, decided Suslev. Not that he was taking any chances. There was a freighter called the *Marriv* due in port on the twelfth. There wasn't anyone in Haifa named Hanan Cohen, though. It didn't matter; he was sure they wouldn't think of double-checking. There was no reason for them to do so. They trusted him.

*   *   *

Edward Makimber determined against telling the rest of the SWAPO command of the difficulties involving the *Bellicose*. That had all been resolved, so the only effect would be to make them uneasy. And they were nervous enough as it was.

"From what I saw in Marseilles, I estimate it will take two days to unload," he said. "It didn't take that long to put the stuff aboard in France, but the port facilities were better there. I think we should truck them directly inland, to the dispersal points. If we allow three days for that, then we can commence on the fifteenth and launch the attack on the seventeenth."

"Exactly on schedule," said Arthur Kapuuo, the overall military commander.

"It's going to be a spectacular success," said Makimber confidently. He wished he could understand why the Russians had warned him about the interception in Dakar. He would have thought it more in their interest to let the consignment be turned back, to prove the unreliability of outside suppliers. It was the only uncertainty in an otherwise perfect operation. And Makimber didn't like uncertainties.

Karen sat silently listening to Levy's account of the argument in the downstairs room. When he finished she said, "I'm sorry for causing difficulties."

He smiled, reaching out to touch her face. "It isn't your fault," he said. "Don't be silly."

"Is it a problem?"

"No," said Levy at once. "Leiberwitz has always been jealous of my being in command. He thinks he should have been chosen in Israel."

"Why wasn't he?"

"He's too impulsive. He doesn't think things through."

"Just like us," said Karen.

31

The package was brought aboard on the evening mail run from the harbour master's office, the two photographs protected by hard cardboard and carefully sealed. Grearson unwrapped them and laid them before his employer. The boy was holding the newspaper, staring straight at the camera; the woman was looking to one side, obviously distracted by something or someone. From the drawer of one of the large bureaux Azziz took out the first ransom picture, putting it next to the new ones for comparison. He leaned forward as if caught by something, groping into the drawer for a magnifying glass and adjusting it over the prints.

"He's thinner," said Azziz. "And they've beaten him." He offered the lawyer the glass. "Look," he said. "There's bruising on his face."

"It's very faint," said Grearson. "It might be some fault in the printing."

"Beaten," insisted Azziz. "The pigs have kept him short of food and beaten him."

"But at least we know he's alive," said Grearson. He indicated the copy of *Nice Matin*. "And close."

"Not close enough," said Azziz. He brought the photographs together like a man collecting playing cards. "The navigating officer had made the calculations," he said. "According to the supposed speed of the *Bellicose*, it should be just north of Casablanca. That's about a day and a half from Algiers.''

"Time for the *Hydra Star* to sail?" said Grearson.

Azziz nodded. "Are Evans and his people ready?"

"Absolutely."

"Evans knows to expect a message off Algiers?"

"Yes," said Grearson. "There's no radio-telephone communication, so it will have to be by cable. There's no way they will be able to know it isn't Deaken replying."

Azziz looked at the collection of tapes. "On your next contact we should get the handover instructions then?"

"Right."

"I want you to be the one who collects him," said Azziz. "Personally."

Grearson hesitated and then said, "Of course."

"You'll need someone to act as a liaison," said Azziz suddenly. "There can't be any response from the men on the boat until we've got the boy back."

"Evans would be the obvious candidate," said Grearson.

Azziz shook his head. "There needs to be a command on the boat. Take one of the others."

"I'll arrange it," said Grearson.

Azziz looked down at the most recent pictures showing the fading traces of his son's beating, then up at the lawyer. "I want them hurt," he said quietly. "Make sure Evans understands that. They've hurt my son and now I want them hurt in return."

They were all assembled at the villa on the Aubagne road when the lawyer arrived. He took the photographs, wanting them all to know what the boy looked like if the handover was made anywhere near the supposed weapons' exchange. Evans studied them first, then passed them round to the assembled group.

"Do you think they're marks of a beating?" asked Grearson.

"Could be," said Evans.

"Mr. Azziz wants retribution."

"Sure," said Evans. "You've already made that clear."

"There was to be half payment in advance," reminded Marinetti, forever practical.

Grearson unclipped the briefcase and passed around the envelopes. To Marinetti he said, "There'll be little need for any expert explosive use?"

"It wouldn't seem so," said Evans.

"So I'll have Marinetti as the liaison," decided the lawyer. "He can come back with me to the yacht and be with me when we exchange the boy."

Marinetti smiled around at the others. "I'll be thinking of you guys cramped up in that shitty old barge," he said.

"Getting the boy back safely is the most important part of the operation," said Grearson.

The smile was wiped from Marinetti's face. "We'll get him back," he said.

Evans stood, a signal for the rest. As they started to file from the room Grearson said, "Good luck."

"Luck hasn't got anything to do with it," said Evans.

The photographs had to be developed, so it was not until evening that they were brought to the Hotel Negresco. By then there had already been protracted telephone conversations with Muller, in Pretoria, about the location of the kidnap house and of the second arms-carrying freighter. Aware of Deaken's concern, Swart let him examine them first. Deaken stared down at Karen, blinking the mistiness from his eyes. Neither picture was perfectly in focus and each was obscured by the blurred foliage in the immediate foreground of the shubbery through which they were taken. Karen didn't look as Deaken had expected her to. He had anticipated that the strain of captivity would show; that she would look as rigid-faced as the boy. Instead she appeared relaxed, almost carefree.

He looked up at Swart, white-faced, and said, "The promise was to help me get her out."

"Not yet."

"What do you mean, not yet!"

Swart nodded towards the telephone. "My instructions are to find out a little more first . . . we don't understand enough."

The difference of interest, remembered Deaken. "Fuck understanding enough," he said. "We know where she is . . . where they both are. Let's get them out."

"No."

"I don't need you," said Deaken.

"Don't be ridiculous," said Swart. "You can't do anything by yourself. You'd be killed . . . and get your wife and the boy killed as well."

"Help me, then!"

"We will," said Swart. "But not yet. We know she's all right . . . that they're both all right. Wait."

"How the hell can you expect me to wait?"

Swart looked at the photographs of his own family. "No," he said distantly. "How can I expect you to?"

Deaken was about to speak when the telephone rang. It was a short conversation. As he replaced the receiver, Swart said, "The ship has sailed from Marseilles. Some men went aboard at the last moment. And then it sailed. Half an hour ago."

32

They maintained the separation of Rixheim, Levy taking his meals with Karen and the boy, while everyone else ate in the kitchen. That night Azziz said he felt too unwell to eat, so it was just the two of them at dinner, a subdued, awkward meal, with long silences between them.

"What is it?" said Karen at last. She pushed her plate away, revolving her wine glass between her hands.

"I hope he isn't going to become ill again," said the Israeli.

"I don't think he is." Karen hadn't told him about her escape conversation with Azziz. If the boy got away it would upset whatever it was they were planning, possibly extend the time she could be with the man she loved.

He looked at her curiously. "Why do you say that?"

"I looked in," she said. "There's no fever." She paused then and said, "It's not just the boy, is it?"

"No," he admitted.

"What then?"

"There was some other discussion today, apart from the row. Everything is almost ready." He couldn't look at her.

"When?"

"Tomorrow. We've got to be ready for tomorrow."

She felt sick and a weakness seemed to permeate her body, numbing her legs. "What's going to happen?"

"The weapons we're getting from Azziz are on a boat.

It'll be here very soon now. When we get the shipment, the boy is to be returned to his father.''

"What about me?"

"Both of you," said Levy. He reached out to grasp her hand.

"What are we going to do?"

He didn't answer. She took her hand away. "Tell me what we're going to do."

"I don't know," he said, empty-voiced and still not looking at her.

"Do you want me?"

"You know the answer to that."

"Do you want me?"

"Yes."

"But you want Rebecca as well?"

He humped his shoulders, a gesture of helplessness. "It's more than that," he said. "There's the protest about the settlements. There's got to be the protest."

"But it's Rebecca as well, isn't it?" she persisted. "You love her, don't you?"

"Yes," he said shortly. "Shit! Why's it got to be like this?"

"I don't want to go back to Richard," she said. "It's not his child; it's yours. I *won't* go back to him." Karen knew she was being irrational, ridiculous. But everything that happened to her was irrational and ridiculous. She refused to be shaken awake from the dream.

"I don't want you to go back to Richard."

"So tell me the alternative."

"There's no way we can stay together, not immediately anyway."

She snatched at the straw. "Not immediately?"

"You didn't think I was going to abandon you, did you?"

Karen was near to tears. "Something like that," she said.

He raised his hand to caress her cheek. "Fool," he said softly.

She bit at his fingers, enjoying his touch. "I love you so much," she said.

"I don't know how, not yet," he said. "Or how long it will take. But it won't end tomorrow or the next day. I'll make something work."

Karen smiled. Whatever it was he decided, however difficult, she would go along with it. She was consumed by him, indifferent to anything or anyone else.

Four hundred yards from where Karen sat, her husband drove slowly by the house, straining through the darkness to make out its shape, managing only to locate the tiny squares of light at various windows.

"There's no purpose in everyone losing sleep," decided Swart. "The observation will be in shifts; the rest of us can try to get some rest in Sisteron."

"All right," said Deaken. He screwed around in the seat for a final look. Soon, my darling, he thought, very soon now.

The maps and the blackboard were still in place, but only Deaken's father was in the room with Muller. The intelligence chief tapped his pointer against the map and said, "The *Bellicose* seems to have stopped off Benguela: the last reconnaissance report says she's turned back upon herself and is steaming in circles."

"Waiting for contact?"

"That's what it seems like."

"There's to be a final meeting, but the consensus in the cabinet is for a preemptive strike—an interception at sea."

"I know," said Muller.

"Nothing more from Europe?"

"Not since the other freighter sailed."

"The timing is important, isn't it?" said Piet Deaken. "If we have to intercept the *Bellicose* in advance of any exchange in Europe, my daughter-in-law could be killed."

"Yes," admitted Muller.

The old man turned away from the dais, looking out over the South African capital. "My vote is for interception," he said.

The South African intelligence service had established their electronic eavesdropping headquarters at Ondangua, as near to the Angolan border as possible, with equipment sufficiently sophisticated and powerful to intercept all commercial wavelengths, as well as dial searches for clandestine transmissions. Edward Makimber's contact with the *Bellicose* was on a normal commercial link, giving them perfect reception.

"Victory," muttered Muller when the coded message was brought to him. He looked up, shaking his head at the theatricality. There was going to be a victory, but not the sort they imagined.

Evans knocked politely at the door, looking through the glass for Papas's nod of agreement before going out onto the bridge. The captain of the *Hydra Star* stood in front of the helmsman, close to the radar screen. "We should be approaching Algiers soon after dawn," he said.

"And then we wait," said Evans.

"I control this ship at all times," said the captain firmly.

"You made that clear from the start."

"I'm making it clear again, so there'll be no misunderstandings."

"There won't be."

"I know what sort of men you are," said Papas. "Know what you do. I'm not having my ship endangered, no matter what instructions I get from Athens."

Evans hoped Papas wasn't going to become a nuisance.

33

The interception of the guerrilla communiqué to the *Bellicose* reached the South African cabinet towards the end of its discussion when the decision had already been practically made, but the confirmation of SWAPO involvement made the vote unanimous. The order to the Army, Navy and Air Force was accorded top-security classification and a second cabinet meeting was scheduled for the afternoon to consider the country's reaction to the inevitable international protest.

By the time the order reached Admiral Hertzog, he already had two freighters and a cruiser carrying a helicopter squadron of marine commandos off Moçmedes, but well outside any recognized limit of territorial jurisdiction. He immediately signalled the speed to be increased from cruising to full and for the course to be altered northeast.

The air and army strength in Namibia was already high because of the conflict, but three additional detachments of commandos were airlifted into Walvis Bay in C-130s, on standby readiness. The Air Force had maintained a permanent high-altitude reconnaissance over the *Bellicose* but now an additional and specially equipped C-130 was sent into position. It was, in fact, a flying laboratory, utilizing technology developed by Israeli scientists and capable of completely immobilizing the electrical capability of any given target. The target was the *Bellicose*.

Captain Erlander frowned at the radar screen which he had been watching for the approach of Makimber's launch and said, "Bloody thing's fogged."

Edmunson, who had been attempting visual sighting from the wing, came back into the bridge housing, but before he reached the screen the rear door opened from the radio shack and the operator said, "Trouble, sir. Radio is out."

"What about the secondary set?" demanded the first officer.

"That too."

"A sunspot?" suggested Erlander.

"Don't see what else it could be," said the radio operator. "Indications aren't the same, though."

Edmunson looked briefly at the snowed image. "Never seen a sunspot do that either," he said.

Both men stared in the direction of the unseen Angolan coast. The skyline was hazed with dawn mist, the sea flat and unbroken. "Think there will be repair facilities ashore?" said Edmunson.

"We don't know the port," reminded Erlander.

"It's got to be Benguela, surely?"

"Then why all this nonsense of cruising off and awaiting the arrival of a launch?" said the captain. "Why couldn't we have gone straight in?"

"What time did Makimber give?" asked the first officer.

"He estimated nine—said he was leaving at dawn."

The African had kept to his timing and the departure had been monitored by the reconnaissance plane. Its signal to Walvis Bay was relayed at once to the approaching ships. The reconnaissance aircraft kept up a steady flow of information, enabling Hertzog's navigating officers to chart both course and speed for Makimber's launch so they could achieve the blocking position their commander-in-chief wanted.

"There he is," said Edmunson, pointing to starboard. The captain stood alongside the first officer and watched as a black smudge on the horizon formed into the recognizable shape of a launch. It was large, maybe forty tons, and moving fast through the water. Both men went out onto the wing to look through glasses.

"Quite a deputation," said Erlander, counting the other Africans grouped around Makimber.

"I'll be glad when we've offloaded and are underway again," said Edmunson with a sailor's superstition. "This has been a funny trip from the very beginning."

From inside the bridge the radio operator said, "I've checked right back to the radio mast itself. Can't find anything wrong at all."

"Check again," said Erlander. "I don't want to be at sea with dead electrics." He signalled dead slow and gave the course so that the bulk of his ship would provide some lee for the smaller launch. It maintained its speed flamboyantly, finishing with a wide arc to bring itself alongside the *Bellicose*. Makimber led the way aboard, followed by four other Africans. Makimber was clearly pleased with himself, his face lit by a constant smile.

"You're on time," he said. "It is good. Very good."

"Are there docking facilities?" asked Erlander.

"Everything," assured Makimber.

"Benguela?"

"Dombe Grande," said Makimber. "There's a river anchorage."

"I've got some heavy stuff," said Erlander. "I need to be alongside."

"Everything will be okay. Everything," said Makimber in a voice that lacked confidence.

"What about repair facilities?"

"Repair facilities?"

"We seem to have some radio trouble," said Erlander. "We might need some electricians."

"Not at Dombe Grande," said Makimber.

"We could go into Benguela afterwards," suggested Edmunson to Erlander.

"We'd like to inspect the cargo," said Makimber.

Erlander led the way to a lower stairway, bringing them out on the open deck again. Several of them were suddenly aware of the noise, but it was Edmunson who spoke, gesturing over the stem of the ship. "What the hell . . . ?"

The helicopters were coming in low, practically at wavetop level and out of the rising sun, like a swarm of black insects. The formation split at the last moment, arcing out of the direct line of the freighter but pulling into a tight circle. Erlander realized the four Africans with Makimber had pistols in their hands and that two were supporting themselves against the deck rail, taking aim.

"Don't be bloody ridiculous," he shouted. "They're gunships, for Christ's sake!"

The helicopters were circling sufficiently close for the cannon to be visible through the cutaway sides, heavy-calibre weapons with their bandoliers of tracers looped at the ready. There was an operator and armourer at every opening.

One of the Africans began shooting wildly, hand bucking with the recoil from his pistol. The answering fire was deafening, timed bursts coming from each helicopter as it reached the bridge area. Shells from the first ricocheted harmlessly from the flat decking at the stern. The others were aimed intentionally wide as well, either in the air or plucking up a churn of spray from the head or sides of the vessel. Erlander and Edmunson threw themselves below the rail line.

"What can we do?" said Edmunson frantically.

"Nothing," said Erlander. He had always known it would happen one day; he wondered how difficult it was going to be from now on.

Makimber crawled up alongside. "There are rockets in the cargo," he said. "Get us down to the holds."

"Don't be stupid," said Erlander wearily. "There are eight of them up there. Where do you think they came from? There's obvious backup. We don't stand a chance."

"Look," said Edmunson in confirmation.

Through the rail venting, the warships could be seen, approaching in line-abreast formation.

"I want the rockets!" shouted Makimber.

Erlander screwed around so that he could sit with his back to the rail. "We're in international waters," he said. "We stand a chance if we argue. If we try to fight, they'll blow us out of the water."

"We're sending men aboard," announced a metallic voice, echoing across the water from a bullhorn. "If there's any resistance, the next shot won't be fired wide."

Erlander and Edmunson stood up, and at the captain's gesture distanced themselves from the still-crouching Africans. Six of the helicopters maintained the encirclement but the remaining two dropped low again, flattening the water with their downdraught. Erlander watched as the rubberized dinghies flopped into the water, to self-inflate before the wet-suited men splashed alongside, immediately hauling themselves aboard. It was expert and quick, outboard engines starting almost at once. Still unsure whether there would be any further firing from the *Bellicose*, the dinghies split wide and approached from different angles. Overhead the gunships stopped circling, hovering instead in an uneven but solid line, their cannon trained upon the *Bellicose*.

"Jesus!" said Edmunson, his voice a mixture of horror and admiration.

The commando group was ten strong. They came alongside the launch, occupying that first. Four spread out along its deck, covering the higher superstructure of the freighter with 9-mm. machine guns to enable the remaining six to climb up the rope ladder that Makimber and his party had used earlier.

They had kept their rubber suits on, even the hoods, so there was no designation of rank.

"My ship is in international waters," said Erlander.

"Right," agreed the unidentified leader, a muscular, moustachioed man.

"So you have no lawful authority for this attack. You're committing an act of piracy."

"Right again," said the man.

Erlander felt a lurch of despair as he recognized the accent. "Get off my ship!" he said.

"Bollocks," said the man.

"And so it comes to a happy conclusion!"

"I hope so," said Grearson. Instinctively he gazed from the kiosk towards the surrounding buildings, wondering where the bastard was: he hoped he would be present at the exchange and get his ass burned by Evans.

"I'm glad you were sensible in the end and did everything we wanted."

"Shouldn't we be finalizing things?" said Grearson impatiently.

"We've got to be careful."

"Set it out," demanded Grearson.

"It may be that you have something in mind for the handover. A little surprise for us. So we've got to take precautions against that. We're going to split them up, Tewfik and the woman. He's going to be taken to an address and left there. He'll be quite safe and unharmed—just unable to move about. Only the girl will know the address. The people who come to meet the freighter won't, so there'll be no point in seizing them. If the exchange goes according to plan, then you'll be told where the girl is. Get to her and then you get to the boy."

"No," said Grearson at once. "That doesn't give us any guarantee at all."

"It gives you what you want, the boy back. But on our terms. And they've always been our terms, haven't they?"

Azziz wasn't going to like this tape, the lawyer knew. The pendulum had swung, greatly to his disadvantage. "How soon after the exchange?" he said.

"As soon as we've made sure that the weapons are there . . . that there's no stupidity, then you'll get the address of the woman, the same way as you got the two sets of photographs, through the harbour master's delivery. She's quite close, maybe an hour away. You should have the boy back two hours after we get what we want."

He didn't have a choice, realized Grearson. "All right," he said.

"No stupidity," repeated the man. "The boy is going to be shackled in the cellar of an empty house. It's in its own grounds, so he wouldn't be heard, even if he were able to call out—which he won't be, because he'll be gagged. Behave properly and he'll be free in two hours. Do anything silly and he'll starve to death. Do you understand?"

"Yes," said Grearson. "I understand."

"It's been a pleasure doing business with you," said the Russian, replacing the telephone. He had other calls to make. He still hadn't sent the instructions to the ship off Algiers.

And when everything was arranged, there were the French police to be alerted.

"We're sure the *Bellicose* didn't get a message out before the seizure," said Muller.

"Thank you," said Piet Deaken.

"So your daughter-in-law should still be safe."

"How long can you keep it under wraps?" asked the old man.

"As long as we want," said the security chief. "Days, if necessary."

"I hope to God it doesn't go on for days," said Deaken. "That girl must be going through hell."

34

The noise of revving engines beyond the shuttered windows awoke Karen. She lay momentarily disoriented and then turned sideways, realizing that she was alone in the bed; she hadn't been aware of Levy leaving. She was dressed and waiting when Leiberwitz came for her, gloatingly hostile.

"It's over," he said.

Karen stared back, saying nothing. Levy would keep his promise not to abandon her—she was sure of it. She wished he had woken her up earlier.

"You're to come now," said Leiberwitz.

Azziz was already at the table when she got downstairs, with Kahane standing guard at the door. It was open and through it she could see lorries lined in the driveway.

"They're taking me somewhere," said Azziz.

"What?"

"Another house," said the boy.

"Why?"

He shrugged. "I don't know."

Levy entered hurriedly from the garden, flushed and obviously excited; his demeanour altered when he saw her and she got the impression that he was embarrassed. He said something to Kahane and Leiberwitz which she didn't catch and then came farther into the room.

To the boy he said, "Ready?"

The Arab stood uncertainly, and Kahane called from the doorway, "We'll take you to the car."

Levy waited until Azziz had left with the two men and then said to her, "I'll be back."

"When?"

"Soon. Maybe an hour."

"Leiberwitz said it was over, sneered at me."

"I said I'd find a way."

"Hurry back."

"Sure." He reached out awkwardly, touching her hand, and then appeared to change his mind, turning abruptly from the house. She stayed alone for several moments, then followed to the doorway. The lorries prevented her seeing which car he had gone to. It was only when it reversed out onto the road that she saw he was alone with Azziz and remembered the boy's determination to escape.

"Stop!" she called, but Levy was too far away to hear. The car turned left, heading towards the coast road.

Azziz sat uncomfortably, his left wrist handcuffed to the securing clip of the car seat belt, his right hand clenched into a fist of frustration. There was a Browning automatic pistol in the luggage shelf in front of Levy instead of the earlier Magnum.

"By tonight it should all be over; you'll be with your father," said Levy.

"He'll get you," said Azziz. "He won't be beaten by you."

"Maybe he'll try," said Levy. But the Arab wouldn't succeed; it was an extremely clever idea, to sail to Haifa. They had been fortunate, establishing links with Underberg so early in the protest movement.

Beside him Azziz was concentrating upon the road. He saw the sign to Pertuis and then, almost at once, the turning towards Aix-en-Provence and felt a stab of satisfaction at having guessed where they were during his conversation with Karen. "How much farther?" he said.

"Not far," said Levy. He looked quickly to the boy, then away again. "You're going to be left by yourself," he said. "When we've got what we want, your father will be told where you are. You won't be in any danger. I promise you he'll be told."

Levy skirted Aix, slowing at the signposts for the indication to Allauch that Underberg had identified at his briefing. He found it at last, turning to the left and driving with the directions Underberg had given him held against the wheel. The villa was to the right, just off the road, the high wall and metal gates exactly as the man had described. The padlock on the gate was well oiled and opened easily to the key Underberg had provided. Carefully Levy took the car through and then locked the gate behind him. The house was just visible, at the end of the curving drive.

"I could die, left here," protested the boy.

"I said your father would be told."

"What happens if something goes wrong?"

"It won't."

The driveway curved smoothly up to the villa, which was shuttered and closed. Levy was still reluctant to leave Azziz by himself. He tried to suppress the doubt, realizing there was nothing he could do to alter arrangements now. He took the Browning from the front compartment and got out of the car, leaving the driver's door open. He tossed two keys separately onto the seat and said, "The first unlocks the handcuffs—release yourself. The second is to the front door."

Azziz twisted across the car, freeing himself. He got out of the vehicle massaging his wrist, the handcuff still dangling from it.

"Into the house," said Levy, gesturing with the gun.

Azziz looked at him contemptuously and then moved ahead towards the villa. He fumbled at the door, appearing to have difficulty inserting the key, and then pushed into the house.

Levy followed too quickly and it was then that the boy

made his move. As Levy came in, Azziz slammed the
door back abruptly, so that the edge caught the Israeli's
gun hand. Levy felt a moment of agony in his wrist, then
numbness. The gun skittered away across the darkened
hallway. Azziz was already on the attack, the handcuff
chain between his fingers, swinging the free armlet as a
weapon. He caught Levy high on the forehead, a glancing,
insubstantial blow but sufficient to bring tears to his eyes,
blinding him. He lashed out, hitting Azziz in the shoulder.
The Arab staggered, momentarily off-balanced, but recovered almost at once. He was fit, from the sports regime at
the Ecole Gagner. He swept the handcuff towards Levy
again but it was a feint. As Levy tried to dodge, Azziz
swung with his right hand, all the anger and frustration of
the past days put into the punch. It caught Levy high on
the side of the head and he grunted from the stinging pain
that reverberated through his skull. He crashed back against
the door, causing it to slam shut. The action shut off any
immediate chance of escape for Azziz but put the hallway
in greater darkness.

Through his blurred vision Levy saw Azziz staring wildly
around, trying to locate the gun. As the boy moved, Levy
lashed out with his foot. It was a desperate but lucky kick,
thumping in just below the boy's knee. Azziz screamed
with pain, stumbling, but kept going towards the gun.
Levy could see it now, right against the stairway which
arced up around the wall of the high-domed vestibule.
Azziz reached it seconds ahead of Levy, his fingers actually grasping the butt before the Israeli dived on him,
seizing his wrist. Azziz tried to use the dangling handcuff
again as a weapon, but they were too close now, rolling
and grappling over the tiled floor, clawing and gouging at
each other. Azziz tried to bring his knee up into Levy's
groin, but missed, striking his thigh instead. Sensation was
returning to Levy's numbed arm. He thrust upwards, getting the heel of his hand beneath the boy's chin, forcing
his head upwards, at the same time clutching the wrist of

the gun hand; he could feel Azziz's teeth grating under the pressure. The boy clubbed wildly with the handcuff, pounding Levy on the neck and shoulders and twisting desperately to free his upthrust chin. When he did so he snapped down, trying to bite Levy's fingers. The Israeli rolled away to avoid the teeth, and his grip momentarily loosened on Azziz's wrist. Levy found himself trapped against the bottom step, his shoulder caught beneath its lip. The boy had secured his hold upon the gun and was bringing the barrel around towards him. Levy slashed out with a chopping motion that knocked the gun against the step. And with unthinking ferocity he used his foot again, stamping down on the tightly clenched hand. He heard the crunch as Azziz's fingers splintered between his heel and the metal of the automatic. The boy screamed. The gun clattered back against the marble and Levy grabbed it, rolling farther away and then swivelling back to point it at the Arab.

"Fool!" he gasped. "You stupid bloody little fool."

Azziz was crouched doubled over, trying not to cry, his crushed hand pressed against his stomach. "You've broken it," he groaned. "You've broken my hand."

"Let me see."

Azziz stayed bent over.

"I said let me see!"

Azziz reluctantly extended his right hand, the wrist supported in the palm of his left. The index finger was bent awkwardly, broken, and the one alongside was already swelling, blackly discoloured.

"You can't leave me like this," said the boy.

"I've got to," said Levy.

They were all nervous and excited, laughing too easily and too loudly; only Leiberwitz showed any control, remaining with her in the main living room after Levy had gone. Karen knew he wanted her to make some request, like being allowed into the garden, so that he would have the pleasure of refusing her. Instead, Karen got up from the table and started to walk towards the stairs. "Where are you going?" said the bearded Israeli.

"To my room."

"You didn't ask."

"Please may I go to my room?" she said with weary disdain.

Leiberwitz considered for a moment, for effect, then said, "OK."

Karen sat slump-shouldered on the bed, staring down at the floor. It seemed inconceivable that soon, in hours or maybe days, she would be reunited with Richard; be kissed by him, having to pretend she wanted him.

She wouldn't pretend, she decided; couldn't pretend. She'd tell him as soon as they met. Apologize for the hurt. Beg his forgiveness even. But she wouldn't pretend. Maybe he wouldn't be too surprised, not for long anyway. There had been too many arguments over the last few months for him not to know she was fed up. Inevitable that they would separate. Peculiar though the circumstances might be, what had happened was just bringing it all to a head. She looked up at movement from the doorway.

"I know his wife," said Leiberwitz. "I know Rebecca."

"I suppose you would."

"I'm godfather, to Yatzik."

"He's told me about Rebecca. And the children," said Karen.

"He's sacrificed the right to expect to be in charge."

"Why are you telling me this?"

"I want you to know what you've cost him."

"But he is still in charge, isn't he?"

"Here maybe," said Leiberwitz. "He might not be later."

Four miles away, in the Grand Hotel du Cours in the town of Sisteron, Deaken looked angrily at Swart and said, "They're moving, for Christ's sake! The freighter's gone and now they've got lorries at the villa. How much longer are we going to wait?"

''Soon now,'' soothed the South African, unhappy at the way they were using the man.

Mitri came with his customary discreet quietness into the stateroom to give Azziz the message that had been relayed from the *Hydra Star*. The Arab scanned it, then looked up at Grearson and Marinetti. ''They've received instructions,'' he said. ''They've got to go to Toulon. A berth has been scheduled for them there.''

''They won't do anything until they're sure the boy's OK,'' said Marinetti. ''They're the best trained group of guys I've come across.''

Grearson turned at the sound of the departing tender.

''Carole and the other girls talked about spending a couple of days ashore shopping,'' said Azziz. ''I thought it best to get them out of the way.''

Grearson hoped Carole wouldn't be gone too long; after this was over, he wanted to relax.

35

Kahane was facing the door and saw him first, starting up with concern, then the others turned and Greening said, ''What happened?''

On the way back to Sisteron the cut over Levy's eye had begun to bleed again and he had completed the journey with a handkerchief over the wound.

''He made a break,'' said Levy.

"So you needed help there too?" said Leiberwitz.

"He's where he should be, waiting to be freed," said Levy, irritated by the constant challenging. Azziz had started to cry when he had realized that he was to be left alone without help, the defiance going at last. Levy couldn't shake off the feeling of sickness at abandoning him. His only concern was to hurry now, so that the boy could be released.

"Everything's ready," said Kahane. "Lorries gassed up . . . everything."

"Where's the woman?"

"She's safe and untouched," said Leiberwitz. He paused and then said, "No one else wanted to."

Levy moved forward, instantly aware of Leiberwitz tensing, wanting a physical confrontation. He stopped, fighting for control. Leiberwitz smiled, as aware as everyone else in the room of the retreat.

"She's necessary for what is to happen," said Levy.

"We know how necessary she is," sneered Leiberwitz.

It was a childlike exchange but he was losing ground, Levy realized, and there was already sufficient disarray among them. "The freighter is coming into Toulon," he announced.

There was a stir among the group, breaking the tension between Levy and Leiberwitz.

Levy went on, "We only want the small arms, rifles, the rockets and the launchers. According to Underberg, the *Marriv* is at berth thirty-eight. There'll be people there waiting. Underberg's people. The guns are coming into berth twenty."

The attention upon him now was absolute and Levy decided they were back under control—everyone except Leiberwitz.

"Will there be any resistance?" asked Greening.

Levy shook his head. "That's why the boy's been moved; and why only the girl is going to know where he is. Azziz has been warned that you don't know anything . . . that it would be pointless putting up a fight, because only his son will suffer.''

"*You* know," said Leiberwitz. "Aren't you coming to the docks?"

"Not immediately," said Levy. "But I'm coming. I don't want anything to start until I get there."

"So who decided you wouldn't break under pressure?"

"Haven't we other people to fight?" said Levy. There was so much more to do and already he felt very tired.

"Sure you'll still be able to?" persisted Leiberwitz.

"Yes," snapped Levy. "I'll be able to." Already the boy had been chained in the house at Allauch for three hours. "Let's get going," he said, trying to indicate an energy he didn't feel.

Obediently they all stood, except Leiberwitz.

"Aren't you up to it?" said Levy, scoring.

The other man hurried to his feet. "We'll see soon enough," he said.

"Remember," warned Levy, stopping them at the door. "I don't want any approach to the freighter until I get there."

Leiberwitz looked to Levy, towards the stairway and then back to Levy again. "I'll be there," he said. "Will you?"

Levy remained in the downstairs room while the lorries reversed out onto the road and then accelerated away. At the foot of the stairway he halted, hand against the balustrade, thinking back to Leiberwitz's question. Throughout all the planning and preparation he had never had any doubts. But now he did. He wasn't sure he wanted to fight.

Levy sighed and began climbing the stairs.

"This is it!" said Swart, as soon as he learned of the lorries' departure. The people with him were already briefed, moving at once to their cars. The man he had sent for Deaken caught up with Swart in the car park.

"He's not in his room, and I can't find him anywhere in the hotel."

"Damn!" said the Director.

"His wife's still at the house," said the observer who had returned with the news about the lorries. "Just one man with her, as far as we could guess."

"We've still got a car at the house?" said Swart.

"Yes."

"It's the weapons shipment that's important. That's what we're here for."

"What about Deaken?"

Swart only hesitated for a moment.

Then he said, "Leave him. Nothing can happen to her if we've got the house covered."

36

Deaken decided he had been stupid to believe their promises. They'd never intended to help him. They just wanted to use him, like every other bastard had wanted to use him since the whole thing began. No one gave a damn about Karen. Not Azziz or Grearson or his father or Muller or Swart. No one. Bastards, all of them. He didn't need them; didn't need any fucking one of them.

Despite the burning anger, Deaken still moved carefully along the road, sure that once Swart noticed his absence from the hotel he would try to intercept, to prevent any interference with their plan of campaign. Bugger them.

There was only one thing that mattered, that had ever mattered. Getting Karen back. He had much to apologize to her for, he knew. The ridiculous, unnecessary delays—days when he should have acted instead of letting other people take control.

He walked, alert to the slightest danger, twice jumping sideways and concealing himself behind the bordering hedge to avoid being spotted by any passing car. On the third occasion a whole cavalcade roared by and when Deaken risked a glance it was too late to confirm whether it was the South Africans looking for him.

He wished he had a gun; but he didn't imagine any of the people he had seen issued with them would have been careless enough to leave one lying around. But then he didn't know how to use a gun. He didn't know anything about safety catches and cocking mechanisms or automatic firing. So how was he going to get her away? Deaken was forced to accept that he didn't know. Just that somehow he would.

The ground dipped and then rose again to provide a vantage point from which to observe the hollow where the house lay. Trees obscured it up to the roofline. The road and the distant knoll from which he knew the South Africans kept observation were completely hidden; but Deaken realized that by cutting away from the road he would be able to make his approach without being visible to anyone. And the gathering darkness would help too.

He hurried, stumbling through the grass, anxious now that he was so close, and slowing only when he got to the ditch and the hedge towering above it. He had to move with the utmost care now, not to make any noise. He didn't risk jumping, slithering instead down one side and then clawing up the other. He was glad the ditch bottom was clean and summer-dried.

Wincing against the sudden snap of a twig beneath his feet, he parted the foliage. Fear stabbed into him when he realized the driveway was empty of lorries. Then he saw the solitary car, and the pendulum swung: if they were moving her, they would be more likely to use the car than the lorries. The lorries had to be for the guns.

He was at the side of the house, the drive and the road beyond to his left, the house almost immediately in front, the rear and the outbuildings to his right. He moved sideways, following the hedge, conscious as he moved that the garden curved to provide even greater concealment from the house. The bank rose again and had it not been so dark Deaken guessed the view of the surrounding countryside would have been impressive. The hedge was sparse here and he had no difficulty pushing through. Deaken bent against the slope of the hill, not wanting to drop noisily downwards into any unseen dip; lights in an upstairs room guided him through the gloom of the garden. His toe stubbed against the edge of the patio at the rear of the house and he slowed further, edging his feet forward, tensed against any noisy collision. At the house he pressed his ear against a darkened downstairs window, listening for sounds. Everything seemed quiet, deserted.

A double door was alongside. Deaken pressed against it to lessen any sound, then cautiously turned the handle. There was the faintest sound, the creak of wooden frames parting from wooden surrounds, and then the door gave.

The Russian looked regretfully around the luxury room at the Bristol Hotel and then for the last time out over the harbour, towards the glittering outline of the *Scheherazade*. He left abruptly, carrying his own luggage down into the foyer. He paid his bill and went through the ritual of assuring the receptionist that he had enjoyed his stay and would come again, wishing it were true. On the front he paused, savouring the warm, scented, nighttime air, and then got into the rented car for the journey along the Corniche. He had purposely left three hours before his flight, wanting to enjoy the drive. He was looking forward to going home.

37

It was the old part of the commercial docks, scheduled for redevelopment and therefore being run down, some wharves and their container sheds already abandoned, cranes like decaying skeletons where they had been half disassembled for their scrap-metal value. Marinetti drove, only using sidelights, even though many of the road lights were out and hadn't been replaced, foot depressed lightly on the throttle so there was only the faintest hum from the engine.

"Could fight a war with cover like this," said Marinetti.

"We aren't going to fight anything or anyone until we get the boy back," reminded Grearson.

"Twenty," identified Marinetti

Grearson strained, just able to pick out the berth number painted on the slanted roof of the wharf shed. It had to be one of the last operational moorings in this part of the docks, he decided. Only three of the five arc lights set into the shed roof were working and in front of them three cranes stood sleeping.

"No stevedores," said Marinetti.

"It's supposed to be engine trouble, with engineers not needed until tomorrow," reminded Grearson, remembering the instructions that had been relayed by Evans from the *Hydra Star*.

Marinetti reversed the vehicle into a shed a full berth away from that designated for the returning freighter, manoeuvring it into the shadow of a high wall. He killed the lights and then wound down the window.

"Put yours down too," he ordered the lawyer.

"What for?" said Grearson.

"Noises," said the soldier. "You can always hear before you can see."

Grearson did what he was told. Far beyond the waiting berth there was the glow of the active section of the docks and he could just detect the distant whine of machinery and the water slapping gently against the sea wall. Unseen in the darkness there was a scuffling movement and Grearson shifted uncomfortably, knowing it was foraging rats.

Marinetti saw the lorries first. "There!" he said softly, pointing.

Leiberwitz was in the lead lorry, with Kahane and Greening beside him in the cab. Katz, Sela and Habel were in the second vehicle immediately behind.

"It's not here yet," said Kahane unnecessarily.

"It's not scheduled for another two hours," said Leiberwitz. He had got in the parting shot but the anger still burned through him over the confrontation with Levy.

"Nice and quiet," said Greening. "It'll be easy to unload."

Kahane peered at his watch. "Wonder how long it'll be before Shimeon gets here?"

"Depends how difficult it is for him to get out of bed," said Leiberwitz.

"Haven't we had enough of that?" said Kahane wearily.

"He doesn't seem to," said Leiberwitz.

All three reacted nervously to the noise, then relaxed when they realized it was Katz and Sela, who had drawn up behind in their lorry and were now standing on the dock.

Leiberwitz wound down the window.

"What happens if Levy doesn't show up?"

"We go ahead," said Leiberwitz.

"That isn't what was agreed," said Katz.

"Have you got a better idea?"

There was no challenge from either Katz or Kahane.

Katz moved away from the lorry, going farther towards the water's edge. From their vantage point Marinetti said, "I count five but I think one stayed in that second lorry."

"Tewfik?" said Grearson.

"No," said Marinetti. "The arrangement set out on the tape was a clever one. I don't think it was a bluff. It would be too much of a risk for them to take, bringing him with them."

"I wonder if there's been any contact with the ship," said the lawyer.

"More people," hissed Marinetti, ignoring the question.

"Where?" said Grearson, squinting into the darkness.

"In the shadows, by the shed. See that broken crane," said Marinetti. "They're very good—they know how to use cover."

Swart was in the lead car with four men, the rest of the group in the one that followed. They had had to move too quickly for any consultation with Muller, and Swart was uneasy at having to make the decision on the spot. And Deaken's disappearance was an additional complication. The order had been to stop the lawyer doing anything that might embarrass his father. He was glad that at least he had covered the house where the woman was being held. He gazed across the intervening water towards the lorries and the men beside them.

"This is where we intercept," said Swart.

"What about the French authorities?" asked one of the men in the back.

"They've let out two shipments," said Swart. "I'm not risking a third."

Where the Israelis expected the ship to dock, Katz, who was nearest the water, realized that what he had imagined to be stationary navigation lights were moving. He hurried back to the first lorry and said, "Something's coming."

"Where's Shimeon?" said the loyal Kahane nervously.

"Where do you think!" said Leiberwitz. He never gave up.

"He said to wait," insisted Kahane.

Aboard the freighter, Harvey Evans stepped from the bridge ladder onto the foredeck. The assembled men turned at his approach and Sneider said, "Looks quiet enough ashore."

"There's plenty of time yet," said Evans.

"Wonder where Marinetti is?" said Melvin, peering towards the deserted dockside. "Unless he's got the boy, there won't be any action."

"The money's just as good," said Sneider. "Why get our asses shot off if we don't have to?"

"There's an awful lot of crew around," said Evans.

"According to my count," said Bartlett, "we're each of us being covered by at least two." He spoke looking towards the hatch area, where twelve crewmen were attempting to look busy heaving tarpaulin off the metal hatch covers.

Evans nodded. "And I've just had another lecture from the captain about the safety of his ship."

"Always had him pegged as a sneaky little bastard," said Sneider.

Evans looked to Hinkler and Bartlett. He said, "I want you two against the offshore rail. Just watch our backs. If we have to move and there's any attempt to stop us, give them a burst over their heads. I don't want to kill anyone— just frighten them."

"What happens if they don't stop?" said Hinkler.

"No one is to be killed," repeated Evans. "Take them out at the legs."

"There she goes," said Jones. The mooring lines snaked out from the ship, to be collected by the escort tender and ferried in to the shore bollards. Fore and aft the engine whined, bringing the freighter gently in against the quay wall. There was an imperceptible bump and they rocked slightly. Hinkler and Bartlett picked up their gunny sacks and moved away to the far rail, and Evans watched as four of the hatchmen detached themselves and followed. He decided the Greek captain was a bloody fool.

Ashore Kahane could not quell a sense of deepening anxiety.

"It's early," he insisted. "It wasn't due for another hour . . . more than another hour."

"What the hell does that matter?" said Greening. "It's here. And Shimeon isn't."

"He said wait," said Kahane.

"You want a vote!" said Leiberwitz. "So let's vote. I say we move."

"With you in charge?" demanded Kahane.

"Somebody's got to be," said Leiberwitz. "Somebody who accepts responsibility."

"I say move," supported Greening.

Leiberwitz stared at Katz and Sela. The men looked at each other, clearly feeling uncomfortable, and Katz said, "I don't see why we should wait; it seems pointless."

Sela shrugged. "The quicker we get it over, the quicker we can be away."

"You're outnumbered," said Leiberwitz to Kahane.

"Habel hasn't voted," said Kahane. He knew it was pointless but it would mean a further delay, no matter how slight.

To Sela Leiberwitz said, "Go and tell him what's happened . . . what we're deciding."

Ahead of them the freighter's derrick stirred into action, swinging the gangway over the side and then manoeuvring it into position through the split rail.

"They don't want to wait," said Leiberwitz.

"They don't have a choice," said Kahane.

"Neither do we!"

Sela came back to the first vehicle and said, "He thinks we should wait."

"Four against two," said Leiberwitz. He looked contemptuously to Kahane and said, "If you want to sit here wetting yourself, you're welcome."

He climbed out of the lorry, leaving the door ajar for Greening to follow. On the quayside the four of them stood for a moment, uncertain what to do next, looking to Leiberwitz for a lead.

"Let's go," he said.

Three hundred yards away Swart raised his hand and said, "Not yet, not yet . . . let them get far enough away from the lorries . . ."

The driver sat hunched forward, fingers ready on the ignition key.

"Now!" said Swart.

The two cars accelerated away, tires howling, headlights glaring, anxious for maximum surprise before the men on the quay could recover.

The four Israelis stood transfixed, immobile with shock. Kahane responded first, thrusting the Uzi machine gun through the cab window and squeezing off a short burst that went hopelessly wide, ricocheting off the concrete quayside.

"What the hell's happening!" screamed Grearson. "They were told not to shoot!"

"It's not coming from the ship," said Marinetti. "They're firing from the dockside."

Aboard the freighter, Evans shouted, "It's a setup; I don't know what's happened, but it's a setup. We'll have to fight our way out."

The men snatched their weapons from gunny sacks and holdalls. Hinkler and Bartlett immediately sprayed warning shots over the heads of the crew who had begun to move when they saw what was happening.

"Face them off," Evans told Melvin.

On the quayside, the Israelis moved into action at last, trying to shield their aim from the blaze of the approaching lights, firing with their handguns. Kahane's second burst was better than his first, shattering the windscreen of the

second South African car. The inrush of glass blinded the
driver who was also shot through the shoulder. He still had
the instinct to haul the wheel to the left, to swerve away
from the hurtling approach to the quay edge and the oily
sea below. They smashed into the second Israeli lorry, the
impact so violent that Habel was hurled out of the vehicle
and shattered his skull against the bordering wall. The
driver died instantly, together with the man beside him and
one in the rear. The fourth broke his neck but retained
consciousness, screaming out in immediate agony and then
continuing wail after agonized wail.

The mercenaries were positioned well, protected by the
metal of the freighter rail. Sneider sprayed the quay with
automatic fire, which was taken up by Evans as soon as
Sneider's ammunition clip was exhausted. By the time
Evans ran out for Jones to begin firing, Sneider had re-
loaded, ready to resume an uninterrupted hail of high-
calibre bullets. Behind him Evans heard more shooting,
close from Melvin, and then farther away from Hinkler
and Bartlett. And then screams as the crew were brought
down. The captain was a stupid bastard, he thought again.
One of Jones's bursts caught the protruding Israeli lorry,
shattering the windscreen and decapitating Kahane. Then
one of the rounds penetrated the fuel line, and the vehicle
erupted in a violent white and orange explosion.

Swart's car had slewed around thirty yards from the
Israelis, and everyone had got out, using it for protection
to shoot at the four men who were trying to crab sideways
from their totally exposed position towards the compara-
tive safety of the shed. Two had turned to answer the
concentrated and calculated fire from the freighter, and as
he watched Swart saw one, then the other, literally blasted
off the ground from the avalanche of bullets.

And then the French ambush erupted.

The blackened quay was suddenly flooded with blinding
white light as the supposedly broken shed lights and then
at least ten more ancillary search beams were switched on.

Car and lorry headlights in a solid, practically unbroken line came on in unison to encircle the berth. In the sudden break in the shooting the clatter of squads of soldiers running was momentarily the only sound. From the sea as well as from inland a flurry of helicopters arrived, with more lights focusing downwards upon the fighting. And then the announcements demanding surrender, amplified metallic voices in French, then in English, saying that they were completely surrounded by police, antiterrorist squads, CRS and a French army detachment.

Calling Hinkler and Bartlett to the shore rail to join with Melvin and Sneider, Evans scurried with Jones, bent double, towards the bridge ladder. A crewman saw them and moved to intervene. The black man shot him almost carelessly, the automatic rifle balanced in his right hand. He waited until Evans had climbed to the top, then scrambled up after him. Side by side they dashed into the bridge housing. Papas was crouched rigid against the storm rail, staring down at the quayside battlefield. Evans snatched at his shoulder.

"Cast off!" he yelled. "Cut the line and get us out of here!"

Papas blinked, like a man awakening from a deep sleep.

"I said get us out of here!" repeated Evans. "Cut the mooring lines."

"You're mad," said the Greek, broken-voiced. "Utterly mad. Don't you imagine they'll have sealed the harbour entrance against us. They've got helicopters overhead, soldiers on land. I can't go anywhere."

Evans swung around, absorbing at once the stupidity of his demand. Below, his men had started shooting again, but at once were answered by equally professional, coordinated fire, blasting out simultaneously from at least five different spots and scything into the ship's side. Even with the protection of their elevation, Evans saw Hinkler clutch upwards and then fall backwards, his face pulped red. As he stood crying, Bartlett was hit.

"They've got a tripod-mounted cannon down there!" said Jones. "Nine-millimetre, at least."

A phosphorous flare, then another, exploded lazily from a helicopter hovering directly above and floated gently down, completely illuminating the deck. At once, still from above, automatic fire rained down on them. Sneider and Melvin died instantly. And the already wounded and dying crewmen twitched and jumped under the relentless downpour.

"Bastards!" screamed Evans. He ran out onto the bridge wing, conscious of Jones behind him. Squinting against the light still above them, they both began firing, using the recoil blast of the overhead guns as markers. Suddenly there was an explosion more violent than that of the Israeli lorry, as their bullets caught a helicopter fuel tank. There was a red and black roar, a searing, skin-scorching blast of heat and then the helicopter plunged downwards, lodged for a moment at the very stern of the freighter and then toppled, hissing, into the sea.

Far below the two remaining Israelis ran forward, arms high above their heads in surrender. Leiberwitz was caught in the stomach by a blast from one of the French machine-gun emplacements, practically cutting him in two, before any-one realized what they were doing.

To the men around him beside the car, Swart shouted, "Stop firing. Stay down but keep your hands visible."

On the bridge, Jones aimed at the quay but only managed a short burst before a second helicopter arrived, flattening them against the deck with its downdraught. It released a flare, which blinded them, so neither Evans nor Jones ever saw the momentary black flecks of the three dropped grenades set to five-second time fuses. The explosion killed both of them as well as Papas, and split the bridge wing from its main housing.

Grearson obeyed Marinetti's instruction, keeping his hands visible and stretched out against the car dashboard when they were surrounded. Black, hooded figures hauled open the doors to drag them out.

Seconds before it happened, the lawyer said, distant-voiced, "What happened? For God's sake, what happened?"

"We lost," said Marinetti.

38

Levy's concern was entirely for the boy, refusing to let Karen even look at his bloody cuts or the bruising until she had repeated and then repeated again his instructions on how to guide the police to the villa where Azziz was held.

"Sure you've got it right?" he said.

"Positive," she said. "Now let me clean you up."

Levy shook her off, his voice far away as if he couldn't believe what he had done. "I had to leave him handcuffed to some piping in the cellar of some empty bloody house. He was crying, asking me to help him, and instead I walked away!"

Levy snatched the Browning automatic from the waist-band of his trousers and slammed it onto a chest near the bedroom door. "I never want to see a bloody gun again," he said.

"He'll be all right," said Karen. "I'll see to it he's all right. Please let me help you."

"I haven't time," said the Israeli. "The ship's due."

"You can't drive like that," she said. "It was a wonder you weren't stopped by the police coming here."

He allowed her to lead him to a chair near the bed, where she eased off his bloodstained jacket and examined the deepest cut.

"It should be stitched," she said. "It's very deep."

"Just bind it—try to stop it bleeding."

Karen poured water into a bowl from the pitcher and set it down at his feet, aware as she cleaned away the caked blood how pale Levy's face was; it made the bruising around his cheek and eye appear even more prominent. "Poor darling," she said. "My poor darling."

"Stop it!" he snapped. "After what I did to that kid, stop it."

Karen made a pad from a clean handkerchief and then tore the sheet on her bed for a strip to tie against the gash. Almost at once it began to stain from the unstaunched blood.

She smiled feebly, close to tears. "You look odd," she said. "Like someone dressed up for a fancy-dress party."

"It doesn't feel like a party to me," he said.

She snatched out, cupping his face between her hands. "Don't go!"

He snorted at the absurdity of her plea. "They might expect me to do that; Leiberwitz at least."

"You'll be killed," she blurted, eyes flooding. "If not here, back in Israel."

Levy shook his head. "Israel would never turn the army against its own people! It couldn't do that and survive. It'll be compromise, like politics always is."

He stood, pulling her to her feet. "I have to handcuff you," he said. "The police will cut you free, once we've unloaded the ship and I've told them where you are . . ."

Levy took the wrist bands from his coat and stood staring down at them. "I can't," he said.

"It doesn't matter."

"Yes, it does," he insisted. "There mustn't be anything against you . . . any suspicion."

He looked around the room and said, "The bed frame, I suppose."

Karen sat demurely, offering her arm. He clamped on the handcuffs, running his finger round the inner rim to ensure it wasn't tight. "Just wait until they cut it off," he said. "Azziz moved around—that's why he got sore."

When he had connected the other band to the metal bedhead he said, "I have to leave you now."

Karen bit her lip, not wanting to break down but knowing she was going to. She reached out for his hand, not able to speak.

"I meant it," he said. "About finding a way."

"Yes."

"It'll take time."

He bent to kiss her and the tears broke, flooding uncontrolled down her face.

"I love you," he said.

Which was what Deaken heard as he came through the door.

The fury surged through him, so strong there was a brief moment of faintness. And then he saw the discarded gun.

"Get away from her!"

Deaken moved as he screamed out the demand, plunging into the room and snatching up the automatic.

"Get away!" he said again. There was no hysteria in his anger. He was icily controlled—illogically almost detached—the gun he didn't know how to use steady and unwavering in his hand. They were very close, only feet apart, and the man seemed to fill Deaken's vision, magnifying his impression of a strained, scratched and bruised face, the shirt splattered with blood. She had obviously put up a fight.

"No!" said Karen, her voice jagged.

"It's all right, darling. All right," said Deaken, eyes fixed upon Levy. "I'm here now. It's going to be all right."

"No," shouted Karen. "Leave him."

"I'd like to kill you," said Deaken. He aimed the gun with both hands at Levy. "But I want to hurt you more than that. I'm going to see you locked up forever. I'm going to invoke every law and every statute under every international or national legal convention. I'm going to see that you spend the rest of your life living through the sort of agony you've put her through . . . put me through . . ."

"I love him." Karen didn't raise her voice. It was a calm, positive assertion.

He stared at her, not understanding.

"I love him and I'm going to have his child."

Deaken blinked against another spasm of faintness, bringing his other hand to steady the gun. God, how he'd make this bastard suffer if her breakdown was permanent.

"And I love her," said Levy.

"What?" said Deaken. His voice was suddenly weak and unsure.

"We're going to have a baby," said the woman. "We're going to stay together somehow." Karen hesitated and then she said "I don't want to be with you anymore, Richard."

Deaken never remembered making a positive decision; even any contraction of his fingers. There was a sudden, blasting roar and the gun kicked wildly in his hand so that he almost dropped it. The shot caught Levy fully in the chest, kicking him backwards onto the bottom of the bed and then onto the floor.

Karen's cry was beyond hysteria, animallike. She threw herself sideways, jerked short by her handcuffed wrist, fingers of her free hand clawing out as she tried to touch Levy's crumpled body. She threw herself again and again until the blood began to drip from her stripped arm and then she stopped, whimpering in her frustration at not being able to reach him.

She stared up at her husband.

"Bastard!" she said. "You bastard!"

Epilogue

Suslev was waiting for her knock. When it came he hurried to the apartment door, opening it wide to admit her. Excitement churned through him at the first sight of his wife. So beautiful, he thought, so radiant.

"How are you?" he said.

"Fine."

"Sure?"

"Positive."

He stood back for her to enter. The apartment was just off Kalinin Prospekt but still with a view of the Kremlin and far more spacious than Suslev had ever expected. He led her around it, like a rich child with a toy no other child could afford, showing her the kitchen quite separate from the dining area, a full-sized room where they could entertain, and the third bedroom, which could be used on the rare occasions when they had guests. The bathroom was equipped with a shower, which he turned proudly on and off to prove that it worked.

"Sergei's at the academy," he said. "There's going to be an acceptance ceremony in a week's time." Suslev took a square of pasteboard from a dresser and said, "Here's our invitation."

She smiled, enjoying his excitement. Beside the invitation was his official citation, confirming his promotion to full colonel.

"Very impressive," she said, picking it up. She felt a great weariness and wished she could share his excitement.

"They're calling it one of the most successful disinformation operations ever," said Suslev. "There's even talk of it being included in the training manual."

"That's wonderful" she said. She hoped the conceit wouldn't last. It was going to be difficult enough to learn how to love him again without additional barriers.

"It's nice to be properly recognized," he said.

"I hope you're right," she said.

He seemed to miss the point. "I got worried that it took Deaken so long to go to South Africa," Suslev admitted. "I think that was the greatest uncertainty, the delay involving his father and the South African intelligence service. I didn't expect to have to manoeuvre him there, with all that bullshit about Dakar and boarding the ship."

"What about the second boat?" She yearned to deflate his pride.

"That was a surprise," he conceded. "I knew there'd be something and guessed it would be mercenaries. In the event, two ships gave us a better propaganda result, because of the seizure of the *Bellicose*."

"How could you be sure of being identified?" she said.

He shook his head. "I knew I'd be on the South African security files: I spent most of my time in Angola making myself obvious—I even saw them photographing me. It was logical that when Deaken, with his family connections, got to Pretoria with his story they'd check out the Underbergs in security, try descriptions and end up with me. That was the lure, the bait I knew they'd have to follow, because of their neurosis about Russian involvement in Angola and Namibia."

"You'd have been in trouble if they'd extended the search beyond their own security service."

"But they didn't!" he said triumphantly. "South Africa has even paraded the real Rupert Underberg at press conferences and insisted he's nothing more than a senior clerk in their Foreign Office . . .'' He sniggered. "And got the rest right! They actually identify his visit to the Seychelles as the time when we got all the passport details to make our own copy. And been laughed at and condemned for trying to avoid the truth. The French have retrieved my hotel registration in Monaco, with the passport number . . . Underberg's passport number . . . and directly accused Pretoria of lying. I used it for all the car- and lorry-rental registration forms too. And for hiring the last villa to hide the boy in. South Africa's illegal seizure of the *Bellicose,* as well as their involvement in the carnage at Toulon, makes the evidence against them overwhelming. It's years since they've been hurt so badly internationally.''

"Did Israel work out as well?''

"Absolutely,'' he said, enjoying the boasting. "Up to now there's been an incredibly close business liaison between Israel and South Africa. Israel's largest export is the polished diamonds it gets rough cut from South Africa and that's only a small part of the business and commercial ties. Now it's damaged, probably forever. It'll certainly be years before either Jerusalem or Pretoria trust each other. I used the same Underberg passport going in and out of Israel, so again there's official registration on airline immigration forms and hotel documents. As far as Israel is concerned, it's incontrovertible proof of a South African government employee stirring up a dissident, anti-government group and using them in an operation to smuggle weapons through to an area where they're involved in conflict. And by exposing Azziz, a Saudi Arabian with direct links to the court as the supplier of those weapons, and having him made look foolish by the Israeli involvement, whether by dissidents or not, puts back for years any chance of the Saudi peace plan for the Middle East and any recognition of Israel. The Saudis have lost face and Israel has been shown to be a country treating its settlers so roughly they'll try armed resistance rather than look for the Promised Land.''

Suslev paused, splaying his fingers. "We've made fools of South Africa internationally, and split them from one of their closest allies, Israel. We've made Israel and Saudi Arabia turn away from each other and run back into their corners. And we've strengthened our position in Angola by convincing SWAPO and every other nationalist group on the entire African continent that they shouldn't trust any other arms supplier but Moscow."

The woman looked sadly away. "What about Deaken?" she said.

"He's a hero. He killed the terrorist who kidnapped and murdered his wife. That's the official version anyway—that she was shot during the struggle."

She shrugged. "I thought he was a nice man; gentle, frightened and nice." She paused, wanting to make the point. Then she said, "He loved his wife very much . . . didn't want her used . . ."

"Sure you're all right?" he said, reverting to his earlier question.

"Shouldn't I be?" she said. "People pay thousands for that sort of vacation."

"None of it would have worked without you," insisted Suslev.

"Didn't it upset you?" she demanded.

He felt foolish at having been carried away by his own euphoria. He came forward, pulling her into his chest, excited by the feel of her closeness. "You know it did," he said softly. "We talked about it before it ever started and agreed it wouldn't matter . . . that it wouldn't count."

She pushed away from him, looking up into his face, wanting to feel some emotion at his touch and failing completely. They had lost too, she decided.

To break the moment between them, he took the false duplicate passport of Rupert Underberg from his pocket and tossed it onto the dresser, alongside the citation certificate.

"It's gone on for so long," he said, "that I think I'm going to miss not being Rupert Underberg."

"I'm not," said the woman. "I hated being Carole, being a whore. I just want to be myself again." She didn't think it was ever going to be possible.

BESTSELLING BOOKS FROM TOR

☐ 58725-1 *Gardens of Stone* by Nicholas Proffitt $3.95
  58726-X   Canada $4.50

☐ 51650-8 *Incarnate* by Ramsey Campbell $3.95
  51651-6   Canada $4.50

☐ 51050-X *Kahawa* by Donald E. Westlake $3.95
  51051-8   Canada $4.50

☐ 52750-X *A Manhattan Ghost Story* by T.M. Wright
                                            $3.95
  52751-8   Canada $4.50

☐ 52191-9 *Ikon* by Graham Masterton $3.95
  52192-7   Canada $4.50

☐ 54550-8 *Prince Ombra* by Roderick MacLeish $3.50
  54551-6   Canada $3.95

☐ 50284-1 *The Vietnam Legacy* by Brian Freemantle
                                            $3.50
  50285-X   Canada $3.95

☐ 50487-9 *Siskiyou* by Richard Hoyt $3.50
  50488-7   Canada $3.95

Buy them at your local bookstore or use this handy coupon:
Clip and mail this page with your order

TOR BOOKS—Reader Service Dept.
P.O. Box 690, Rockville Centre,·N.Y. 11571

Please send me the book(s) I have checked above. I am enclosing $_____ (please add $1.00 to cover postage and handling). Send check or money order only—no cash or C.O.D.'s.

Mr./Mrs./Miss _____

Address _____.

City _____ State/Zip _____

Please allow six weeks for delivery. Prices subject to change without notice.

MORE BESTSELLERS FROM TOR

☐ 58827-4 *Cry Havoc* by Barry Sadler $3.50
    58828-2   Canada $3.95

☐ 51025-9 *Designated Hitter* by Walter Wager $3.50
    51026-7   Canada $3.95

☐ 51600-1 *The Inheritor* by Marion Zimmer Bradley $3.50
    51601-X   Canada $3.95

☐ 50282-5 *The Kremlin Connection* by Jonathan Evans $3.95
    50283-3   Canada $4.50

☐ 58250-0 *The Lost American* by Brian Freemantle $3.50
    58251-9   Canada $3.95

☐ 58825-8 *Phu Nham* by Barry Sadler $3.50
    58826-6   Canada $3.95

☐ 58552-6 *Wake-in Darkness* by Donald E. McQuinn $3.95
    58553-4   Canada $4.50

☐ 50279-5 *The Solitary Man* by Jonathan Evans $3.95
    50280-9   Canada $4.50

☐ 51858-6 *Shadoweyes* by Kathryn Ptacek $3.50
    51859-4   Canada $3.95

☐ 52543-4 *Cast a Cold Eye* by Alan Ryan $3.95
    52544-2   Canada $4.50

☐ 52193-5 *The Pariah* by Graham Masterton $3.50
    52194-3   Canada $3.95

Buy them at your local bookstore or use this handy coupon:
Clip and mail this page with your order

TOR BOOKS—Reader Service Dept.
P.O. Box 690, Rockville Centre, N.Y. 11571

**Please send me the book(s) I have checked above. I am enclosing
$_____ (please add $1.00 to cover postage and handling).
Send check or money order only—no cash or C.O.D.'s.**

Mr./Mrs./Miss _____

Address _____

City _____ State/Zip _____

**Please allow six weeks for delivery. Prices subject to change without
notice.**